The Bodyguard and the Bombshell

Also From Lexi Blake

ROMANTIC SUSPENSE

Masters and Mercenaries
The Dom Who Loved Me
The Men With The Golden Cuffs
A Dom is Forever
On Her Master's Secret Service
Sanctum: A Masters and Mercenaries Novella
Love and Let Die
Unconditional: A Masters and Mercenaries Novella
Dungeon Royale
Dungeon Games: A Masters and Mercenaries Novella
A View to a Thrill
Cherished: A Masters and Mercenaries Novella
You Only Love Twice
Luscious: Masters and Mercenaries~Topped
Adored: A Masters and Mercenaries Novella
Master No
Just One Taste: Masters and Mercenaries~Topped 2
From Sanctum with Love
Devoted: A Masters and Mercenaries Novella
Dominance Never Dies
Submission is Not Enough
Master Bits and Mercenary Bites~The Secret Recipes of Topped
Perfectly Paired: Masters and Mercenaries~Topped 3
For His Eyes Only
Arranged: A Masters and Mercenaries Novella
Love Another Day
At Your Service: Masters and Mercenaries~Topped 4
Master Bits and Mercenary Bites~Girls Night
Nobody Does It Better
Close Cover
Protected: A Masters and Mercenaries Novella
Enchanted: A Masters and Mercenaries Novella
Charmed: A Masters and Mercenaries Novella
Treasured: A Masters and Mercenaries Novella
Delighted: A Masters and Mercenaries Novella
Tempted: A Masters and Mercenaries Novella
The Bodyguard and the Bombshell: A Masters and Mercenaries: New Recruits Novella

Masters and Mercenaries: The Forgotten
Lost Hearts (Memento Mori)
Lost and Found
Lost in You
Long Lost
No Love Lost

Masters and Mercenaries: Reloaded
Submission Impossible
The Dom Identity
The Man from Sanctum
No Time to Lie
The Dom Who Came in from the Cold

Masters and Mercenaries: New Recruits
Love the Way You Spy
Live, Love, Spy
Sweet Little Spies, Coming September 17, 2024

Park Avenue Promise
Start Us Up
My Royal Showmance

Butterfly Bayou
Butterfly Bayou
Bayou Baby
Bayou Dreaming
Bayou Beauty
Bayou Sweetheart
Bayou Beloved

Lawless
Ruthless
Satisfaction
Revenge

Courting Justice
Order of Protection
Evidence of Desire

Masters Of Ménage (by Shayla Black and Lexi Blake)
Their Virgin Captive
Their Virgin's Secret
Their Virgin Concubine

Their Virgin Princess
Their Virgin Hostage
Their Virgin Secretary
Their Virgin Mistress

The Perfect Gentlemen (by Shayla Black and Lexi Blake)
Scandal Never Sleeps
Seduction in Session
Big Easy Temptation
Smoke and Sin
At the Pleasure of the President

URBAN FANTASY

Thieves
Steal the Light
Steal the Day
Steal the Moon
Steal the Sun
Steal the Night
Ripper
Addict
Sleeper
Outcast
Stealing Summer
The Rebel Queen
The Rebel Guardian
The Rebel Witch

LEXI BLAKE WRITING AS SOPHIE OAK

Texas Sirens
Small Town Siren
Siren in the City
Siren Enslaved
Siren Beloved
Siren in Waiting
Siren in Bloom
Siren Unleashed
Siren Reborn

Texas Sirens: Legacy
The Accidental Siren

Nights in Bliss, Colorado
Three to Ride
Two to Love
One to Keep
Lost in Bliss
Found in Bliss
Pure Bliss
Chasing Bliss
Once Upon a Time in Bliss
Back in Bliss
Sirens in Bliss
Happily Ever After in Bliss
Far from Bliss
Unexpected Bliss

A Faery Story
Bound
Beast
Beauty

Standalone
Away From Me
Snowed In

The Bodyguard and the Bombshell

A Masters and Mercenaries: New Recruits Novella

By Lexi Blake

1001 DARK NIGHTS
PRESS

The Bodyguard and the Bombshell
A Masters and Mercenaries: New Recruits Novella
By Lexi Blake

1001 Dark Nights

Copyright 2024 DLZ Entertainment, LLC
ISBN: 979-8-88542-070-9

Masters and Mercenaries ® is registered in the U.S. Patent and Trademark Office.

Foreword: Copyright 2014 M. J. Rose

Published by 1001 Dark Nights Press, an imprint of Evil Eye Concepts, Incorporated

All rights reserved. No part of this book may be reproduced, scanned, or distributed in any printed or electronic form without permission. Please do not participate in or encourage piracy of copyrighted materials in violation of the author's rights.

This is a work of fiction. Names, places, characters and incidents are the product of the author's imagination and are fictitious. Any resemblance to actual persons, living or dead, events or establishments is solely coincidental.

Acknowledgments from the Author

I had the best time writing this book. Nate and Daisy were fun, but they came from a story that could have been a tragedy. If you've read *A Dom is Forever*, you know how close these two came to not existing. The choice Avery O'Donnell makes when she's faced with true darkness forms one of the central themes that runs through many of these stories. We cannot control what happens to us sometimes, but we can control how we handle it. We can choose light even when faced with unimaginable darkness. And when we get through those times, there is love and joy and the best kind of chaos waiting for us…

One Thousand and One Dark Nights

Once upon a time, in the future...

I was a student fascinated with stories and learning. I studied philosophy, poetry, history, the occult, and the art and science of love and magic. I had a vast library at my father's home and collected thousands of volumes of fantastic tales.

I learned all about ancient races and bygone times. About myths and legends and dreams of all people through the millennium. And the more I read the stronger my imagination grew until I discovered that I was able to travel into the stories... to actually become part of them.

I wish I could say that I listened to my teacher and respected my gift, as I ought to have. If I had, I would not be telling you this tale now. But I was foolhardy and confused, showing off with bravery.

One afternoon, curious about the myth of the Arabian Nights, I traveled back to ancient Persia to see for myself if it was true that every day Shahryar (Persian: شهریار, "king") married a new virgin, and then sent yesterday's wife to be beheaded. It was written and I had read that by the time he met Scheherazade, the vizier's daughter, he'd killed one thousand women.

Something went wrong with my efforts. I arrived in the midst of the story and somehow exchanged places with Scheherazade — a phenomena that had never occurred before and that still to this day, I cannot explain.

Now I am trapped in that ancient past. I have taken on Scheherazade's life and the only way I can protect myself and stay alive is to do what she did to protect herself and stay alive.

Every night the King calls for me and listens as I spin tales. And when the evening ends and dawn breaks, I stop at a point that leaves him breathless and yearning for more. And so the King spares my life for one more day, so that he might hear the rest of my dark tale.

As soon as I finish a story... I begin a new one... like the one that you, dear reader, have before you now.

Family Trees

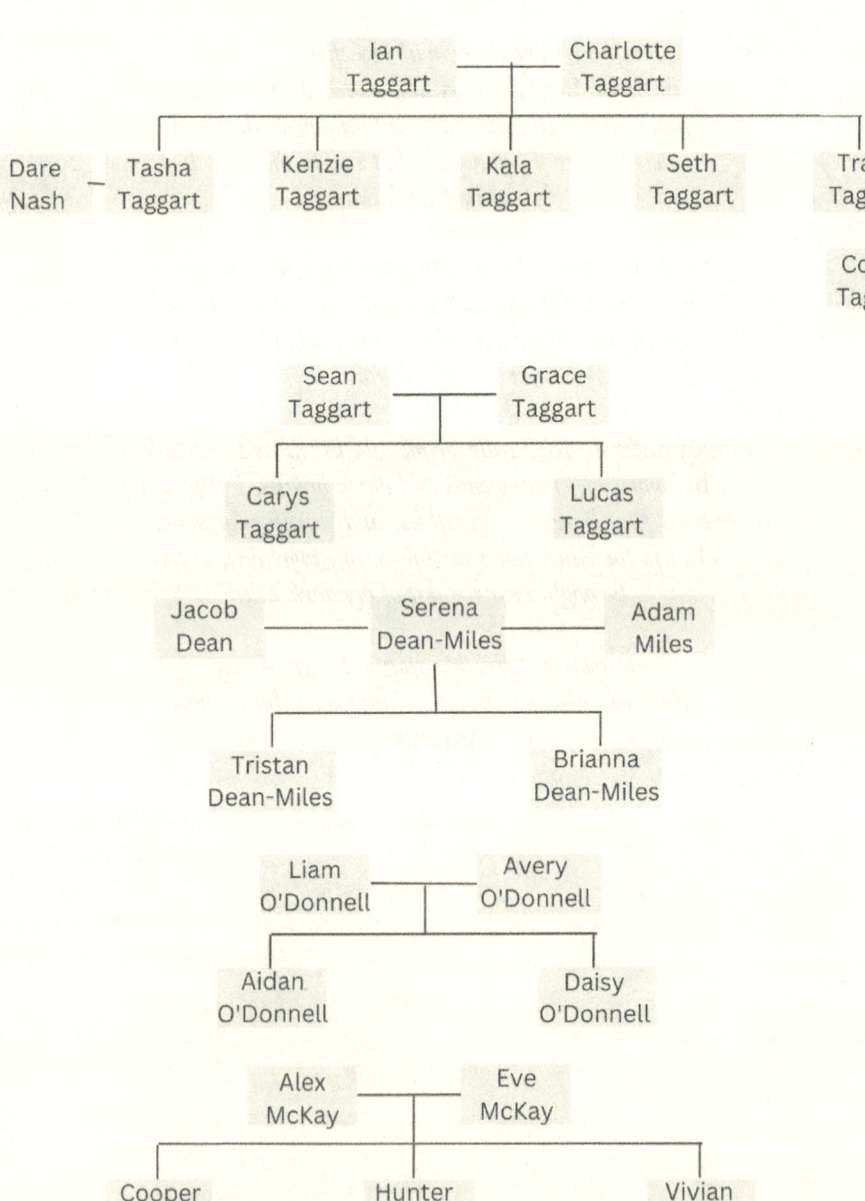

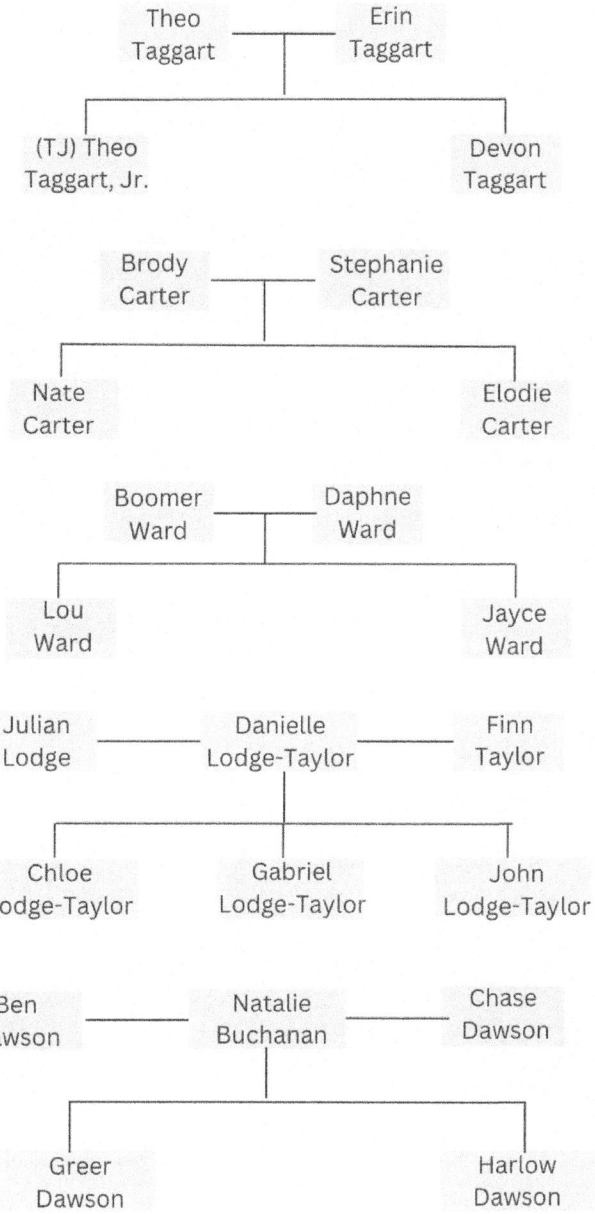

Chapter One

Australia

Nate Carter stood on the big lawn of the house he'd spent his teenaged years in and wondered why it no longer felt like home. It wasn't like he didn't love the big ranch house, didn't have fond memories of riding horses across the rambling station with his sister, Elodie, or spending evenings with his parents watching movies.

His parents weren't the problem. His sister was still the same obnoxious, loving woman she'd always been.

He was the problem.

"Are you sure you want to do this?" a deep voice asked.

He turned and saw his father standing on the big wraparound porch where he would sit with his sister, swinging and talking about what was going on in their lives.

He'd been home for six months and he made excuse after excuse why he wouldn't sit there with Elodie. He was busy. There was work to be done.

He never once told her the real reason. He was scared he would sit there and have absolutely nothing to say.

Elodie had known what she wanted to do with her life since she was five years old. He was twenty-six and had no idea where his place was in the world.

Which was why he was changing things up. "Moving to the States or working for Big Tag?"

His father wore his normal uniform of jeans and a T-shirt and looked more like a cowboy than the soldier he'd been in his younger years. Brody Carter was a legend in the security business. He'd gone from Aussie Special Forces to working for an international security company. He'd married a woman he'd met on what he would call an "op" but what Nate kind of thought was really fate. All of his life he'd looked up to this man, and Nate was so worried he was letting him down. "Both, I suppose. You know Damon would love to have you."

Before they'd moved back to Australia, his family had been based in London. Elodie barely remembered living in the place called The Garden, but Nate did. Nate remembered growing up with Damon Knight's kids and all the others.

"I need something new." It was nothing less than the truth. Since he'd left the military, he'd been drifting. Nothing had been able to shake this sense of... He hesitated to use the word *ennui*. Ennui sounded like something that happened to way smarter people than him.

"Are you sure you're not following one of the Taggart girls?" His father's brows had risen. "Because I worry you would be making a mistake, son. Tasha's getting married and the twins... Well, I don't know how any man handles those twins of Tag's."

Nate laughed. It felt good to laugh. He'd been kind of numb for the last couple of months. "Absolutely not. And I'm not trailing after Lou, either. There is no woman involved in this decision of mine. I'm doing this for me."

He wasn't going to mention he'd been thinking a lot about Daisy O'Donnell lately. He wouldn't pursue her or anything. When they'd been kids, she'd followed him around and he'd known about her crush. He hadn't minded, though he also hadn't touched her. It made him wonder what she was up to these days.

His father nodded and stepped down, joining him on the lawn. "I suppose my question is what you're going to get out of the experience. You told me you didn't think you wanted to work security."

"It seems to be the only thing I'm halfway good at." Which was precisely the problem.

"Ah, so you're feeling the pressure, are you?" his father asked.

"Pressure? No one puts pressure on me. I come home and tell you I've left SASR and Mum simply gets my old room ready and you put me on the schedule. I thought the military was going to be my career."

His father shrugged. "There's no pressure from me or your mum. You want to help me around the station, I'm happy to have you. You want to go work at Mum's clinic, she would love it. Your uncle's business is the only one I'm going to ask you to stay out of, and you know damn well why."

Because Uncle Alfi worked on the outer edges of morality. He'd been a fun guy to have around, but he could get into the wildest scrapes. "I don't think he's looking for a partner."

His father snorted. "He's always looking for a partner. I suppose I'm just wishing you didn't have to go so far away to find yourself. This is the pressure I'm talking about."

"I don't understand."

"Ah, but I do understand you," his father said with a sigh. "I was you, son. I was the rather normal man madly in love with a brilliant woman who I couldn't believe I deserved."

His parents were some of the most solid people he'd ever known. While his friends' folks were splitting up or taking breaks, his parents were obnoxiously in love.

He'd never felt romantic love either. Elodie fell in and out of love so easily, and he'd never felt more than some affection for the women he'd been with. Friendship and good sex had been the height of his relationships. "I think Mum would disagree."

"Oh, she did, and I was a stubborn arse for a long time," his dad admitted. "I let my insecurities put you and Mum in a very bad position. This is why I talk about pressure. You have been raised around extraordinary women. Women who have sparks of talent they can't deny."

His mother was a doctor. She was driven and practically glowed with purpose.

His sister had started dancing at the age of five. Most kids outgrew it, but not Elodie. She was attending a prestigious university and expected to join a company when she graduated.

He'd had his shot at the career he'd thought he'd been destined for, and it hadn't worked out. "I'm very proud of them both."

"But you wish you had that spark," his father prompted.

Nate shook his head. "No, I wish I knew where I belong. Don't think I'm not grateful, Dad. I love my family, but I don't belong here anymore. At least when I was working with the team I felt some sense of purpose."

He'd been called in to help with an op Tag's daughters and their team had been running in Sydney. Naturally it had all gone to hell, but it had been the one thing in months that made him feel like he mattered.

"You won't be working with the Agency," his father pointed out. "You're going into the bodyguard unit. It's not the same. Do you want to be an investigator? Because Damon probably has more room for you to move around."

"I've lived in London. I want something new. I want to try this. Like I said, I don't mean to hurt you or Mum."

"We'll be fine. I simply want to make sure you're not running away for the wrong reasons."

"I don't think I'm running away at all. I've been drifting. I don't want to work the station the rest of my life," Nate admitted.

His father's arms crossed over his chest as he looked out across the lawn. "I don't have a problem with you wanting out. Your sister wants another life, too. We came back to help your grandmother. She's gone now, and we'll probably sell the place. Your mum has a hankering to travel again."

His mother's version of travel would be to go to the world's forgotten places and try to make them better. His father would be right beside her. "She wants to open another clinic?"

He'd been born in a clinic his mother had run outside of Sierra Leone.

"Her kids are grown and I think she wants to do more good in the world. And I'll be honest, I'm looking forward to having time with her, but I worry what happens if we're out wandering the world and you need us. Am I wrong to not keep a place for you to come home to?"

Damn, but he loved this man. "You and Mum and Elodie are my home. Not some space. I know if I ever need you, you'll be there. I'm trying to be brave, Dad. It would be easy to stay here and work this station and marry someone from town, but it's not what's in my heart."

"Then you have to go into the world and figure it out," his father said, putting a hand on his shoulder. "Find your passion and don't let it go. But I want you to consider what I'm about to say to you. Sometimes the passion we need isn't a career. It's a person. It's a family. I'm not ever going to be as smart as your mum, but I learned my place long ago. It's to love her and build this family with her. To support her and you and your sister. I wouldn't take it back for anything in the world. Certainly not for some high-powered career. It's the best job for me. Be open to what the universe offers you. And know no matter where we are, we're here for you."

The door opened and his mother stepped out. "We should get on the road if we're going to make it to the airport in time." She strode down the steps and joined them. "Oh, I'm going to miss you. All my babies are flying out of the nest. You should know I've already called Avery, and she's going to make sure you have everything you need. Are you sure you don't want to wait until you find an apartment?"

He was staying with friends. Well, with people he knew back when he was a kid. He'd known Aidan O'Donnell since they were babies. Their parents were friends who would get together every couple of years.

"I want to get a feel for the city," he explained. He would be living with Aidan and two of his friends. Their extra room would work until he decided where he wanted to live.

The fact the room was also close to a BDSM club Aidan and his friends ran was a plus. He'd been raised around lifestylers, but the clubs were few and far between here in the outback, and he hadn't had occasion to play during his time in the military. Unless he went to Sydney, he didn't play, and Sydney was so far away.

But that wouldn't be a problem in Dallas. There were several clubs he would have easy access to. He would go and figure his life out. And maybe spend some time with a pretty sub or two.

"Let's get going then," his father said.

He took his mum's hand and moved to the truck so he could start his future.

* * * *

Dallas, TX
One week later

Daisy O'Donnell was ready.

Real estate hadn't worked out for her, but she was all right. She wasn't meant for the restaurant world either. The fifth time she'd dropped a platter of five-star food had proven she was not a perfect server. She'd never actually seen her Uncle Sean cry before. The man was serious about food.

She'd moved through a series of jobs, but nothing had stuck yet.

Until today.

"So you think you know how to use the phone system?" Her brand spanking new boss was named Harlow Dawson, and she was twelve kinds of awesome. She ran the Dawson-Lockwood Agency along with her business partner, Ruby Lockwood.

Harlow handled the rough stuff while Ruby was the kickass hacker who no firewall could keep out.

An all-women private investigation firm. Yes, this was right where she belonged. After all, her beloved Da was one of the world's best investigators, so it was probably in her genes.

"I think I got it." She sat down behind the desk. Her desk. The small space consisted of a reception area, two offices for the founders, a baby break room, and a single bathroom she was apparently responsible for as well.

She could handle it. Her mother had always kept a neat house. That was in her genes, too.

Harlow was roughly the same age as Daisy, though she seemed older since she was tough as nails and had some way cool scars Daisy had only seen because she played at The Hideout, a club Daisy belonged to. Although she hadn't had any fun there lately. It was tough when all the Doms considered her a little sister.

"Are you sure? It can be tricky," Harlow said, tucking back a strand of electric blue hair.

"It's not tricky." Ruby walked out of her office. "You're terrible with tech. Daisy, the right button puts the call on hold, and then you send the caller to either of our offices. I'm one and Harlow's two. When you go to lunch, you put the whole thing in *away* mode which sends the caller to our voice mail box. When you get back, check the voice mail and send us any messages we need to reply to. When the system is in *answer*, the button goes red. Easy-peasy."

Totally easy. "I can handle it. I'm so grateful to you both for this opportunity. I was surprised when the boutique I was working at went under so quickly. I appreciate the job. The last thing I want to do is move back in with my parents. I love them, but my da can be a lot to handle. He has an unrealistic vision of me."

Her sweet da firmly believed she could do no wrong. Not true. She could fuck up majorly—re: that time she was helping a friend with a demo of her condo and accidently took down a load-bearing wall…and then the condo—but everyone got out and insurance paid for some of it. Also, he didn't think she understood the word fuck or its many uses. Despite actually using the word around him.

Her mom had asked her to clean up the potty mouth, but where did her mom think she'd first heard the word from?

"As a woman whose dad is up my ass twenty-four seven, I'm happy to save you from a terrible fate." Harlow looked down at her watch. "Speaking of, he usually comes around right before lunch. You want to grab something before we meet with the client?"

Ruby was slightly older, but she fit right in with the twenty-somethings in her chicly ripped jeans and a concert T-shirt. She obviously hadn't gotten the memo explaining she must look professional at all times. Daisy's da still wore a suit and tie when meeting with clients.

Ruby looked way more comfy.

"Let's do it," Ruby said. "Daisy, feel free to take a nice long lunch. We won't be back this afternoon. Close up when you leave, and make sure the security system is on. I put the code and instructions on your desk. Call if you have any questions, but seriously, this shouldn't be hard for you. Unless you're here when her dad comes by. Then you'll get a full dose of paranoid."

"Only one of them," Harlow corrected. "Dad One is great. Dad Two got a double dose of weirdo."

Harlow came from an alternative-lifestyle family, but Daisy was used to that. She'd figured out pretty early on her da and mom's Friday night meetings weren't about playing canasta but doing the nasty. Actually, she still wasn't sure what canasta was, but she did understand BDSM. Not in Da's version of reality, though.

And wasn't that kind of sexist? He'd sent Aidan to a club for training, but had anyone thought to get her a corset and heels and teach her how to submit to a Dominant partner in exchange for a bunch of orgasms and a deeply intimate relationship? No. She'd had to wait until after college and take the course The Hideout offered.

"It's in the eyes," Ruby was saying. "That's how you know. Ben Dawson has normal dad eyes. You can totally see the rage of paranoia in Chase's."

Because Harlow's dads were twins who shared her mom.

Maybe she should consider a threesome. It would make rent easier.

"So you know what you're doing?" Harlow didn't seem entirely certain.

The good news was, Daisy always looked on the positive side. She would figure it out. "Absolutely. I'm ready to handle this. You have a great afternoon."

Ruby slung her big bag over her shoulder. "Come on. We can grab a sandwich at the café. It's close to the meeting spot. Daisy, we'll see you in the morning."

Harlow still looked reluctant but followed her business partner out.

Thus began her first day as a private investigator. Well, receptionist to a private investigation firm, but this was it. This was going to be her calling.

She managed to answer the phones and deal with Harlow's Dad Two—because she was right. The man was intense. It was easy because she'd told him they were grabbing sandwiches at a café. She'd learned it was important to stick as close to the truth as possible when lying. It threw the person she was lying to off. Dad Two had totally bought it because it was super true. Surely there were a lot of cafés around. The man couldn't check all of them.

Right before she was about to head to lunch, a chiming sound rang through the office as the door opened and a young woman walked in. She was petite, with long blonde hair and tears in her eyes.

Daisy's heart immediately melted. There was a woman in trouble. This was what her new firm did. They helped. "Welcome to the Dawson-Lockwood Agency. We're here for you."

She should write that down. It might be a good slogan. It had more heart than the current: *New investigations for a new age*.

"Hi, I need a private investigator. I think…" She sniffled. "I think my boyfriend is cheating on me, but I'm too scared to go check all by myself. It's happening right now, I think. Once a month he goes to this building, and I'm sure he's seeing someone there. It's like clockwork. He should be there now. I'm supposed to marry him in six weeks. I don't know what to do."

Daisy stood. Ruby and Harlow would be gone all afternoon, and this woman would have to wait another month to find out if her honey had another honey? It wasn't happening. Not on Daisy's watch.

"I'll go with you." Daisy got her purse and made sure her cell phone was fully charged. The camera on her cell would have to do for today. She would need to invest in more sophisticated equipment as she moved more heavily into her new career. The good news? Her birthday was coming up.

"You're a detective?" the young woman asked.

She was now. Besides, this was an easy job, and she was here to make life easy for her bosses. She set the phone system to *away* mode. At least she thought she did. She was pretty sure. Then she set the alarm system. The light went green. Green was the universal sign for go. Well, at least it was here in America.

"Absolutely. Now let's go find your fiancé and put your mind at ease." She followed the woman out, using her keys to lock the door. "I'm sure this is all a misunderstanding. He's probably not cheating on you."

He wasn't. It was far, far worse.

Chapter Two

"Let me get this straight," Liam O'Donnell began, sitting in the big conference room at his place of business. "I want to make sure I've got everything down."

Daisy O'Donnell had spent her whole life coming up to this building where her da worked. She'd played with her brother in the daycare, and later she'd done her homework in her da's office while she waited for him to drive her home. She knew this building like the back of her hand. It was practically her second home.

So why did it feel so weird to be sitting in the conference room? It was probably the fact that she wasn't alone with her da. Her mother was up here, too, looking worried and patting her da's hand from time to time. The big boss, Ian Taggart, and his wife, Charlotte, were at the head of the table, along with Mitch Bradford. She wasn't sure why John's dad was here, but he was a lawyer.

She didn't need a lawyer. Did she?

"I was helping out a client," she began.

"Uhm, Mr. Taggart, I would like to make it clear we didn't hire Daisy as a private investigator." Her bosses were here, too. Harlow and Ruby sat at the opposite end of the table, and Harlow seemed to be the one who wanted to set the record straight.

"She was supposed to answer the phones." Ruby frowned her way.

She was going to have to soothe her bosses. Things had done what they so often did in Daisy's life. They had gone awry.

To top things off, her brother was somewhere in the building. Aidan had been the one to drive her up, and he'd told her he needed to go talk to his newest roommate.

Nathan Carter. Big, gorgeous Nathan Carter, who'd barely known she'd existed past being his friend's obnoxious sister.

She hadn't seen Nate in years. Was he still stunning? He probably had a girlfriend.

"Daisy?" Her mother's voice brought her out of her reverie. "Uncle Ian asked you a question."

Of all the grave faces around the table, it was her aunt and uncle who broke the mold and looked highly amused.

"I asked how you went from answering the phones to taking down a drug cartel," Uncle Ian said, his lips curling up. He leaned in like he was ready for this story.

Her da made a sound and held his heart like it was breaking. "My poor girl."

Her mother got up and moved to the big table where there were drinks and snacks laid out. "I'm going to make you some tea."

"He's going to need something stronger," Aunt Charlotte said. "I brought out the good whiskey."

"Oh, you know what…" Daisy began, but then the look from her sweet mother could have frozen lava in its tracks. Well, she'd had a rough twenty-four hours, too. Still, when her mom looked like that it was best to follow her lead. And she could hit the bar at The Hideout later on. "Tea sounds great. Now, before I tell the story you should know I took every precaution."

"Which ones?" Ruby asked, her eyes narrowing. "Like the one where you pushed in the security code and then didn't ask it to set?"

"There was a green light." It had been an honest mistake. "And I did lock the doors."

"Yeah, well, someone broke in and we didn't get a notification because the light should have been red," Harlow pointed out. "Now Dad Two thinks we should move the whole office. Well, he thinks we should shut it down. Also, I'm still trying to figure out how he found me at the café. I was almost late for my meeting because I was dealing with my dad. Mr. Taggart, do you have like a wand or something? I think my dad LoJacked me."

"I do, actually." Uncle Ian had the biggest smile on his face.

Maybe telling Chase Dawson they were getting sandwiches at a café wasn't the smartest thing. She hadn't told him the name of the café. Weren't there like a hundred in Dallas? "I'm sorry. I thought green meant it was set."

"You totally got the answering machine right," Harlow said.

Daisy sat up straighter. "I'm glad. I wouldn't want to miss a single message."

"Yes," Ruby agreed. "It was how we knew you were being held by the police as a material witness to federal crimes."

"Just drink." Her mom put the whiskey in her da's hand very quickly. And he drained it.

Yep, she was driving her sweet da to drink.

"I still don't quite understand what happened," Aunt Charlotte said.

She'd gone over this again and again in the last twenty-four hours. "So the woman came in and she's getting married to this guy but she thinks her fiancé is cheating on her because once a month he goes to this building downtown. She's followed him before but she's never gone in, and she said when he would come out hours later he looked super satisfied. Like when they had sex."

"I'm so glad she can expertly read facial expressions." Uncle Ian looked like he was ready to giggle.

They always underestimated the younger generation. They had good instincts, too, though not in this case. "Anyway, so I thought he probably wasn't cheating because she seemed sweet, you know. Like if some guy's cheating on her then we're all in trouble."

"Yes, we are all in trouble," Harlow agreed.

"So I thought we would go down and maybe he was planning a surprise for their wedding," Daisy explained.

Her da shook his head as her mom passed him another glass. "My poor, sweet, naïve girl."

She wasn't naïve. "Well, he wasn't cheating. Turns out he was checking on a shipment from his employer."

"A shipment of what, Daisy?" Ruby asked.

As a boss, she was going to be the unrelenting one. "At first I thought it was maybe, like, powder."

She could have sworn her da had tears in his eyes. "She wouldn't know what cocaine is, much less what it looks like. My god, girl, you could have been killed."

"I mostly kept my distance, but then my client was angry and she rushed out of the spot where we were hiding," Daisy continued.

"You went into the building?" her da asked, horror evident in his tone.

"Of course. How else would I have gotten the pictures of her fiancé meeting with the head of the cartel? They were good pictures, too. Who says cell phones can't take excellent pictures? When I realized this was like my first case, I even thought to get a selfie with the drug lord in the background." It had been an excellent picture. "But the police made me take it down. I was getting good reach and everything."

Now her uncle simply laughed his ass off. "She put it on Instagram."

"You looked good, sweetie," Aunt Charlotte said. "You got a great angle."

"Do not encourage her." Her mother was not amused.

"Like I said, I kind of thought it was all okay until Bri texted me. She told me she thought it was probably cocaine and I should get out of there before the cartel people killed me." Her friends always looked out for her. She'd gotten several *you're about to die* texts, and Cooper McKay had shown up with her brother in tow just in time to watch her get carted off by the police.

Law and Order made interrogations look glamourous. They had kept her there for hours, and the snacks had been terrible.

"It's me fault," her da was saying. "I should never have let her out in the world alone."

He didn't understand. "Like I said, Da, I wasn't alone. The client was with me. And she got upset and yelled, and that was how the people figured out we were hiding. I got into the building through a window they left open. I didn't think I could wriggle through, but I totally did. I think I'm truly cut out for this line of work."

"I do, too, kiddo," Uncle Ian said.

It was good to know at least one person believed in her.

Mitch Bradford had been quiet the whole time, but he leaned forward now. "Ian, this is serious. I don't want to think about what would have happened if she hadn't posted a dumbass pic to social media. Her friends figured out where she was and called the police immediately."

"Oh, I had a locator on. It can help with engagement," she explained.

Which Ian thought was hysterical, but her da simply went even paler. Not even Irishmen should be able to go so white.

"We're all thankful for the quick thinking of her friends." Her mother sat beside her father, and she'd poured her own whiskey. "The question is what happens now? Was everyone arrested? Is my daughter in trouble?"

Mitch sat back. "Daisy is not in any trouble with the police. She is a material witness, however. Everyone was arrested, and they're being held for questioning right now. The problem is if they make bail, Daisy is technically the only witness they can count on."

"But the client was with me," Daisy argued. She'd been the one to cause all the trouble when she'd revealed their hiding spot because she was pissed at her boyfriend.

She'd gone from crying because he might be cheating to yelling because he was obviously withholding funds from his secret job.

"Heidi Groverson is now claiming she believes her boyfriend when he says he got sent to the address to deliver a lunch order and had nothing to do with the operation ongoing there," Mitch explained.

"So she's lying," her da accused.

"I think she's trying to protect her boyfriend," Ruby added. "I'm already working on it. Ronnie Wilson is registered with a company called Meals To You. They're a group of gig workers who run food. I think I might be able to prove it's also a front for moving drugs. According to Daisy's account, Ronnie went once a month. I think he's likely the go-between for the cartel and their lower-level dealers."

So she'd busted up a dangerous drug ring on her very first case. "We can take them all down."

"Very likely," Mitch agreed. "But first you have to go to trial. With Heidi changing her story, you're the star witness."

"A cartel is going to want to kill me darling girl." Her da always sounded more Irish when he was emotional. He'd been born in Dublin but had lived most of his adult life right here in Dallas. Not that his accent showed the time he'd spent here. He was a handsome man with green eyes and dark hair. So many women would look his way even now, but he only ever seemed to see her mother.

She wanted the kind of love her parents had. Deep and true. Steadfast.

"We're not going to let someone kill Daisy," her uncle said. Ian Taggart wasn't related to her by blood. Or rather not the kind that normally made a family. She'd heard the stories. The men and women of McKay-Taggart had bled for each other over the years, and they'd formed bonds as tight as any family. It meant she had a ton of overly protective aunties and uncles. One of them seemed to finally be getting serious. "Ruby, I would appreciate you sharing anything you find out with us, but know we're going to work this from our end, too, and we'll obviously handle getting her a bodyguard."

Ruby seemed to breathe a sigh of relief. "Thank you, Mr. Taggart."

"Yes, my dad will likely chill if he knows you're handling it." There was a bitterness to Harlow's words. Maybe her relationship with her dad was worse than she'd thought.

Daisy could work on that. She was good with parental units. Perhaps Mr. Dawson simply needed to see how competent his daughter was. If anyone knew how to handle an overly protective father, it was her. She was already thinking of ways to help out her boss.

"She should probably move home for the time being," her uncle said.

She loved her parents, but the thought of leaving her house made her sad. And there was the issue of her employment. She knew he wasn't talking about simply sleeping in her old bed at night. Her da would go for the full lock-down. "I can't. I have to work."

"About that," Ruby began.

Daisy felt tears well. Not again. She'd tried so hard. She'd been good at it. Mostly. Sort of good. She could be better, but she needed time. "But I just started."

Harlow's head shook. "Sorry, man. It was a hell of a first day, so it needs to be your last day."

Tears pierced her eyes. She'd worked so hard to afford the down payment on her ramshackle little home. "But I won't be able to afford my house."

She expected her da to tell her to move back in, but he reached out and put a hand over hers.

"Don't worry, me darlin'. You'll come to work right here. We'll find you a place," her da promised.

"I'm getting the Scotch, babe." Aunt Charlotte was on her feet in an instant.

Uncle Ian had gone pale, and a distant look hit his eyes. Like he'd gone someplace else.

It was weird. She often saw that look in men's eyes.

But her natural positivity was already taking over. This could be good. Maybe she was too extra for what was essentially a two-person show. Here at McKay-Taggart she would be joining the big time. "I can help you, Da."

Now her da paled. "Or you can work at reception. Or bookkeeping. We'll find you a place. Don't worry about it."

And she would work her way up.

It would be okay. Although what had they said? "What did you mean I need a bodyguard?"

* * * *

Nate Carter had been working at McKay-Taggart for exactly one week, and he was fitting in well. It was good to be around the men and women of the bodyguard unit, good to feel this brotherhood thing they had going.

It wasn't the lightning bolt he wanted, but it was enough for now.

He was about to finish up his first week on the job, and tonight was his first night at The Hideout. He planned to spend his weekend settling into his new space.

"Hey, I thought I'd come down and hang with you while my sister is being interrogated for her latest adventure." Aidan O'Donnell strode up to the desk Nate had been assigned. "It's a doozy."

He'd heard a lot about the ball of chaos known as Daisy O'Donnell. "What's she up to this time?"

She was a mystery. He hadn't seen a picture of her since he didn't do social media, and Aidan was packing up to move in with his fiancée, so his part of the house was looking pretty sparse. He hadn't seen his other roommates yet since Cooper McKay and Tristan Dean-Miles were... He had no idea where they were since it was classified.

He'd worked with both young men on a CIA op in Sydney a few months back, so he was certain he could hang with the guys. Though everyone had thought Tristan would be moving out with Aidan since they'd been involved with Carys Taggart since they were kids. For reasons he didn't understand, Aidan was marrying Carys in a few short weeks, and Tristan was out of the relationship.

It was a lot of drama, but they were all blokes so they dealt with it by drinking beer and not talking about anything but sports.

"So my sister recently took a job as a receptionist for a private investigation firm." Aidan sat in the chair across from Nate's assigned desk. He was in the back of the floor, fairly close to the boss's office. He and Aidan had fallen back into an easy friendship. Like the years between them hadn't mattered at all. It was comforting to be around Aidan.

"I thought she was going into real estate." He'd heard many stories of the chaos that seemed to follow Aidan's baby sister. She was a complete mess, but it was obvious her brother adored her.

"Yeah, real estate did not work out. She passed the test and everything, but then she put the wrong keys in all the lockboxes they use and mistakenly put in some list prices she said seemed more in line with the neighborhood." Aidan shook his head. "She lives in her own world."

She sounded like a hoot. "So now she's a receptionist. How much trouble could she get into there?"

Aidan's eyes went wide. "She managed to uncover a cocaine distribution organization."

Nate felt his jaw drop. "She did what? How? How does answering the phone lead to exposing criminals?"

Broad shoulders shrugged. "I have no idea how she does it. She should have a patent or something. Anyway, to hear her describe it there was a client looking for her cheating boyfriend and the new bosses were out for lunch, so she took the case."

"But she was the receptionist."

"My sister has a confidence only Hollywood stars have. The men, I mean. Daisy plows through life never understanding how dangerous the world can be, probably because our da chased after her making sure she never had to deal with anything. Don't get me wrong. My sister is a wonderful woman. She would do anything for a friend. She'll literally give you the shirt off her back. She did it one time when this woman she met had been dumped by her boyfriend at the lake and he'd taken off with her clothes. She was in a bikini and crying. Daisy told the girl she spends half her life in fet wear, so walking around in her bra wasn't a problem."

Nate tried to wrap his head around the idea. "She'd just met the girl?"

"Yup, and she managed to find the girl a ride home and talk her parents down from grounding her because she wasn't supposed to be out late," Aidan explained. "All while wearing short shorts and a pushup bra."

He was rapidly becoming fascinated with the idea of Daisy. "So did she get hurt? When she exposed the cartel? I assume she called the police."

"No, she was too busy not understanding what she was doing. She was taking a selfie memorializing her first 'case' as a detective." Aidan used air quotes around the word *case*. "Her best friend caught it when she posted it on Instagram and Brianna called the police. Luckily she'd tagged her location. So now she's a material witness against a drug lord. Just another day in the life of Daisy O'Donnell. Not even her worst day."

"Is your dad freaking out?" Liam was famous for having a distorted view of his daughter. He claimed she was a saint most of the time. When he'd seen the man the last few years, Liam would always announce his Daisy was the sweetest, most perfect child in the world and Aidan… Aidan was a boy.

Aidan nodded. "Beyond freaking out. It's why I spent last night at Daisy's. Carys and I had to be with her because my da wouldn't let her stay alone. Daisy loves her little house. It's a dump, by the way, but she bought it for a song, and for some reason she's obsessed with living on her own. Though if the meeting goes the way I think it is going to, she'll be coming back to our place tonight."

"Why?" He didn't mind. In fact, he was curious. If she was anything like she was when she was a kid, she would be pleasant to be around. She used to tell him how smart she thought he was, how much she liked being around him. He'd only been a year older than she was, but he'd been so big physically the age difference seemed larger. "I thought we were going to the club. Isn't there a party tonight?"

"There is, and we wouldn't miss it. It's our annual masked ball." Aidan's lips curved up in a devilish grin. "It's the best night since everyone's in a mask and you can pretend to not know you're playing with the sub you've always wanted to play with. It's fun." He sat up. "I mean that in a watch the drama way. Not in an I participate way. Trust me. I know exactly what Carys will be wearing. But it's funny to watch the others fumble their way through. My cousin Lucas likes it because he can pretend he's sleeping with someone new. He has to pretend since he's gone through most of the available subs already. Seth will try to find Chloe Lodge because he wants her so bad, but he wants to pretend like he doesn't want her at all. Chloe will stay away because she's the smart one. I won't even go into what Kala and Coop would do. They won't be here because they're saving the world or something. But it will still be a crazy night."

He was looking forward to it. Not because he would play tonight. He intended to take it slow, to get into the groove of the club before looking for a play partner. He would put on his leathers and the mask Aidan supplied him with and sit in the lounge for most of the night. He might watch some scenes. "So what's Daisy doing while we're playing?"

"She usually sits in the locker room," Aidan explained. "She doesn't mind. She'll grab a bottle of wine from the lounge and pop some popcorn and watch bad reality shows on her tablet. You need a ride? I was planning on going home and grabbing my kit and Carys before picking up baby sis."

It seemed like Aidan had a lot on his hands. "I'll drive myself. No worries. So is she going to be hanging around the place for a bit? I take it you're worried about Daisy's safety. Is there a plan?"

"There's always a plan and it always goes awry. I think Da wants Brian Langton to shadow Daisy for a couple of weeks," Aidan explained. "They're friends, and he's married with a couple of kids so he's pretty sure Brian won't perv on her. Da will probably try to get her to move back home for a while, but my sister can be stubborn. We don't know a lot about the people she exposed, so we don't know how serious it is yet. If Daisy runs true, I would bet the head of the cartel will try to blow us all up."

Now some things made sense. "Brian's on assignment and doesn't get back in until Monday."

"So we've got Daisy watching this weekend. She'll probably spend most of it with Brianna at her parents' house. Having Brianna's dads around means mine won't freak out about her safety. And I've got a double shift this weekend, so you'll have the place to yourself." Aidan studied him for a moment. "You going to be okay on your own?"

He would have told anyone he would love being on his own, but he wasn't looking forward to the quiet. The quiet reminded him how alone he felt. But then he'd felt alone even when he was surrounded by a loving family. Even when he'd known he wasn't. "Yeah, I'll probably hang out at the club Saturday night, too, but otherwise I'll be chilling at home. Leave me a list of whatever I need to do."

"We're pretty low maintenance," Aidan replied. "Coop and Tristan are always on the road, and I work constantly. I have no idea how Carys is planning this wedding. Even with help from the moms, it's a lot. I'm lucky I know when to show up."

"You're going through with it?" Nate wasn't sure how to bring this up, wasn't sure he even should. It was weird to think of Carys and Aidan without Tristan. They were a threesome. Always had been. He'd thought they always would be. It wouldn't be the first time they'd put off the wedding because of Tristan's job.

A grim look came over his friend's face. "I'm going through with it no matter what this time. I'm not letting her down again. If Tristan's work is more important than our wife, then he's made his choice."

Somehow he thought there was more to the situation, but he didn't think he was the guy Aidan was going to talk to. "Well, I'll be there."

"Of course you will. You're one of my groomsmen." Aidan got a wistful smile on his face. "We'll go get our tuxes fitted next week. It'll be fun."

"You let me know and I'll be there." And he would be there tonight. Maybe he would even meet Daisy again. It would be fun to see how the pixie had grown up. She'd been an awkward child, all gangly and skinny, with braces and untamable hair.

She would remind him of his childhood. Remind him of when he thought he knew what he wanted to do with his life.

Maybe a friendship with her would be good for him. And apparently amusing since she was a ball of chaos.

Aidan glanced down at his watch. "They should be done soon. I'm going back upstairs. I bet I get to either babysit my sister or come back at five and pick her up. Either way, my father will lecture me on how it's my sacred duty to ensure no harm befalls Saint Daisy. The man's blinders are strong. See you at the club tonight."

He waved and then got back to work.

Tonight he would figure out if he could reconnect with a lifestyle he'd once loved.

Or he would sit and drink in the bar. Yeah, that was probably how his night would go.

Chapter Three

Daisy sat in the locker room at The Hideout. It was one of her favorite places on the planet, but tonight she felt antsy.

It had been a genuinely terrible day, and Aidan being willing to take her in for the night was the only reason she wasn't locked in her parents' house.

Come tomorrow she would have a bodyguard on her twenty-four seven. She'd done it again. She'd upturned everyone's lives when all she'd wanted to do was help.

Should she give in and go home? Was she causing more trouble than she was worth?

It was kind of the question that plagued her life.

"Hey, you okay?"

She looked up and Carys Taggart was already dressed in an emerald green corset and matching boy shorts. She had an elaborate mask in her hand. It wouldn't cover up the pile of glorious auburn hair on her head. Her hair would give her away at a party like the one going on in the club this evening. It wouldn't matter. She only wanted to play with Aidan.

Well, Aidan and Tristan, but it looked like Carys was going to be permanently down a Dom.

So naturally she was here checking on Daisy. "I'm fine. I guess everyone heard."

Carys sat down on the bench next to Daisy. "About you being a badass and taking down a cartel? Yup."

She should have known her future sister-in-law would have her back. Carys was the best. "I don't think that's the way my da saw it. I probably didn't make things easier for myself by posting a selfie. My parents do not understand the importance of social media."

Carys chuckled. "I'm sure they don't. You know if you hadn't posted the social media pic, no one would have known where you were. Think about it. Now, the parental units are not here tonight, so you're just talking to me. Not your brother, either. Are you okay?"

"I guess I feel dumb." She was feeling beyond dumb. She felt useless. "I'll be better tomorrow, I'm sure."

Though maybe she was being overly optimistic since tomorrow she would wake up at her brother's place and start the new job her father had basically forced her into. Forced her upon everyone else.

She'd overheard the deep discussion between Uncle Ian and Uncle Alex about how much more insurance they would need and whether or not she would find a way to burn down the building.

She wouldn't. Not intentionally at least.

Carys was a gorgeous young woman who looked so much like her mother, Grace Taggart. Carys was everything Daisy wished she could be. Smart. Successful. A doctor. Carys knew what she wanted to do with her life, what she was good at. She reached out and put her hand over Daisy's. "You are anything but dumb. You are a light in the world, Daisy O'Donnell, and don't let anyone tell you otherwise. What you did yesterday was brave."

"That's not what my da says. Or my brother." She'd gotten a hearty lecture from her brother and pleading from her da not to kill herself, thereby destroying his soul or something.

"Your father has issues when it comes to you. He was raised with a brother. His mother was significantly tougher than you or your mother. I mean that in a physical sense," Carys said. "You're tough and so is your mom, but what your da sees is his sweet girl getting eaten up by the world."

"So I don't ever get eaten up by anyone at all?" She sniffled, feeling sorry for herself. It wasn't her usual mood, which was probably why it hit her so hard.

"Ah, I do see where the two are connected. You haven't found the right guy yet," Carys said with a sigh. "I know it's easy for me to say. I found the right ones… I found your brother when I was very young. You have to give it some time."

Daisy turned so she could look Carys in the eyes. "I'm not looking for the right one. I'm looking for anyone at this point. I want to ask you a question, and I need you to be honest. Is there something wrong with me?"

A brow rose over Carys's eyes. "Why would you say that?"

"Because this is literally a sex club, and I can't get laid." It was the saddest part of her world. She had great friends, a wonderful family, a wide-open world career wise. Mostly. But on the romantic front she couldn't seem to find a groove. She wasn't looking for anything serious. Not right now. She wanted to play, and no one would play with her here. It was hard watching other subs get picked night after night while she sat in the lounge.

She'd taken all the classes, but even her training Dom had treated her like a kid sister. While her classmates were indulging in discovering the pleasures of D/s, she'd get lectures about how dangerous the world could be.

She'd thought it would change when she graduated, but it was more of the same. Even the new guys—the ones she hadn't grown up with—avoided her.

Carys seemed to think for a moment. "The problem might be that you already know everyone here. We're bringing in new members next month. People you didn't grow up with."

"I didn't grow up with the guys from The Club," Daisy pointed out. The Hideout had been started by the group of friends they were supposed to pretend didn't work for the Central Intelligence Agency, and Julian Lodge's kids. The Lodge gang had brought in a group of their friends, and Daisy liked them all.

Not a one of them would play with her.

It made a girl think.

Carys frowned. "None of this seems right. I'm sorry. I've been caught up in my own drama and I haven't been checking in with the people who are important to me. I know how my brother and cousins view you."

Daisy did, too. "As a kid sister."

Carys nodded. "Sorry, they can't help it. But the others shouldn't. Are you telling me you haven't had a single D/s encounter since you became a member here?"

"I had a couple of scenes in the beginning, but I know Aidan asked the Doms to run them with me. They didn't have any interest in me physically." It bugged her and quite frankly brought down her body positivity. "It's weird because I ran through some dick in college, if you know what I mean. I'm so not a virgin. Despite what my da thinks. But I suspect I would like it even more if it was D/s sex."

Carys's head shook. "Seriously? You haven't had sex in the club? I thought everyone had sex in the club."

"Brianna doesn't because she never took the class. Devi doesn't because she's pining after someone." That wasn't her story to tell. "Do you think it's because my best friends are all sexless and stuff? Does everyone see me and think I don't want sex? I mean, I'm not terrible to look at."

"You're freaking gorgeous, Dais," Carys said and seemed genuinely stumped at her predicament. "You are what the older generation would call a bombshell. I need to think about this. It might be time to look for another club for you. Sanctum runs a bit older, but they have new people coming in. Some of the new staff at Top are taking the training class right now. And one of the bodyguards at MT. I only know him because his dad has run Top Fort Worth for years. I don't think you've met Landon Vail yet. He's cute. Is this why you hide out in the locker room?"

"It feels better than sitting in the lounge knowing everyone is looking at me and wondering why I bother." It was better than sitting home alone, and at least then she had her friends around her. Devi and Bri weren't here tonight, so it would be super lonely all the way around. Everyone would be out partying and exploring, and she would be watching crap videos on her tablet waiting for her brother to be done.

Only one thing about staying the night at Aidan's place sparked her interest.

Nate Carter was living there now. He'd been there for a week, and she was finally going to get to see him.

"No one thinks that way. No one. I assure you, you belong here, but if it's not what you need, then we'll find a new place. Or import some tops who didn't watch you grow up." Carys had her "I'm plotting" expression on her face. Carys was a good plotter. "You know we've got a couple of visitors tonight and a new member."

"I didn't know anyone had taken the class recently."

"He didn't have to," Carys explained. "He had a membership to a club in Australia."

Yes, there it was. Just the word *Australia* could make her heart thump.

Nathan Carter. He was here? She'd thought she would meet him tonight or maybe over breakfast in the morning. "Are you talking about Nate?"

Carys's shoulders slumped. "Damn. I forgot. You know him."

"I haven't seen him in person in years. I used to follow him around like a puppy. I had the biggest crush on him," she admitted. "And I was Aidan's obnoxious kid sister to him."

"But you wouldn't be tonight," Carys pointed out, her lips tugging up in a kind of evil grin.

"I assure you I'm always his kid sister. Aidan's the doctor and Daisy's the screw-up." Her father was the only person in the world who didn't seem to see the truth.

"You're not a screw-up," Carys insisted. "You simply haven't found your place yet, but it doesn't mean you're a screw-up. You did great in college."

After she spent five years trying to figure out what she wanted to do. She'd gone from majoring in theater to business to philosophy, finally ending with a degree in psychology and then rapidly figuring out there was nothing she wanted to do in psychology.

Carys had enough to worry about. "Maybe I will look into another club," Daisy said.

But she loved this one. She loved the fact The Hideout wasn't elegant like Gabriel's father's club, or sleek and modern like Sanctum. It was a little run-down and needed some care, but it was theirs. They were building it.

Well, her brother and his friends were. They got nervous when she wanted to help with anything but bringing them beers. She hadn't meant to nearly bring down a whole wall.

"I have an interesting idea." Carys had the biggest smile on her face. It was a smile Daisy hadn't seen on her friend in weeks. "Tonight you don't have to find a new club. It's masquerade night and we have visitors. We have Doms you've never met before."

And Nathan Carter, who hadn't seen her in years. He'd probably seen pictures of her, but she didn't take great pics most of the time. It was why it had hurt to dump the one with the cartel. She'd gotten in the right light… She was drifting.

She *had* seen pictures of Nate. She followed his mom and sister on social media, even though the gorgeous weirdo didn't have a single page of his own. He was still the most beautiful man she'd ever seen.

He might know her. He might take one look at her and laugh.

But she was curious. There was only one problem. "I don't have any fet wear here. It's all at the cleaners." She didn't own much in the first place. "I wasn't expecting to play anytime soon, much less attend a masked party."

Carys seemed to think for a moment. "I would loan you some of mine, but…"

"My boobs are way too big. My hips, too." She was a curvy girl, and there wasn't anything she seemed to be able to do about it. She worried her ample curves were one of the reasons the Doms weren't rushing in to play with her.

Carys's eyes narrowed. "Sure. They're too big. Like I said you're gorgeous and sexy as hell. I don't know what's going on. But you're right. What I have on hand won't fit you, but the twins were planning on attending so I would bet they've got fet wear in their lockers. Let me check real quick. Kenzie is smaller than you, but she wears a lot of stretchy fabrics."

"I thought they were…on assignment for McKay-Taggart." She'd been taught never to say the words *central* and *intelligence* or *Agency* when referring to the twins or Cooper or Tristan. Or Zach, even though he wasn't on the payroll at MT.

Carys snorted. "Sure they are." She pulled out her cell and popped in a number, pressing the screen to put it on speaker phone.

"Hey, Carys. What's going on?" a familiar voice said.

"Oooo, it's Carys? Ask her about the bachelorette party," another voice said.

The first had been Kenzie Taggart and the second Louisa Ward.

"I don't think I'm up for it, Lou," Carys said with a sigh. "This rotation is kicking my ass, and I barely have time to get ready for the wedding."

"Then we'll call it a girls hang," Kenzie offered. "I promise no wild strippers. I will keep Kala away from all the planning. Lou will handle it and Kala will handle Lou's, and I'll make sure Tasha's is in Vegas and we all act out *The Hangover*. Who would have guessed marriage would be so fun? Hey, sis, you've got someone coming up on your left. Yeah, he's definitely armed."

Were they actually working an op right now? "Uh, maybe we should call back."

"Is that Dais? Hey, Daisy. You doing okay?" Kenzie's tone had changed from bouncy to sympathetic.

Yeah, she got sympathy from all the girls. Especially the ones who were a little older than she was. Carys's crowd tended to take on big sister roles. "I'm great."

"She's not," Carys corrected. "She's lonely and wants to play tonight."

"I wanted to play tonight," Kenzie grumbled. "But no, I have to go to work. Have to save the world. Just once I wish I could save the world on, say, a Monday night. Yeah, Zach, he's coming your way. Wow, that is a big knife. You should avoid getting stabbed today. Lou, can you cut the lights to the last room on the second floor in the east wing?"

"On it," Lou said.

Yep, they were definitely working an op. Apparently Kenzie was excellent at multitasking. "I don't have to play."

She'd probably caused enough trouble for one day.

Carys shushed her. "Yeah, about that. Did you have what you were going to wear in your locker? Dais doesn't have any fet wear here, and it's not like after today she can go out on her own and grab some. Did Coop fill you in?"

"Yes," Kenzie replied. "He almost missed the plane. Zach gave him hell until he found out why. You know everyone loves you, Dais. And yes, I totally have my costume. It should fit her. There's a mask to go with it. I wish I was there. There are a couple of new guys I would love to introduce Daisy to. Oh, shit. Uh, we've got a big problem. Yes, that's a bomb. Guys, I'm going to have to call back. No. Not you, Coop. I'm talking to Dais and Carys. Zach, that is rude, and yes, I'm hanging up. The mask is on the top shelf. Dais, have a blast. Kala, do not cut the blue wire…"

The line went dead.

"Do you think they're okay?"

Carys stood up and went to Kenzie's locker. She put the code in and opened it, pulling out an angelic-looking corset and a white feathered mask. "They'll be fine. They always are. It's just Kala thinks she knows how to defuse bombs better than she actually does. Or so I've heard. A long time ago." Carys frowned. "Maybe pretend I didn't say anything."

She wasn't sure what was going on, but she also knew better than to ask about Tristan. The threesome seemed to have split up over some vague reason they weren't talking about, but she was almost certain Aidan still talked to Tris on a regular basis. Instead she stared at the corset in Carys's hands.

Could she pretend to be someone else for a night? Someone who didn't screw everything up. Someone who could tempt a Dom into play for a night.

"Do you think it'll work?" Daisy stood up. Kenzie had excellent taste. The corset was gorgeous. The mask would cover most of her face and might look good against her dark hair.

"I think you'll have the new guys panting after you," Carys replied. "Let's get you ready. Daisy, you're gorgeous, and you should know you deserve to have a night of fun. I just want…"

Daisy groaned. "I'm on birth control. Haven't needed it lately, but I'm on it. And I'll use a condom. If it comes to it. Which it probably won't. But maybe it would be better if my brother didn't know. I worry he'll try to vet anyone who wants to play with me."

"They've already been vetted." Carys started working the stays on the corset. "But you're right. He will want to know who the guy is, and that's not the point of tonight. So I'll go out first, and then you can make your grand entrance after I've distracted him. Though if he asks me, I have to tell him."

"He won't." Her brother would think she was staying far from the dungeon. And he would take Carys to a privacy room most likely. It would be a free-for-all in the dungeon. He wouldn't risk some other Dom touching his precious sub.

But it might be exactly what Daisy needed.

Things were suddenly looking up.

She really hoped the twins dealt with that bomb though.

* * * *

Nate stood at the back of the lounge staring out over the dungeon floor. The Hideout was one of the smaller clubs he'd played at, and it was definitely the most stripped down. The Hideout, he'd been told, was a work in progress. It was open Thursday, Friday, and Saturday nights, and on weekend days a bunch of the members worked on the renovations they were making.

"How's it going?" a deep voice asked. "You must be Aidan's friend from Australia."

He glanced over, and there was a man in dark leathers, a black mask on his face. Nate was wearing one of those himself. The face mask felt weird, but he felt comfortable in leathers. Putting on a set of leathers helped him transition his mindset. It allowed him to let go of his everyday worries.

When he put on leathers and walked into a club, he felt like he belonged.

So why hadn't he found the familiar peace here tonight?

Nate held a hand out. "Nate Carter."

"Seth Taggart," the other man said, shaking his hand.

"Ah, you must be one of Ian's." Nate stepped back, settling against the railing that demarked the lounge area from the dungeon. The lounge was on the second floor, so whoever was occupying the space could look out over the dungeon.

A bloke could stare out over the sea of gorgeous subs and wonder why none of them called to him.

"Yep, he's my dad. I hear you're his new hire," Seth said, taking a sip of the beer in his hand. "Good luck. All of my siblings and most of my cousins have worked at McKay-Taggart at one point or another. Mostly as summer jobs. I lasted maybe a month before I begged to wash dishes at my uncle's restaurant. My dad is a sarcastic asshole. I love him but I cannot work for the man."

"I suppose I'm used to the type. Spent some time in the Army," Nate replied. "Also, I'm in the bodyguard unit, so I don't see much of the upstairs folk. At least not yet. My boss is Tessa Hawthorne."

Seth nodded. "Yeah. She took over when Wade Rycroft got an executive job at Lodge Corp. To say my dad was unhappy would be like saying a nuclear bomb causes a little mess. At least they didn't take his assistant. I don't know what my father would do without Genny Rycroft. But Tessa's awesome. She's much easier to get along with than my father. The key with my dad is to pretend like nothing bothers you. Ever. Nod and agree with him, and then go do whatever you were going to do in the first place. It's how I survived my childhood."

Nate had to chuckle at the thought. "I grew up around a group very much like the one here in Dallas."

"That's right. Aidan was telling me you spent most of your childhood in London, right? Your dad worked for Damon Knight," Seth said. "I'm sure we've met at some point."

"Probably, though we were much younger. We moved back to Australia when I was eleven, and our visits here became more infrequent." He'd lost touch with some of his closest friends from childhood. He'd heard Oliver Knight was working with his dad. He'd been close to Oliver and his brother, Archie, and their sister, Samantha, had been around Elodie's age.

It was his mom's relationship with Avery O'Donnell that had kept him close to Aidan, and even they had gotten distant when he'd gone into the Army and Aidan had gone into college and then medical school.

It was odd how easily they'd fallen back in.

"Yeah, life catches up to you, doesn't it? I live close to a bunch of the kids I grew up with, but sometimes I only seem to see them on nights like this. Starting this club actually kept us all together. Huh. I always thought it was because my sisters and their friends were perverts," Seth said thoughtfully. "Now I have to wonder. Not about Kala, but Kenzie might have thought this was a way to keep us all together."

"Are you the older son or the younger one?" Aidan had been on an opposite schedule the week since Nate had gotten in, and honestly, he'd been trying to adjust to his new American time zone. It would be good to start putting names to faces.

Like Daisy O'Donnell, who he would meet later tonight when he got home.

"Older," Seth explained. "You might have seen my younger brother, Travis. He was the dude asleep on the couch in the locker room."

He'd wondered about the bloke snoring away earlier in the evening. The men's locker room wasn't elegant, but it had its charms, including a big living room area with a TV and game systems and a couple of couches, one of which had been occupied by a sleeping Taggart. "Is he okay?"

Seth stared out over the dungeon floor as though looking for someone. "It depends on your definition of the word okay. He's a third-year law student and a single dad with an infant. This is the night my parents agreed to watch his son so he could have some form of a social life, and what does he do? He falls asleep in the locker room during the wildest party of the year. Didn't even manage to get a beer in. I knew he likely wouldn't indulge in the sex part of the evening, but I thought he would at least get a little drunk."

Poor guy probably wasn't sleeping at all between school and parenting. He felt for Travis Taggart.

He checked his pocket. Yes. The condoms he'd snagged were in there. Just in case.

"Is there a reason you're not down there? It really is a wild time," Seth said. "We only do it once a year, though it gets talked about for months after. The couples of the group tend to either skip this party or sit up here and watch the chaos."

Aidan had taken one look at Carys and swept her away, picking her up and carrying her toward the privacy rooms. He'd told Nate he would see him at home.

"I don't know." He wasn't sure this was the right night to make his debut at The Hideout. The idea of some giant orgy wasn't appealing.

Of course an orgy wasn't what was happening. It was more like a slow rotation of Doms around subs before one of the Doms would gently move in and separate his selected treat for the evening from the crowd.

He understood what a party like this was for. Exploration. It was for indulging in something that in this group wouldn't come back to bite a bloke in the arse.

A couple was already playing on the main stage. A big Dom in all black had a tiny sub tied to a St. Andrew's Cross, and he was using a violet wand on her nipples.

It should have him aroused, but he was still strangely numb.

He wanted to blame it all on jet lag, but he was over it. And the numbness was exactly why he'd taken the job in the first place. It wasn't working.

"Then this is not your night because the chaos is part of the fun. It's also a great way for a smart woman to indulge in self-delusion." Seth stared out as a couple of subs walked in from the locker room. One of them was a petite sub in a red catsuit and matching mask, dark hair piled high on her head. She was whispering to her blonde friend and seeming to look around for someone. "I think I'm going to go downstairs. Hope you find what you're looking for. I'm going after what I need tonight."

Seth strode toward the stairs. He obviously knew what he wanted. Nate stared out again, trying to figure out which gorgeous sub had caught Taggart's eye, but before Taggart came into view a woman in white stepped out from the hallway leading to the locker rooms, and Nate felt like the world slowed down.

Long, dark hair caressed rounded shoulders, tumbling over a set of truly gorgeous breasts. They were offered up by the pure white corset that cinched in her waist and flowed over hips he could hold on to. She stopped at the edge of the crowd, staring out as though trying to decide if she would join them. The white boy shorts she wore barely covered a spectacular arse.

She was a beauty, and he felt a rip of pure lust go through him, making his cock tighten and sparking his dominant instincts.

A Dom approached her, his every move seemingly predatory. His lips curled as he moved in close. She turned her chin up and said something. The Dom suddenly stepped back as though shocked. His hands came to his chest, palms out, and he backed away.

The pretty sub's face fell. She glanced around the dungeon and seemed to realize there were a lot of eyes on her, but now the first Dom was talking to another, and they all seemed to ease away from her. One of the subs moved in, but she shook her off. Her head came up and he watched as she pasted a smile on her face and squared her shoulders. She leaned over to the other sub who nodded, and then the gorgeous woman turned to the stairs.

She was coming up here. What the hell had happened? Why had that asshole taken one look at her and rejected her? She was simply the most stunning woman in the place.

He turned, watching as she climbed the stairs in her stilettos. She moved as though she was used to walking in what had to be five-inch heels. He would bet she was quite petite, but those heels brought her close to being as tall as most of the men around her.

She might come to his shoulders. Maybe.

His gaze caught on her as she stepped into the lounge. She smiled at the bartender, who seemed to know her, but she waved him off and started toward the railing.

Then stopped and simply stared his way.

Low and sexy hip-hop played through the whole space, forming a soundtrack that could absolutely be used for sex, but it all faded into the background as he got his first good look at her.

She was every bit as gorgeous as he'd suspected.

She turned suddenly, and he realized he wasn't going to let her go. This was the most he'd felt in forever, and he wasn't willing to end it. He could be intimidating, but he could also charm a lady. He suddenly really wanted to charm this one.

Before he could take a step toward her, she turned again, and there was determination in the way she strode toward him.

"Hello, Sir." She stood in front of him, her shoulders back and chin up. "You must be new around here. I wanted to welcome you to The Hideout. If you have any questions, I'll be hanging around tonight. I know the place very well."

So she was a regular. It made him wonder what kind of drama was going on with her that the other Doms seemed to back away. And then he had to admit he didn't give a shit. She was standing there, and it was obvious it had taken some courage for her to get rejected and try again.

Brave sub. Gorgeous sub.

There it was. His cock tightened for the first time in forever, and for a moment it felt like he could breathe again. He hadn't realized how tight his life had become, how like a vise it felt around his chest until this moment.

She'd asked him to come to her if he had questions. He had one for her.

"Do you have a partner for the night?" Nate asked.

Gorgeous green eyes flared behind her elaborate white mask. "Do I… No. I don't."

"Would you like one?" He could feel the fucking heat between them.

He had to hope the heat he felt seared them both.

Her head nodded. "Yeah. Yes, I would, Sir. If you're the partner, I would like very much to play."

He held a hand out, and when she placed hers in it, he knew the night would change everything.

Chapter Four

Daisy looked up at the man who could only be Nathan Carter and placed her hand in his. Her breath had caught the minute she'd seen him, and she'd been a freaking teenaged girl with a crush all over again.

She knew she should tell him who she was, but names were optional tonight. If he'd wanted to get to know a woman, he would have come on a night when they didn't all wear masks.

Though the mask hadn't helped her with Gabriel Lodge. He'd moved in and started to ask her to play when he'd realized who she was.

Nate didn't seem to have the same instincts. Of course he hadn't spent almost every Saturday night with her for the last couple of years.

"You can call me Sir. What should I call you, sweetheart?" His hand enveloped hers.

That accent went straight to her pussy, or maybe it was how heat sizzled along her skin where he touched her. He was so big and strong he made the other men look like boys. "You can call me Dee."

She wasn't about to say *Hey, I'm Daisy O'Donnell. You remember the awkward kid who followed you around and wrote our names together in notebooks with hearts and arrows?* No way.

She wasn't Daisy O'Donnell tonight. Tonight she was Dee, an eager to please sub who might get an orgasm from the big bad Dom this evening.

Though Daisy was always an optimist, she had no delusions Nate Carter would fall in love with her. He might be horrified if he ever put two and two together, but after her talk with Carys tonight, this might be her last hurrah at The Hideout. When Gabe had looked horrified to even see her, she'd made the decision to change clubs. She needed somewhere people didn't view her as a joke.

So she had tonight, and she was going to make it count.

"How long have you been in the lifestyle, Dee?" Nate asked, his eyes trailing over her.

It felt good to have someone look at her like she was beautiful, like she was sexy and he couldn't wait to get his hands on her. "A few years now, but I've never had a permanent Dominant partner. I've taken all the classes, but I haven't played much. I usually hang out in the lounge."

"Do the Doms here not have bloody eyes?" Nate muttered the question under his breath but seemed to push the thought away. "Well, there's some luck for me then. I've been in the lifestyle for a long time, was raised in it. My parents are a D/s couple. I know a lot of the members here grew up in the lifestyle. My parents aren't 24/7, but they do bring a bit of it into their normal lives."

"My parents pretty much keep it to the club and the bedroom." Her parents were an excellent example of true partners. Her mother took care of the things her da wasn't good at, and he shouldered the load she was weaker on. "But that's all a way of saying even though I haven't practiced a lot, I'm not a newbie. We don't need a contract for tonight. I use the stoplight system for safe words. I enjoy bondage and a pretty big bite of pain. Humiliation play is a hard no for me."

One hand moved up her arm, sending sparks through her. "I enjoy tying a pretty sub up. How do you feel about getting naked at some point in time?"

Shedding her clothes for this man wouldn't be a hardship. "I'm good with it. You should know I react well to praise. Despite what people around here will tell you, I'm not a heinous brat. I would rather please you."

A brow rose over seriously blue eyes. "Do you have a problem with the Doms here? Am I getting involved with a sub with a reputation?"

Not the kind she wanted. She had to blink because emotion welled inside her. She was going to miss this place, but maybe it had been too much to think she could fit in at this club. She was always going to be Aidan's kid sister at The Hideout. Somehow it didn't come into play with the others, but the Doms couldn't see past it when it came to her. "It hasn't worked out for me here. It's a great club, but this is my last night. I'm moving to another club. I was hoping to make some memories tonight."

"I'm struggling to figure out why you didn't have ten Doms on top of you the minute you walked onto the dungeon floor." He tugged her closer, his hand going to her chin to tilt it up. "You're a stunner, love."

She wasn't about to tell him why the Doms wouldn't play with her.

The truth was she didn't understand it herself. Devi didn't have the same trouble she did. She didn't play, but there were always Doms trying to tempt her to come out on the dungeon floor.

No one had ever asked her except the two cowboy Doms who came in from time to time, and they'd changed their minds before she could have a session with them.

"I think I'm trouble, Sir. But you can play with me for a night and not get pulled into my drama. Are you planning on making this your home club?"

"Yes. I'm new in town. I recently took a job at McKay-Taggart," he said, but the words felt absent since his eyes wouldn't leave their slow perusal of her body. "I know some of the board members here, so I expect they'll accept my membership."

She was absolutely certain of it, and now that she'd seen him it was probably for the best she changed clubs. He thought she was hot right now because he didn't know her. When he got to know her, he would likely put her right back in the sister bin and pant after the twins or her ex-bosses. Harlow and Ruby played here from time to time. Precisely how she'd gotten the job. They were elegant and competent, and chaos didn't seem to follow them. "You'll like it here. I take it you've had a tour?"

"I have, but I will admit I didn't spend nearly enough time in the privacy suites."

That sounded promising. Privacy would suit her purposes quite nicely. The last thing she needed was one of the Doms seeing her sceneing with this gorgeous man. They might feel the need to warn him. "What are you up for, Sir? The night's young, so most of the rooms should still be open. I happen to know the spanking room is open. And the bondage playroom. I think the medical playroom is occupied."

His nose wrinkled. "I'll pass on the whole doctor-patient thing. My roommate talks way too much about his profession. Even more than my mum. I'd like to tie you up, Dee. I agree to use the stoplight system. I propose we run a bondage scene. I prefer rope. When I have you tied up, I'd like to do some edging play, and can we both agree we're open to the idea of actual sex? I have condoms."

Her whole body tightened at the thought. She knew she should play this cooler but damn it, she didn't want to. The day had been awful, and she was looking at having her freedom curtailed for weeks. She had to find a new club, and the prospect was equal parts scary and depressing. Why couldn't she have one night? One night to indulge. One night to pretend. The next time she saw him she would be Aidan's little sister again, and he wouldn't look at her the same way. "I agree to your terms, Sir."

"Then lead the way, sub." He stepped back, but his hand was on hers again.

She led the way through the back of the lounge to where a bank of privacy rooms were located. And also a dungeon monitor. A familiar-looking Dom.

Hunter McKay was dressed for the party, but it was obvious he was working. He gave her a once-over. The same one Gabriel Lodge had given. Hunter was six foot four and built like a linebacker, so it was odd to see how small he was in comparison to Nate Carter.

"Hello, gorgeous," he began and then seemed to recognize her. "Whoa. Sorry about that. Hey, does A…"

She let go of Nate's hand and moved in closer. "I would like to remind you what night it is," she said quietly. "The rules are in play, Hunter. Are you going to break them? Why does my brother need to know what his adult sister is doing in a club she holds a membership to? Should I have a talk with your mother? I'm feeling the need for a session or two about how the men in my life treat me."

Even in the low light she could see the way Hunter paled. His mother was Eve McKay, and she would be pissed if she thought her son was infantilizing the perfectly capable adult women around him. The aunties in her life were pretty kick ass, and she would invoke their names now to get what she wanted.

One hot night with the Dom of her dreams.

"Which room were you thinking of?" Hunter asked politely. "They're all open except four."

"We're going to use room two, thank you," she said, and stepped back to allow Nate to take the key from Hunter.

Hunter put the key in Nate's hands. "Go with god, man."

Daisy tugged him toward the room.

"Okay, that was weird," Nate said, following along.

"He likes to joke." She stopped at the door, turning his way. "Everyone's sarcastic around here." Her heart fell as she realized he was glancing back at Hunter, a wary look on his face. Had Nate heard her threaten Hunter with Aunt Eve? Probably not the sexiest thing she could have done. "It's okay if you changed your mind."

He turned back to her. "I haven't changed my mind. Not about you, but I'm starting to wonder about the club. I feel like there's something going on I don't understand. I don't like how they're treating you."

"They're joking," she said quietly. "But if it bothers you, we don't have to go any further. I will understand, Sir. This night is supposed to be easy. No names if you don't want them. No expectations. No drama. One night of pleasure. You don't have to worry about anything except pleasing me, and I'll do the same for you. But if you're worried I'll drag you into some kind of…"

She wasn't even sure what she would call it, but he stopped her.

"I'm not worried about getting dragged into something. I'm rather worried I won't be. But you're right. It's one night, and I want to spend it with you. I don't think you understand how much." He got into her space again, his body brushing hers. "I'm getting in my head, and I'm pretty sure overthinking could fuck me over tonight."

"Don't think tonight, Sir. Just feel." It was what she wanted to do. It was the only thing she wanted to do. Tomorrow she would go into the office and he would be one floor beneath her and so far away it would hurt. She would watch him from the shadows after tonight, so she wanted to make it count.

"I'm going to kiss you," he said, his voice low.

The truth was the words formed a sort of question. They were a warning so she could use one of those safe words if she wanted to. She simply lifted her chin and went on her toes, thanking the universe Kenzie Taggart loved high heels and they wore the same size shoe.

How long had it been since she'd been kissed? Over a year? Her heart rate ticked up as he lowered his head to hers, and then heat sparked through her. He was overwhelming. There was no soft, sweet brushing of lips. He placed his hands on either side of her face and gently held her while he devoured her mouth.

Longing welled inside her, warring with the outrageous sexual desire she felt for this man. Her body felt electric for the first time in…for the first time. She let her hands find his waist, touching the warm skin covering his muscular body. He was so big. It would be easy to drown in him. And she would do it willingly.

When he opened the door, she followed him. It didn't matter if she was likely making a terrible mistake. She was going to take this time with him, and then she would be done.

* * * *

Nate wasn't sure what the dungeon monitor had been on about, but the mystery of how all the Doms seemed to treat this particular submissive would have to wait.

He closed the door behind them and watched as she ran a hand over the big bed in the corner of the room. The instinct to simply throw her on it and have her was almost overwhelming.

It felt fucking good to feel anything at all. Like someone had switched him back on the minute she'd walked into the room.

He wasn't going to question it. If it was a mistake, then he would make it happily and take it to the outer edges of way too far.

He set his kit on the table by the door. The room had a St. Andrew's Cross and multiple hooks and apparatuses to accommodate bondage and rigging. There was a dresser he was sure was stocked with helpful items should a Dom find himself ill prepared.

Nate was a freaking Boy Scout.

"Where would you like me, Sir?"

Her every word went straight to his cock. It would be so easy to do what she said she wanted—keep this simple. Play and sex and nothing else.

He didn't want simple. "Tell me one thing about yourself."

Her eyes widened behind the elaborate mask on her face. "I thought this was a moment out of time."

She was wary. He could work with that. "Sure. So in this moment out of time, tell me something about yourself."

She bit her plump bottom lip and looked a wee bit nervous. "What kind of thing about myself? Like where I went to high school or college? What my favorite color is?"

He rather thought she was trying to point out how silly he was being when they were here for play. She would be an unconscionable brat. Perhaps that was what had gone wrong with the Doms here. They couldn't handle her. She didn't have to leave her home club. She'd found the right Dom.

It occurred to Nate how oddly he was behaving. He wasn't this guy. He didn't walk into a room, point to his chosen woman of the night, and carry her away. He was thoughtful. He planned. He didn't throw himself into anything.

But this felt right.

She looked gorgeous, like the sweetest, sexiest treat he'd ever been offered. She was petite but had solid curves. "Come here."

She moved across the room, joining him.

"Turn around and place your hands flat on the bench, arse in the air."

Her mouth came open. "What?"

It was good to know he could surprise her. "It's ten right now. Do you want to make it twenty? I assure you I can spank you for however long it takes."

"Takes to what?"

He intended to make things plain to her. "Get you to understand I'm the Dom in this room and you don't have to hide behind sarcasm. I asked for something of you, something that costs you nothing. You could tell me anything. You could tell me a lie, though I would prefer you didn't. I asked you politely."

"You did not. You didn't ask at all," she shot back, and then her nose wrinkled. "Fine. You want to know something about me? I didn't plan on playing tonight. I had to borrow these clothes from a friend."

She turned and did as he'd asked, leaning over the bench and placing her palms down on the padding. She wore a pair of boy shorts barely covering her luscious backside.

His cock tightened, and he moved in behind her. "Why were you here if you didn't want to play?"

He let his hand find the curve of her cheeks, running over them before delving right past the hem of the shorts.

A gasp came out of her mouth. "I spend a lot of nights hanging out in the lounge or the locker room. My friends are usually here."

He brought his hand back and then slapped her ass. Hard. It would be better if she was naked and he could see the way her flesh pinkened up, but the way her breathing hitched and her hands clutched the bench was more than enough. "Then why would you leave? If your friends are here?"

"This isn't fair, Sir. You said one thing." She'd turned her face toward him, a stubborn expression in her eyes. "Now I'm getting the spanking and all the questions."

He slapped her cheeks again, sending a low groan through her. "Fine. Ask me something."

"Why did you leave Australia?"

Another hard smack. She couldn't know it, but it was precisely the question he didn't want to answer. But she'd been honest with him. "I was in the Army. I thought I would be there for life. It turned out to not be what I needed, so I worked my parents' station for a while. You would call it a ranch. Being a cowboy wasn't for me either. So why did I leave Australia? I suppose I'm trying to find myself, though it sounds ridiculous."

Her head dropped forward when he smacked her right cheek. "No, it doesn't. It sounds real. Thank you for sharing with me, Sir. I'm leaving the club for the same reasons. I thought I could find what I needed here, but I didn't. All I found was frustration."

He didn't get it. She was fucking gorgeous. If he'd taken her into the club in Sydney, he would have to fight to keep the damn Doms off her. "You'll find frustration tonight, but I want you to trust it'll pay off. I promise. You can curse my name, love, but you'll be calling it out by the end of the evening."

He peppered her ass with three quick slaps, moving them around.

"It already is better than anything I've had, Sir. I didn't…I didn't realize how much I needed this," she said, her voice shaky. "I haven't gotten spanked since my training, and it didn't feel like this."

The only reason to come to a club like this was to serve a need deep inside, to find acceptance inside a community of like-minded people. What had happened to Dee? He wanted to push her, to figure out her situation, but that served his needs, not hers.

If he gave her what she required, would she dismiss him at the end of the night? Or would she take the mask off and get real with him.

Was this feeling what he'd been chasing all his life?

Another two smacks. He kept a careful count. "I've had a sub before, but it was more about training. I was the one being trained, of course."

Her lips curled up, and then she huffed out a laugh as he spanked her again. "I like how open you are. Sometimes Doms don't admit they need any training at all. Like they were born knowing how to spank a girl."

"Or a guy." He slowed down because they were approaching the end of her punishment. One more smack, and this time he held his hand to her cheek, feeling the ample curve of her arse. "I trained with her for six months and then I bounced around. Being in the Army isn't conducive to having a D/s relationship in a long-term sense. One more, love. Are you ready?"

"If I say no, will you keep going?" she asked.

He smacked her pretty cheek hard, sending a shiver through her. "No, because there's something else I need. I want you naked and bound. I want to frustrate you in the sweetest way. You say you haven't experienced what you should have. Well, I'm going to change that tonight. Stand."

She raised herself up. Her skin was flushed, and her hair mussed. She looked like sex to him. "You're a bossy man."

He wasn't. He was an easygoing man. He'd learned from a young age his size alone intimidated people, so he had to carefully control himself. He kept his anger in check along with all those other pesky emotions. He was the guy who never let anything shake his calm. Calm was getting boring. "You remember what I said. Turn around and I'll get you out of your corset. Unless you want me to cut it off you. I've got a wicked-sharp knife. It would be quicker."

She seemed to take the threat seriously, turning and holding her arms out so he could easily get at the stays. "Not my corset. I'm already going to have to have it cleaned. I would prefer not to have to replace it. I'm afraid things haven't been easy on the job front."

He quickly worked the ties, a skill he'd learned at the hands of his training sub. She'd been slightly older and kind. He'd enjoyed his relationship with her, including some fairly filthy sex.

But nothing had ever sparked him the way Dee did.

"Then I'll be careful." He wanted to ask her about her job, but he'd pushed her enough on the question front. It was easy to see the woman was wary. As he had no intention of this being some damn moment out of time, he needed to show her what he could offer.

Pleasure.

She wanted D/s sex, he could give it to her.

He eased the corset over her head and set it aside. He pushed her hair back and did what came naturally, running his hands along her shoulders before lowering his mouth to kiss the nape of her neck. "You are the most gorgeous woman I've ever seen. You walked into the room and there was no one else in it for me."

A slow breath shuddered through her. "Thank you, Sir. I'm afraid I haven't been my normal, confident self lately. Thank you for giving that back to me. If it helps, you should know when I saw you in the lounge, I knew you were a tree I wanted to climb."

The words sent a chuckle through him, and he allowed his hands to move around her torso, cupping her breasts. She leaned back in against him.

He went to kiss her cheek, but the mask was in the way. "Can we get rid of these masks, Dee? I don't think we need them."

She went stiff in his arms. "It's not allowed."

"We're alone, and the rules are adaptable." It was the nature of D/s. They made their own rules.

She stepped away from him. "I want to keep mine, Sir. I'm playing a part tonight, one I don't ever get to play."

"It's not a role. It's a part of you."

"It feels very much like a role. I can't..." she began.

He was pushing when she needed his patience. "Put your hands in front of you. Clasp them together. Like a prayer."

She hesitated. "Sir..."

"You want to play a role? You're my sub for the night. I won't touch the mask. I'll leave mine on, but it's nothing more than a flimsy piece of armor, love. You keep it on all you like, but I'll get underneath your skin. I don't think you need another club. You simply need the right top. Do as I asked or it's twenty this time."

She looked so fucking innocent standing there with her pretty tits on display, still wearing white boy shorts and those fuck-me heels. How did she manage to look like a fucking angel? Her arms came out, and he knew they'd passed the crisis. Now all he had to do was convince Dee.

He took out his rope and began to bind her.

Chapter Five

Daisy took a deep breath, trying to adjust to being hung from a hook in the ceiling. Her feet were barely on the ground, her body strung out like a fiddle the man planned on playing.

He'd taken his time binding her hands together and then easing her on the hook of his choice. He'd stared at her for long moments, making her feel like a work of art.

She'd been so tempted to take off her mask when he'd asked about it. To rip it off and ask him to call her Daisy and to be her Dom forever.

And then she'd remembered.

It was better this way.

He was making her crazy. He was just standing there looking at her.

She started to open her mouth and a brow rose above his eyes, a serious expression that sent her subby self a stark warning.

Her butt still ached. Not in a bad way. In a kind of cool way, but she also wasn't some hard bottom used to getting her ass smacked for hours. It was the kind of thing a girl worked up to. Training. She needed more training. With him.

Nope. She wasn't going there. She was going to use this beautiful man and then get away with her whole heart.

And her whole ass.

"Good choice, love." The words rumbled out of his mouth. He was so sexy standing there in his leathers. The mask made him look slightly sinister, and it did something for her.

It made her almost forget what she knew about him. How calm he was, how easygoing.

Pretty much the opposite of her. The kind of man who would want some peace in his life, who would see her as flaky and ridiculous.

"These are coming off." He dropped to his knees but somehow still managed to be on the same level as her very excited nipples.

All of her pink parts were singing. She was going to have to replace the boy shorts because while the corset could be cleaned, she wasn't sure she could do the same for the shorts. They were soaked through after his spanking had brought her to new heights of arousal.

He eased the shorts down her legs, his mouth so close to her breasts. It was maddening. He was right there.

Well, he'd told her she would be frustrated. When he'd mentioned edging, she'd gotten excited. It wasn't something she'd tried before, but it sounded fun.

She might have to rethink the idea.

"I'll leave you the shoes."

It was good because without them she would be dangling. Still, she'd learned one lesson with him. When this man was in top space, she should rethink her sarcastic bent. "Thank you, Sir."

He stood, and the bastard brought her shorts right up to his nose, breathing in the scent. "You liked your spanking."

She was naked and bound. It was kind of everything she'd hoped for when she'd started this journey. To trust someone enough to try anything with him, to push all her boundaries. To take sex and her own pleasure seriously. "Yes, I did, Sir. Far more than I thought I would."

"You've never been spanked? What kind of training program are they running here?"

The kind where her training Dom used to play with her. With dolls and on playground equipment. Jamie Murdoch was the sweetest guy, but he hadn't put a lot of force behind his spankings. Which was weird since some of the other subs talked about what a hardass he could be. "I don't think my training Dom thought I could handle anything rough. I like it rough."

"You responded to it beautifully. I suspect you would like a lot of forms of impact play. Like flogging and paddling and getting a whip taken to your backside so you feel it all the next day." Every word out of his mouth was pure seduction. "If you were my submissive, I would train you all over again. I would make sure you understood every single filthy thing I want to do to you now that I have you wrapped in my ropes."

She felt her nipples tighten. "I think you should show me, Sir."

His lips curled up in the sexiest smirk. "I think you're right. We should begin."

An hour later, Daisy was absolutely certain she was going to die. "Sir, please. Please."

"I am pleased," he replied, holding the vibrator in his hand and watching as she writhed on the bench.

He'd started his torture with a damn feather. He'd run it over her skin, leaving a trail of arousal everywhere he'd gone. He'd balanced it with a violet wand, sparking it across her skin and making her squirm. Every now and then he would touch the wand to her nipples, and she would bite back a scream. Then he would lean over and lick her and she would forget to breathe.

After a while, he'd brought her off the hook and tied her to the bench, her ass in the air and leaving her so fucking vulnerable to him. That was when he'd brought out the cane. It had been flexible and thin, and it had cracked over her like a revelation.

He would give her a few swats and then the man dropped to his knees and gave her a few licks. With his tongue. On her pussy. He would lick her until she was so close to heaven and then she would feel him move away and the pain would flare over her skin and he would start the process all over again.

And again.

And again.

After a while on the bench, he'd picked her up like she weighed nothing and moved her over to the bed.

Then he'd brought out the vibrator.

"I'm very pleased, love," Nate said, his fingers trailing down her torso. He circled her right nipple before giving it a nasty tweak. "You've taken everything I've given you."

"You could give me more." She'd been on the edge of orgasm more times than she could count. Every time she thought she would go off, he pulled away. Like he knew. Like he truly saw her. Like they were connected somehow.

He flicked the body wand on, the sound making her pussy clench. He stared at her for a moment as though memorizing the way her body looked, how it felt to be in this moment.

Needy. Wanton. Anticipation filling her whole world.

This was what she'd needed for so long, and now that she had it she wondered how she was ever going to live without it.

He moved in. "I want you to give me everything you have, Dee. I want all of it, and then tell me I can have you."

Again, not a question, but as much as she would get from a top like him. "Please, Sir. Please have me."

She wanted his cock more than she wanted her next breath, but beyond that she wanted connection to this man. Being here with him fulfilled so damn many of her fantasies. It would have to be enough since they only got this one night. She would dream about him for the rest of her life.

"Spread your legs wider."

Her arms were over her head, wrists still bound, and now she was as taut as a bowstring, every muscle waiting to go off. She spread her legs for him and felt the sweet pang of vulnerability. She couldn't guard herself here. He'd told her the mask was helping her to play a role, but he didn't understand how much of her secret self was here in this bed with him, a piece of herself she'd never shared with anyone else.

She worried she might never be able to share this part again.

Daisy felt the first hum of the vibrator, and it was all she needed. He'd been priming her for this for what felt like hours. All the sweet torture he'd lavished on her body prepped her for an orgasm like none she'd had before. It rolled over her, making her gasp and writhe on the bed as he stroked her clit again and again.

Then he tossed the vibe aside, and she watched as he shoved his leathers down and his cock sprang free. His cock was built to size. Nate Carter was six foot seven and massive and his cock was huge. She wanted to stroke him, to play with that monster cock and make him crazy, but her hands were tied, and it looked like her Sir was done playing.

He rolled a condom on and stepped between her legs. Then he slowly reached up and took off his mask, revealing his handsome, rugged face. "Dee, my name is Nathan. I want you to know I don't have any intention of letting you leave this club."

Before she could protest—she probably wouldn't have in the moment since it felt way too good to have him want her—he started to work his cock inside.

Daisy groaned as he thrust in gentle motions, giving her time to get used to his size. She stared up at him, wishing she could get her arms around him, wishing they could stay in this moment forever. They were too far apart. He was standing at the edge of the bed, tilting her hips for easier access, but she wanted him closer.

It was the sacrifice she would have to make to have this memory because even in the moment she knew she wouldn't be taking off her mask.

She needed it too much.

"You feel so fucking good." His eyes closed as he started to fuck her, holding her hips and finding a rhythm that had her panting all over again.

She'd thought the clitoral stimulation had been incredible, but this was more. He stroked inside her, waking up something that had been sleeping all her life.

Lust. Connection. Satisfaction.

When he went over the edge, she went right there with him.

Nate fell forward but caught himself with one hand. He stayed there for a moment, big chest heaving as he struggled to come down. She could still feel his cock inside her. If he was on top of her, would she feel his heart beating? Would hers synch up with his because they were so in the moment together?

She'd had sex, but it had been nothing like this. Nothing.

Sometimes her friends called her Pandora because chaos seemed to follow her, but now she understood. She'd opened the box, and nothing would be the same again.

Nate took a long breath and stood, gently easing himself out of her. "Stay there, love. I'll be right back."

He moved away, and she heard the door to the bathroom open.

What had she done? It started to crash in on her. She'd had this monumental moment with a man who was close to her family and who she had to pray never found out it had been her.

She'd followed her instincts, and they'd led her to fucking up once again.

Except it was something only she had to know about. She'd worn her mask and hadn't promised the man anything beyond a hot night. She wasn't Daisy O'Donnell here. She was Dee, and Dee was going to find a new club.

Daisy and Dee would both think about Nate Carter for the rest of her life.

"Here. Let me get you out of those and we can talk," he said, his lips curled up in a grin. "Although I have to tell you, you look like heaven, love. I kind of wish I could wrap you up in my ropes and drag you home with me."

Home would be lovely, but she wasn't allowed to go home tonight. Tonight, if she took him with her, Nate would be surprised when she gave him his own address. She had to hope he was an early riser. "I think it might be hard for me to get to my new job with my hands tied like this."

He helped her sit up, and it was weirdly not awkward as he started to untie her.

She didn't want this to end. She also wasn't sure he would simply let her walk away. Her night wasn't over. The only person who'd seen her walk in here with Nate was Hunter, and she had to make sure he understood it was in his best interest to keep his mouth shut. She had to get away without anyone else seeing her with Nate or there would be talk she didn't want to deal with.

She didn't want to leave him.

"Still not ready to take the mask off, eh?" Nate was staring down at her.

"The party's not over." She hoped she sounded way sexier than she felt. "Why don't you settle in and I'll go clean up?"

A big hand came out to smooth back her hair. "All right, love. You can hide for a little while longer. You sure you want to stay here with me? We could go out to the dungeon for a bit if you like. I'm…I don't want to hurt you. If you're sore…"

She could so fall in love with this man. She tilted her head up. "I'm fine. Someone made sure I was ready for him. But, Sir, I don't think I can handle more hours of torture. Maybe we can cuddle and see where the night takes us. I have no desire to leave this room."

Ever. They could lock themselves away, and she wouldn't have to worry about anything but taking care of him. The world wouldn't matter. Only Nathan Carter.

It wasn't going to happen, but they could hide away for now.

"I'm glad." He helped her to her wobbly feet. "I don't want to go anywhere either, love."

He lowered his head and kissed her. Every muscle felt well used and satisfied. Her head felt like she'd had too much champagne.

"Be quick." He laid his gorgeous body out on the bed, turning to his side to watch her as she walked across the room to the bathroom. He yawned like a lazy lion.

Daisy shut the door between them and turned on the shower.

"I'm only going to get you dirty again," he said from the bedroom.

"Then I'll make you clean me up." She found a towel and slipped out of the mask.

What the hell was she doing?

She heard him chuckle as she refixed her hair, ensuring it wouldn't get wet. Her brain was buzzing as she took her shower and dried off, looking for any way out of this trap. She wasn't sure she had the strength to walk out the door and tell Nate she needed to go.

But she needed to go. Aidan would be looking for her, and the last thing she needed was a big reveal "hey, you slept with my baby sister" scene.

Of course, if she stayed in the bathroom much longer, Nate himself would come looking for her.

She settled the mask on her face and wrapped the towel around her.

When she walked back into the room, she realized she didn't have to fight at all.

He was asleep on the bed, his whole body relaxed. He looked younger, carefree.

The idea she would never see him like this again made her heart ache, but she knew what she had to do.

She quickly dressed and forced herself to slip outside. The minute she left the room, the world came back into focus.

She didn't really belong here, and he did. He was starting a new life, and all she would do was complicate it. He was looking for something and it certainly wasn't her. All she would bring the man was trouble, and he'd given her so much.

"Dais?" Hunter had moved from his desk. "You okay? Are you here with the new guy? Dad told me they hired on the dude who used to hang out with you and Aidan. Nate? Nick?"

There was only one way to handle Hunter McKay. Shock and awe. He was a great guy, but he would talk if she didn't scare him out of it. "Aidan doesn't know and neither does Nate. It's masquerade night. You remember what that means?"

"It means Seth might have a shot at getting in Chloe's thong. It means all the subs who wouldn't touch Lucas because he's a manwhore can pretend they don't know what they're doing. I call it delusion night. It's precisely why I'm working the desk," Hunter shot back. "I know the rules, Dais."

She stared him down. He was a year older than she was, but she knew how to handle him. He was a rules guy. "Are you going to follow them?"

His eyes closed and he sighed. "Do you know what you're doing?"

"It doesn't matter. For now, I'm a member of this club, and you owe me discretion," she insisted.

"I know, but Aidan…"

She was sick of this. "Is my brother, not my father. And honestly, even if my father was here, I'm an adult. I have every right to do what I want in this club. Tell me something, if it was Devi or Bri coming out of a privacy room, would you be clutching your pearls and wondering how fast you can bring the patriarchy down on their heads?"

Hunter's hands came up. "I'm so fucking glad my sister is in London. Go on. I was only trying to look out for you."

It was the whole problem with the club. The problem wasn't that someone cared about her, but sometimes their caring became questioning her choices. If she had one more intervention…

"I'm great. Used a condom and everything." She'd one hundred percent protected her body. She wasn't so sure about her heart.

Daisy strode away and didn't look back.

* * * *

"Hey, how'd your night go, big guy? I asked around and no one said they saw you, but I noticed you weren't home when we got here." Aidan sat at the breakfast table, a mug of coffee in front of him.

Nate needed way more than coffee. He needed to find Dee and take his hand to her backside. He hadn't meant to fall asleep. He'd meant to get inside her again. As many times as it took to get her to take the mask off and get real with him.

That was the problem. It had all felt so real. He'd spent one night with the woman, and he was fairly certain he would never forget her.

The good news was Aidan had been a member of The Hideout since its inception, and he tended to be pretty observant. When the dungeon monitor had woken him up, the club had been closing and his Cinderella hadn't even left behind one of her high heels. No clues to track her by except her name. Well, and a couple of facts.

"I met a sub. We decided to play in private. Look, mate, I need to find her. You know a sub named Dee?" Nate got right to the point. He'd driven himself home and the house had been quiet, though he'd seen a light on in the room normally used by Cooper McKay.

Daisy O'Donnell was staying the night. Just yesterday meeting Daisy again after almost twelve years had seemed like it would be the highlight of his week. Now he could barely work up the will to say hi.

Because all he fucking wanted in the world was Dee.

In the course of a few short hours, he'd become obsessed with a woman for the first time in his life.

Aidan sat up. He was in sweats and a T-shirt, his hair still damp from a morning shower, and his gym bag was slung over his chair. "Dee? We have a couple of members with first names that start with D."

"She said her *name* was Dee."

Carys walked in from the kitchen. She was dressed far more formally than her fiancé. She was in slacks and a pretty shirt, her hair up in a neat bun. "Who said her name was Dee? We don't have a Dee. We have a Daisy and a Devon and Denise. But honestly, it was masquerade night so we had some newbies, and almost no one goes by real names."

"It's kind of a free-for-all," Aidan admitted. "The only rule is what happens at masquerade stays at masquerade. It's a decadent, make-bad-choices kind of night."

"It's supposed to be fun." Carys placed a plate of toast down on the table. "I wouldn't know. I've never been because I've pretty much been engaged since I was five."

Aidan's lips kicked up in a grin. "She's right. Tris and I made this ring in art class…" He sobered as though remembering his partner wasn't here and wouldn't be coming home any time soon. "Well, I've never understood the appeal. I did hear Chloe dumped a beer on Seth's head when he tried to hit on her. I kind of wished I'd seen that."

Carys sat down beside her fiancé and put a hand over his. "You were far too busy playing doctor."

"Damn straight I was." Aidan gave her hand a squeeze before turning back to Nate. "So you got lucky last night? Good for you, man."

Had he listened to a word he'd said? "That's where you're wrong. I'm not lucky because I'm the arsehole who fell asleep on the hottest woman I've ever seen, and now I don't know how to get in touch with her."

Aidan chuckled. "Dude, you fell asleep on her? Seriously? So you want to find her again because you didn't get a chance to play with her?"

"Oh, we played. We played for hours, and when we were done she went to clean up, and I was out like a bloody light," he admitted. "When the monitor woke me up, she was gone. Everyone was, actually. I managed to sleep until the club closed."

"Damn, man. I wish I could help you. What did she look like?" Aidan asked.

"She was fucking gorgeous. I mean that woman was sex walking on two legs. Long, dark hair, gorgeous eyes." The sight of her spread out for his pleasure would haunt him until the day he died. Dee was… She was everything he wanted in a woman, in a sub. "I took one look at her and no one else mattered."

Aidan glanced Carys's way. "There are a lot of pretty subs, and a whole bunch who don't usually attend. I know Chloe brought some friends with her last night. They usually play at The Club. It could be one of them."

Carys was suddenly very interested in her phone. "Yeah, it really could be anyone. She could have been wearing a wig and going by a fake name. A lot of the subs do."

He didn't think Dee had been lying to him, and there was zero way all that silk hadn't been her real hair. "She was in all white. She looked like a fucking angel. And her mask had feathers around the eyes. She was in these super-high heels, and her corset had all these rhinestones on them."

"Sounds like Kenz," Aidan said with a chuckle. "Now that would be funny. It's not. I'm talking about Kenzie Taggart. She's somewhere classified. I'm sure she was pissed to miss the party. Chaos is Kenzie's idea of a good time. Also Kenz has pink hair, though she does have a lot of wigs. I always wonder how she gets all her hair under there. You okay, baby?"

Carys had a hand to her mouth. She'd gone a bright pink. "Yep. Yes. Went down the wrong pipe. I need some water."

Carys stood and strode back to the kitchen.

All of Nate's instincts kicked in. She hadn't taken a drink or eaten anything, so there was nothing to get stuck in any of her pipes, and was that the way a doctor should refer to pieces of human anatomy she'd been regularly tested on?

Carys knew something, and she didn't want to tell him.

"I'm intrigued," Aidan was saying. "I can't think of a single sub I would say is super hot. Now I did grow up with most of them, and I'm the weirdo who hasn't taken his eyes off one woman for years, but I can appreciate other women on a purely aesthetic level." He snapped his fingers as though remembering something. "Daphne O'Malley. She's got dark hair. Green eyes. Pretty girl. She might have come in with Chloe. Hey, Car, do you think it could be Daphne?"

A bright smile was on Carys's face as she returned. "That would fit. Yes, it could definitely be Daphne. She doesn't come into town often, but when she does, she usually spends a night at one of the clubs. I'm almost sure I saw her in the locker room last night."

And he was almost sure she was lying. Nate stared at Carys.

The redhead sat down but seemed to feel his gaze on her.

"Nate and Daphne O'Malley." Aidan didn't seem to feel the tension in the room. "I like it. She's actually a good match for you, man. Like I said, you got lucky. Her parents own this organic cattle ranch a couple of hours south of here. You have ranching in common. Now, I will tell you she's the product of one of those crazy threesomes. You might think about that."

Nate never blinked, simply stared at Carys, who tried to look pretty much anywhere but at him.

"I'm joking," Aidan continued. "Not about the threesome part. Her mom is married to two men. Only one of them is a cattle rancher. Lucas is a lawyer. So when you think about it, it resembles your mom and dad. You've got hard physical labor mixed with super smarts. I mean, if you shoved a successful romance writer in there." Aidan stopped, seeming to understand he was missing something. "Uh, dude you look a little crazy right now."

"What do you know, Carys?" He asked the question in the same tone he would use if he was interrogating someone during an investigation.

Aidan sat up straight. "Hey, let's back down. She doesn't know anything."

Carys's jaw tightened.

"Yeah, she does. She knows exactly who I'm talking about. She knew the minute I described what she was wearing." Nate felt it in his bones. "She saw Dee in the locker room, I would bet. You know who I spent last night with. You saw her."

"I don't know what you're talking about." Carys wasn't a good liar. She had many tells, including the fact she couldn't quite meet his eyes. "Besides, what happens in the locker room stays in the locker room."

Aidan was now staring his fiancée's way. "Since when? I was joking about the whole masquerade thing. You know we'll be talking about last night until the next time. The club runs on gossip. Gabe texted me in the middle of a session to ask me if getting beer in his eyes could make Seth blind, and he was not texting for my medical advice."

"Who was she?" Nate didn't care about what had happened last night in any room other than the one where he'd made love to the most gorgeous submissive he'd ever seen.

"There's a reason we wear masks." Carys's pretty face went stubborn. "She has a right to privacy. If she'd wanted you to know who she was, she would have hung around."

"Or she's a scared little sub since something's happening to her at the club," he replied. He'd thought a lot about this.

"What do you mean?" Aidan asked, all of his focus on Nate again.

"I watched her when she walked out. I didn't like the way some of the Doms treated her." He'd been up early this morning, the problem grinding through his brain. He'd arrived at some conclusions. None of them made him feel better. She'd been happy when they were playing. It had been the minute they were done with the initial sex that she'd gotten anxious. Like she'd needed it so badly, needed the affection and pleasure he'd lavished on her, but when it was done the real world had rushed back in.

"How they treated her?" Aidan looked concerned all of the sudden. "I'm going to need some names. If we've got assholes mistreating the subs, I will handle it. I'm having a hard time believing one of our tops would abuse a sub. They're all well trained, and we have some very specific rules about how to behave in the club."

"She told me she's looking for a new club because she doesn't feel welcome at this one," Nate pointed out.

He'd come to the conclusion she might have been shamed for her sexuality. It was an awful thing to think about since the club was exactly the place where she should feel free to explore. He would bet it was about jealousy. She'd likely had some kind of relationship with one or more of the Doms, and they didn't like the fact she didn't want them now. He'd seen it before, and he didn't intend to let it happen to Dee.

He didn't give a bloody hell how many blokes she'd been with. As long as he was the last.

Aidan pulled his cell out of his pocket. "I don't want anyone to feel run out of The Hideout. That's not happening on my watch. I'll call Gabe. We're in charge while Cooper, Tash, and the twins are out of pocket. And Dare. I can call him in. We'll get to the bottom of this."

"I think Gabe is one of the problems." He hated causing trouble when it wasn't necessary. Drama tended to be a thing he avoided, but this was wrong. He'd seen how hurt Dee had been. "He was one of two tops I saw make her uncomfortable."

Aidan stopped as though the thought didn't quite make sense. "You're telling me you saw Gabriel Lodge abuse a sub?"

He was stepping in it now, but he had to speak up. "Well, he wasn't physical with her. I'm not saying he hit her or wouldn't honor her safe word. They were on the dungeon floor. I was watching from the lounge, but I know whatever he said hurt her feelings. And when we went up to the privacy rooms, there was some weird interaction with the monitor. Like he wasn't going to let her go back or something. I couldn't hear everything she said to him, but it felt like she had to force him to let us go back. Again, I feel like whatever he was doing hurt her."

Carys put a hand to her forehead like she had a headache. "Or maybe it was a misunderstanding."

"What kind of misunderstanding could there be?" Aidan was scrolling through his contacts. "I assure you Gabe knows how to communicate, and I know who was working the desk last night. Hunter is about to get a hearty fucking lecture."

"Please don't call him," Carys said, the tight set of her jaw proving she wished she wasn't having this conversation.

A suspicious brow rose over Aidan's eyes. "Why wouldn't I, baby?" His voice had gone Dom deep. "Are you trying to tell me my friend is lying?"

Damn. When Aidan wanted to top a girl, he knew how to do it. Nate felt a little bad for Carys. "I'm not lying."

Carys took a long breath and turned Nate's way. "No, but you also don't understand what's going on. I do know the sub, and she's got a reputation." She shook her head. "Not one she's earned."

"She was being slut shamed?" It was enough to make him see red, but he was going to hold it together because he was so close to finding out her name.

He would go to Dee and ask her why she'd left. He would ask if he could hold her. He would prove to her he wasn't like those other blokes, and they wouldn't step foot in The Hideout again. Even if it cut him off from his only friend.

"No," Carys said quickly. "It's not like that. Look, I can't say who it is. I can only tell you from what I understand every Dom there tries to watch out for her."

"Watch out for who?" a sweet voice said from the kitchen. "Did someone already make toast?"

Aidan sat straight up at the sound. He leaned over, his voice going low. "That's my sister. We'll talk about this later. I promise I'll get Carys to tell me what's happening, but not around Daisy. If Daisy finds out some sub is in trouble, she'll decide to intervene and then the club will burn down."

"I'll help you, Daisy." Carys stood very quickly.

"She means well, but... She can be a lot," Aidan whispered.

Then Daisy O'Donnell was standing there looking adorably sexy in a pencil skirt and flouncy top. She was not the awkward girl he'd known years before. She'd bloomed.

And she was also Dee.

"It's okay. I think I'll get breakfast at the office. Aunt Charlotte always has something in the break room," she said, and then seemed to realize he was there. Her eyes flared with recognition, and he watched as her breath hitched and for a mere moment there was longing in her eyes. Then her expression cleared, and she obviously chose her path. "Hello.

You must be Nathan. It's nice to see you again."

It was odd. There was anger simmering below his surface, but there was also something else. Excitement. An edge of danger.

Damn. He kind of felt alive. He wanted to see how far the little liar was going to take it. "You, too, Dais. Although I will admit, it feels like yesterday."

"Oh, shit," Carys said under her breath.

"Really? It feels like forever to me," Daisy said with a smile. "So you're working at MT now?"

Aidan seemed happy he wasn't pushing it. "He is, but he's going to be on a different floor. Hey, since you're going to the same place, do you mind driving her in? It would save Carys and I twenty minutes."

Daisy's eyes went super wide. Like he'd only seen those eyes on Pokémon before. "Oh, I wouldn't want to bother him."

"Of course." He would love to get her alone. "We're going to the same place."

She just didn't know the place they were going was right back to bed. Or a desktop. Or a broom closet. He was flexible.

Did she seriously think he wouldn't recognize her? The mask had barely concealed some of her face. It hadn't covered her plump lips or the stubborn chin she lifted right before she said something bratty and sassy. It hadn't done a damn thing to cover all that fucking hair he wanted laid out on a bed again.

"I don't..." Carys began.

But Nate was already on his feet. "It would be a pleasure. I'm sure you two need to get to work, and it's been an age since I got to talk to Aidan's sister. The last time I saw you I think you were pretending to be someone you weren't."

"Uh, I did a lot of pretending. I was a kid."

"I do believe you and Elodie were pretending to be pop stars." The memory pierced through him. His sister was much younger, and Daisy had been sweet to play with her. Daisy had been the kid who took care of the other kids, who organized adventures for the little kids at The Garden so the older kids could play video games.

Obvious relief flooded through her, and she proved she did not have any instinct for when a predator was stalking her, planning on eating her alive. "Oh, yes. That. We had fun. I would love to hear how she's doing, but I don't want to be a bother. I can grab an Uber."

That wasn't happening. He knew why she was going in.

Daisy O'Donnell needed a bodyguard.

He happened to be a bodyguard.

The math was simple. One plus one was going to equal that little brat in his bed. "Oh, I'm sure your father would have a problem with you being alone. Come along. We should get in so you can meet your new bodyguard."

"I don't…" Carys began.

"No, you don't"—Nate moved into Daisy's space—"have to do a thing. I'm a trained guard. I'm going to the same place as a young lady who needs protection. I'll deliver her straight to her dad."

"You will?" Daisy asked, looking around like someone would save her.

"Daisy…" Carys kept trying, but it looked like she wasn't completely sure what she thought was going on was actually going on.

"Baby, are you all right?" Aidan asked. "She's fine with Nate. I've known Nate Carter since I was a kid. She's perfectly safe with him. I assure you my father would let Nate watch over her. His parents are my parents' closest friends."

Yeah, he should give his dad a call to let him know he was about to blow their friendship all to hell.

Because she wasn't getting away from him.

"Yeah, I can't think of a reason to not go," Daisy said with a nervous smile. "Like not a single one because we're all friends. So, we should head out."

Trouble. Everyone said Daisy O'Donnell was trouble.

It looked like he was up for a bit of chaos.

Chapter Six

She hadn't been able to think of a reason to not get in the car with the gorgeous man she'd slept with the night before. The man who could never know she was Dee.

It was like she was a heroine in one of her Aunt Serena's books except they always got a happily ever after, and she was not getting one of those.

Tragic. She was a tragic heroine.

Damn, but this was awkward.

She couldn't stand the silence. He hadn't even turned on the radio, simply started driving toward the office once she'd buckled her seat belt. "So, how is your sister doing? It's been years since I saw her. I probably wouldn't even recognize her now."

He chuckled, a deep sound that reminded her of the night before. "Well, since she was only eight the last time you were around, I would definitely say no. When we moved back to Australia, she got into dance. Which is funny since we lived in London for so long and yet she didn't start dancing until she was in a tiny town out in the bush. Miss Addie's Dance Studio. She was one of five girls. She was with Miss Addie for years."

This was much easier. She remembered Elodie as a sweet kid she used to hang out with when they visited. "Mom told me she's probably going to be with a dance troupe. Is it ballet?"

"Mostly, though she does a lot of modern dance. Pretty much any kind. It's been her obsession since she was a kid. I always wonder what it would feel like to know what you're supposed to do," Nate said.

She knew the feeling. "I grew up around a guy who knew he wanted to be a surgeon from the age of seven when he went with Mom to visit your mom's clinic. He came back and all he could talk about was how amazing Aunt Steph is. And she is. I'm pretty sure my da kept waiting for him to get bored with it, but Aidan never did. He had a path in life from a super-young age, and he's followed it. Tris leaving is the only thing that's ever gone sideways for my brother."

"Then why does Liam talk like Aidan doesn't have a brain in his head and you're some kind of saint?" Nate asked.

Daisy let her head fall back against the seat. "I don't know. It's not like I lie to him. I sometimes think it's because he feels bad about how I turned out." She knew her da loved her, but she wondered if he wanted to know her. The Daisy she truly was. "I've been told I can be a handful. I don't try to be. It's hard to compete with a golden boy. I mean in a regular family the whole *I'm going to share my wife with another dude* thing would have helped me out. But no, I had to be born into a kink-friendly family. I know they worry about me. A lot."

"Well, if half the stories I've heard are true, I can't blame them for worrying." He turned at the light. "So you're going to hang around the office?"

She sat beside him, though there was plenty of space in the big cab. His truck was definitely Nate sized. "I'm going to be working there for a while."

But not forever because she was going to figure out her life. Hearing Nate tell her he understood why her parents worried made her feel perfectly secure in her decision to not tell him she was Dee. He would be horrified.

"And you're going to be staying at Aidan's?" He asked the question like he was worried about the response.

At least she could ease his mind about one thing. They wouldn't be stuck together. No forced proximity for them. "Nope. I'm going home tonight. I bought my house a couple of months ago, and I'm working on renovating it."

"All right, I have to ask. How did you afford a house? You're barely twenty-five, and from what I can tell you haven't had a steady job since you left college."

What had he heard about her? She might have to rethink the belief her brother actually liked her. "I've always had a job. It's just I hopped around a lot."

"Did your parents give you the down payment?"

It was another one of those stories she probably shouldn't share with him. But it wasn't like they were dating. "No, they didn't. I came into some money a while back when I happened to stumble on a sex trafficking operation. I saved a couple of young ladies, and their families insisted on giving me a reward. I used it for a down payment on my house, but I still have a mortgage."

Nate's head turned, his jaw dropping. "You did what?"

"It wasn't a big deal. I was dating this guy who turned out to be in the business, so to speak, but I always carry around some strips to test drinks. When he drugged me, I only pretended to be out, and he didn't realize I was carrying one of the twins' phones because they needed to show up as partying downtown to fool some foreign spy agency, so I called and the police raided." She thought about it for a moment. "You know, it's kind of a theme for me."

"I'm sorry. So what you're telling me is the guy you were dating was going to traffick you?"

"I think they called it an auction," she explained. "I didn't get very far into it. Sometimes I wonder what my opening bid would have been."

He shuddered, and his hands tightened on the wheel. "You need a keeper, girl."

She got that a lot. "Anyway, everyone freaked, but I made a couple of friends and I got to give Aunt Serena a good idea for a book, so it all worked out. But I do need a paycheck. I couldn't go home last night because my bodyguard was on vacation. He came back early so he could start the job."

Nate huffed. "So you're making some bloke with a family stay with you twenty-four seven because you refuse to stay with your family?"

She was starting to get the feeling Nate didn't like her very much. "No. My father is making some bloke stay with me. I would be fine on my own. I have a security system. I have had some self-defense training. My father is being overly protective."

"Or you aren't taking the threat seriously enough," Nate replied.

"We don't even know there is a threat. I might not have to testify. We know very little about…" She sighed. "I don't want to argue. I can be quiet until we get to the office. I'll be working on another floor, so you won't have to see me."

He was quiet for a moment. "Why wouldn't I want to see you?"

"I don't know since I thought we were kind of friends. Your parents are pretty much family."

"We're not family, Daisy," he said quickly. "I wouldn't call us old friends either. We don't know each other. Aidan and I kept up. He's come to Australia a couple of times. The one time I visited here, you were out of town."

It had been years before. "It was my senior class trip. Look, I know when I rub a guy wrong. It's cool. You don't like me."

"Never said I didn't like you," he replied.

Not in so many words, but she'd heard him loud and clear. "You literally called me selfish."

"I was merely pointing out that if you stayed at Aidan's, Brian wouldn't have had to cut his holiday short. I could look after you." He said the words casually, like it wouldn't be the end of her world.

It wouldn't be. Not the end of her world. But the end of her peace of mind because she was pretty sure she would make an absolute fool of herself if she was around this man for any amount of time. "Where would I sleep when Cooper eventually comes home?"

"Apparently you could stay in Tristan's room since he hasn't been back in months. You could move right in. It would make your dad feel better. It's not like I'm doing anything."

"Cool, then you can move into my place." She stopped, taking a long breath because she hadn't meant to say that. He was flustering her. "I didn't mean that. I certainly don't think you want to hang around me twenty-four seven. I'll talk to my da. He's being unreasonable."

"So you're going to be stubborn," Nate grumbled.

Maybe he wasn't so gorgeous. "It's nothing you should worry about. Like I said I'll be out of your hair the minute we get to the office. I'm sure my da will be thrilled to give me a ride home."

And numerous lectures on how she was going to give him a heart attack.

"Maybe I should be the one to have a long talk with your da," he muttered under his breath.

He was kind of an ass. At least she could trust her father to take her side. "You do that."

A hush descended over the cab as he continued toward the office.

He'd been so sweet the night before, but she should know better. She wasn't a naïve child. Men could be perfectly nice when they wanted to get into a woman's thong and then jerks when they'd had what they wanted. Or they could seem nice because they meant to auction you off to some dude in Malaysia.

"I heard you were at the club last night. Did you have fun?" Nate asked.

Fun? She wouldn't call it fun. She would call it life changing. A revelation. She could still feel this man's hands on her. She'd sat up in Cooper's bed waiting for the sound of Nate coming home. It had taken everything she had not to be sitting in the living room, ready to confess what she'd done and how she wanted to do it again. "I stayed in the locker room."

"Really? I thought you were a member. Aidan mentioned it, though he did say you never seemed interested in playing. He said it was more of a social club for you." Nate's eyes stayed on the road.

It gave her a chance to study the hard line of his jaw. He was such a gorgeous man. "I wouldn't say I'm not interested. I enjoy the lifestyle." Why was she talking about this? It wasn't any of his business. She wasn't about to whine and cry about the fact that the only Dom she wanted to play with was the one she couldn't have. Well, not the only one since none of them seemed interested. "So you went to the party? Did you have fun?"

"It was all right," he said.

Wow. That hurt. She turned away from him. Had she been this stupid again? Thank the universe she hadn't confessed to anyone. Not even Carys knew what she'd done. She hadn't had a chance to talk to her this morning because Nate had been sitting there.

She wasn't going to cry. "Well, maybe you'll have more fun next time."

How long before she could get out of the truck? Would he insist on walking her all the way up or could she ditch him in the lobby? Maybe in a few weeks she would be able to not want to cry when she saw him, but today she was a mess.

She had to get it together or her da would know something was wrong and she would end up in a session with Aunt Eve.

"I met someone. I thought we made a connection, but it was all one way," he said quietly.

Daisy felt her heart soften. "I can't believe that. I'm sure you misunderstood her. She's probably going through some things."

"Well, she left me sleeping after blowing my bloody mind," he admitted. "She didn't leave a number, so I have to figure it meant way more to me than to her."

Of all the scenarios she'd gone through, she hadn't thought about this one. Where he got hurt. She hadn't meant to hurt him. No wonder he was acting like a wounded bear this morning. His heart was bruised. "I'm sure she had something else she had to do."

He stopped at a red light. "After midnight?"

She could see the MT building up ahead. Only a couple more minutes and they would be safely in the building, and she could run away as fast as her kitten heels would carry her. All she had to do was keep her mouth shut. "Maybe she had an early call at work."

Keeping her mouth shut wasn't one of her talents.

"She could have left a note or given me a real name. I took my mask off, told her real things about myself. Nah, she used me. Not how I wanted to start this whole new life thing off," he said as he eased up when the light changed, but they were stuck behind a sedan trying to turn left without an arrow. "But you know, live and learn."

Okay, this was worse than being hurt herself. Her heart actually ached.

"I came here hoping to start over again." He turned her way and gave her a halfhearted smile. "I've been kind of lost since I left the military, like I don't know where my place in the world is. Last night I guess I felt alive again. But it wasn't real."

Her gut twisted. "It was real."

"It was real for me. Not for her."

She turned Nate's way. Why the hell was she doing this? She was literally one block from freedom, but the stupid traffic was killing her. They were at a dead standstill for some reason.

She didn't have to say anything. Not a damn thing. She didn't owe him. It wasn't like telling him would help him. He would realize he'd screwed his best friend's sister, who he thought was useless and selfish.

So she didn't have to confess to save his delicate masculine sensibilities. Nope.

"It was me."

He turned her way, his eyes narrowing, and then reached out and hauled her down, shoving her torso over as the bullets began to fly.

* * * *

"It was me."

Nate felt a deep sense of satisfaction run through him when the little brat finally admitted the truth.

It didn't last long because when he turned her way, he realized a big SUV in the far right lane beside them had stopped in the middle of the road, and the passenger side window rolled down.

They weren't asking for directions. They had him in a trap, closed in on all sides. He saw the barrel of a gun poke through the open window and did the only thing he could. He reached over and shoved her down, covering her body with his while he tried to keep control of the truck. The sound of glass shattering filled the air as the assassin put three bullets into his brand-new truck, and the world seemed to go chaotic as the people around him panicked.

"Stay down," he ordered as he pulled his SIG. They needed to get to the MT building, and they needed to do it fucking now. The chaos would help, but he needed cover fire. He kept a hand on Daisy's back so she didn't decide to help him as he eased up and fired at the black SUV.

Nate took off, punching the gas and swerving into the oncoming lane. He narrowly avoided hitting a sedan.

The back window of the cab shattered as they fired again, and he heard the sound of tires screeching.

Had they turned so they could keep coming after them?

Nate took a deep breath and punched the gas again.

Daisy started to come up. "What was…"

He shoved her head back down. "Stay down or I swear to god, you'll get the bloody spanking of a lifetime."

"I was only trying to check on you," she grumbled.

"I'm fine." He wasn't. He was pretty sure he'd gotten grazed. He could feel a burning sensation across his right bicep.

It likely wasn't the only time he would be wounded in the service of his submissive.

Adrenaline pumped through his system as he swerved back into the right lane before making a hard turn onto the side street that would lead him to the MT building. Behind him he heard the sound of metal striking metal as two cars hit while trying to flee the scene of the attack.

"Call your dad," he ordered.

He couldn't be sure they wouldn't follow him into the parking garage. They had protocols. He couldn't simply race inside. There was a whole security system in place.

"Tell him we're coming in hot, and we need the entrance gate up," Nate explained as he narrowly avoided an accident. He had to go up on the sidewalk to get past the minivan stopped in front of a grocery store.

He glanced up and winced as the SUV started to gain on him.

"Hey, Da. How are you this morning? Did you get breakfast?"

She was going to make him insane. "Daisy!"

"Nate says I have to tell you we're coming in hot. I don't know what that means, but there is someone shooting at us," she said in a shockingly calm voice. "Yeah, he pushed me down. Yes. He's still driving, but whoever it is keeps coming. I'm not sure what he did to upset them." She gasped. "Da, language. We do not know this has… He went into Irish. I can barely understand him, but I did hear him yelling for Uncle Ian. Oh, should I call the police?"

"Don't bother. I think they'll find us." His arm was starting to ache.

"Hold on, love. And let's hope they get the gate open. When we get inside, you stay down, and you run when I tell you to. You run and don't look back. You get to the security desk."

"I'm not going to leave you."

A sweet thought, but he had to protect her. "You'll do exactly what I tell you to, Dais. I'm not fucking around. Here we go. Hang on."

He swung the truck around, barely missing an oncoming car as he rushed into the parking garage. The guard was there in the booth, obviously trying to get the gate up. He felt the top of it scrape the roof of his truck and heard a volley of gunfire.

He breathed a sigh of relief as he saw Ian and Alex moving toward the gate. The big guys moved like the predators they were, and they were backed up by a whole bunch of guys with guns.

Nate slammed the truck to a stop as a freaked-out Li O'Donnell came charging up.

"Daisy!" Liam opened the passenger side door. "My poor, sweet, Daisy. What happened to you? Are you all right? We should call an ambulance."

Daisy was perfectly fine. Nate was the one bleeding, but did Liam seem to care about his health? Nope. He was too busy looking his precious angel over.

"I kind of hit my head when Nate pushed me down, but I'm fine," Daisy was saying.

"Nathan Carter, you have to be more careful with her," Liam complained.

"They're clear," Ian shouted. "Get MaeBe to pull our security cameras. I want a plate number."

"And get the conference room ready for the police visit we're about to get." Alex had holstered his weapon.

"Come on, my sweet daughter. I'll have a talk with Nathan about how to properly watch after you," Liam was saying.

It was time to start adjusting the whole O'Donnell family to the new dynamic.

He slid out of the truck, slammed the door, and walked straight up to his little brat.

Her eyes widened. "Nate? You're hurt."

He shook his head. "It's nothing. You coming willingly?"

She waved him off. "Oh, I'm fine now. Da's here."

Liam nodded. "I'm here now, and we'll get you a proper guard. You're safe now, my darlin' girl."

The hard way it was then. He leaned over and hauled her up and over his good shoulder, securing her tightly against him.

"Nate," she said with a gasp. "What are you doing?"

"Nathan Carter, you put my daughter down this instant," Liam shouted.

But he was walking away. "When she's in a secure room and she can't get her pretty arse sniped, I'll put her down. She made her choice. She's going to learn to live with it."

"Her choice?" Liam sounded pissed.

"I had a choice?" Daisy asked.

"Oh, you did," he promised.

"Daisy, stay very still. I think I can shoot the little bastard," Liam vowed.

He felt Daisy's arms go out as though trying to protect as much of his back as she could. "Da, don't you dare."

At least she wasn't going to let her father murder him.

Yet.

When she found out his plans for her things might change.

Nate strode to the lifts and walked in as the doors opened. He turned and looked out over the chaos. His truck had several bullet holes, and all his windows had blown. He probably needed a couple of stitches. He was going to spend the next hours of his life with the DPD.

He'd come here for peace, and his mother's best friend's husband was staring at him like he was a monster. Alex and Ian stood on either side of Liam as though they could stop the Irishman from taking out the man stealing his precious saint of a daughter. Alex had a hand on Li's shoulder, while Ian was watching the whole scene play out with a grin.

There was no peace to be found here, but damn it felt good to bloody feel.

"You could put me down, Nate. I think the danger's over," Daisy pointed out.

Before the doors could close, he slapped her arse. "The danger's never over with you, love. I said you needed a keeper. Looks like it's going to be me."

His decision was made. The doors started to close as Liam pointed his way and said something that had Alex trying to calm him down again.

It was going to be a rough day. He was oddly looking forward to it.

Chapter Seven

Maybe he hadn't heard her.

Half an hour later, Daisy was still wondering about those three words she'd said right before the world had exploded.

Nate had carried her up to his desk and set her down, pointing at the chair, telling her in that super Dommy way of his to have a seat.

His boss, Tessa Hawthorne, had ordered him into her office to check his arm and get a report on what had happened. He'd told Daisy to not move a muscle until he got back. He'd been incredibly bossy, and she wished it didn't do something for her.

But then he'd taken a really long time and she needed to see her da, who was probably looking for her, so she'd left him a note and come back upstairs.

After all, she was supposed to report for her job. The phones weren't going to answer themselves.

"Holy crap, Dais. Are you okay?" Devi Taggart walked out of her mom's office. She was dressed casually in jeans and a T-shirt, her red hair in a ponytail. It let Daisy know Devi had likely taken the day off. Devi had a degree in fashion design and was currently interviewing for jobs with big design houses across the country. Until then she was working at Top as a server. "I had breakfast with my mom and I thought I would stop by and say hi to you, but then the whole place went into lock-down and my mom told me not to leave the office."

Daisy stared at her friend. She and Devi and Brianna had grown up together. Her girl gang. She knew them well, and there was something Devi wasn't saying. "You wanted to say hi? Or you heard rumors about last night?"

"Okay, I might have heard something about you going to the masquerade party," Devi admitted.

"And?"

Devi's ponytail shook. "Girl, why are we talking about this when you were apparently just shot at? Are you okay? You didn't get hit?"

"No, and we can't be certain they were shooting at me. It could have been regular, normal street violence." Naturally everyone pointed fingers her way. It wasn't like no one ever got randomly shot at in Dallas. That was a normal Tuesday in Deep Ellum.

"Oh, I think we can definitely say they were shooting at you." MaeBe Hawthorne's head popped up over the walls of her cubicle. Mae was a super-cute thirtysomething with a pair of adorable moppets and a husband who worked in the investigative unit. MaeBe had been in the cybersecurity unit for years. "I pulled the plates, and it didn't take me long to trace that sucker back to a known cartel assassin. I've been on the Dark Web since your dad went nuclear yesterday."

"In the conference room, please." Ian Taggart was striding toward her followed by a couple of what she thought of as the old-school crew, including Devi's mom, Erin Taggart. "Liam, she's here. You can rescue her now."

Her father turned down the hall, his eyes lighting when he saw her. He rushed up to her, putting his hands on her shoulders as he studied her. "Daisy. What the hell is going on, girl? Tell me where the little bastard went. I'm going to send him back Down Under in pieces. I swear it. If he touched a hair on your head…"

Only her da would call a man who outweighed him by at least a hundred pounds of pure muscle and had a half a foot on him height wise a little bastard.

"I'm pretty sure it was her ass he touched," Uncle Ian quipped. "That was a warning slap, Daisy. You should be careful with Aussies. I'm surprised he let you roam around without him."

He was good at that. Sarcasm was fuel for the parental units. Most of the time she found it funny, but she had a da on the edge to deal with. "I'm fine. Nate saved me. He was just a wee bit overstimulated. He wanted to get me to safety as soon as possible, but see, I'm here and I'm perfectly fine."

Erin Taggart had been her father's partner since long before Daisy had been born. She had been the sister her father never had before, and she was usually good at calming him down. "Except for the bullets flying your way and the massive possessive Aussie you've attracted."

Not today. Nope, today her Aunt Erin had chosen violence.

"Possessive?" Her father's brow rose. "What the hell would he be possessive about?"

"Absolutely nothing. Nate was simply saving my brother from having to drive me in. I had to stay at Aidan's last night, and he and Carys had early calls at the hospital this morning. Nate was merely being kind. And then he went through something traumatic. It seems to have disturbed him." Nate had obviously forgotten how to use his words. Or maybe it was a function of his Australianness. He'd barked orders her way, and she could still feel that slap on her ass. He'd meant it. His hard palm had come down on her ass like a promise of retribution for future brattery.

"Is this how you're playing it, kid?" Uncle Ian asked, a brow raised over his blue eyes.

Of all the uncles in her world he was both the most tolerant and the one who saw through twelve feet of bullshit with ease. Still, there wasn't anything to see here. He was also the one who should know what happened at the club should stay at the club. "Playing? Not at all. I was explaining to my da that Nate is new to all the crazy stuff that can happen around here. It takes some getting used to. Not everyone handles things with the cool calm we do."

"He was a bloody commando, Daisy," her da pointed out, also proving he was not in the cool and calm "we" she'd talked about.

Men could be emotional creatures. "I'm sure he's excellent on a battlefield, but traffic is a whole other story. It can be brutal, Da. We have to make allowances."

Devi stood there looking at her, shaking her head. "This might be the Daisiest thing you've ever done."

Aunt Erin leaned against the doorjamb next to her not so mini me. "Nah, calling Liam in the middle of a gunfight and asking him if he's had breakfast this morning before mentioning the whole 'we're being shot at' thing—that's the Daisiest thing she's done today."

"Well, he gets cranky if he doesn't have his breakfast." Her aunt should know that, and when had they started using her name as an adjective? Maybe she should stuff a couple of bangers down her da's throat. He was better when he wasn't hangry.

"My darling girl was being her sweet self and trying to look out for her old man, but I think Nathan has a few things to answer for," her da proclaimed. "He seems to have a mistaken impression of how we handle clients at this company. He's a McKay-Taggart bodyguard, and the minute he agreed to take her to work, she became his client. I'm going to talk to Tessa about her training protocols."

"Oh, I think he's treating her exactly like a client," Uncle Ian said under his breath.

"Hypocrite." Aunt Erin managed to say the word on a cough.

Daisy wasn't sure what was going on, but she needed to get the older generation off this particular topic as quickly as possible. "I am not Nate's client. We're coworkers."

"That's right," her da said with a firm nod. "There's no way I'm letting that youngster anywhere close to my Daisy. He doesn't have the right experience, and it's obvious to me he's got some hormones to deal with. We've got a proper guard for you. A married, stable man."

"Mae, I got your email. Brighton's on his way in," Uncle Ian said, stopping in front of Mae's desk. "Alex is downstairs dealing with the uniforms. Call down and give them a plate. I'm sure the feds will be here soon. It's going to be a fun day."

"Devi, love, would you run downstairs and ask Brian to join us in the conference room?" her da asked. "And bring Tessa up, too. We need a twenty-four-seven watch on Daisy. We might need to bring in some more people. Ian, I'm going to move her to a safe house."

That sounded terrible. "I don't need a safe house. I want to stay at my place."

Her father's head shook. "Not happening. I'll be honest, I'm thinking about shipping you straight to Damon. They can watch you at The Garden."

"Hey, Ian," a masculine voice called out. "I was hoping to talk to you this morning."

Liam sighed in obvious relief as Brian Langton walked in, saving Devi the trip downstairs. "Thank the heavens. Brian, let's go to my office and we'll talk about what we need to keep my Daisy safe."

Langton was in his mid-forties, and he was about as basic as a guy his age got. He had a seemingly never-ending supply of khakis and polo shirts, all in neutral colors. He turned to her father, his face falling as though this was exactly the situation he'd been trying to avoid. "I was... I was... Damn it. Liam, I'm not taking the assignment." He looked Daisy's way, an apologetic expression on his face. "It's nothing against you, Daisy. You're a very nice young lady, but I have three kids. My wife is a stay-at-home mom and honestly, the insurance we have isn't enough if... Well, if the inevitable happens."

What was he trying to say? "What does insurance have to do with it? And what's inevitable?"

Devi leaned in, whispering. "I think he thinks he's going to die."

Brian frowned and turned to Ian. "Look, boss, I like my job, but I like my life more. Daisy O'Donnell is trouble. Send me to protect like a mobster or something. Anyone but her."

Rude. No one had ever died around her. Well, there had been one time, but it hadn't been her fault.

Her father stepped up to her side, his eyes narrow. "It's good to know that now, ain't it? I'll protect her myself. I'll have us on a plane to London in no time. We'll hole up at The Garden, you and me and your mum."

"For how long?" Aunt Erin asked. "Because I don't know if you're aware, but the wheels of the American justice system can grind slowly, my friend. Should I pack up your house? Let Serena know she's losing her assistant?"

Her mother loved her job. She ran the business portion of Serena Dean-Miles's publishing company. It only published Serena's books, but there was a lot of work to do. And the conference season was about to start.

"Of course we're not going to England." She wasn't getting hauled out of the country. This whole thing was spiraling out of control. "Da, we need to be reasonable about this."

Her father's jaw went stubborn, his emerald eyes as hard as stone. "You just got shot at, girl. Don't you think for a second I'm going to be reasonable about that. And if our bodyguards ain't up to the task, then I'll find me own. I'm sure Damon's got some good people."

"Li, come on," Ian said with a long sigh. "I know you're worried, but we need to stay calm."

"Stay calm? What would you do if your girls were being shot at?" her da asked.

Ian shrugged. "Think it was Tuesday and tell them to duck."

"My sweet Daisy don't play dangerous games." Sometimes her da made her sound boring.

"She doesn't have to. She's dangerous simply walking down the street," Brian said.

"Is there a reason you're still here, Brian?" Uncle Ian asked in a tone that had the man slipping away.

It was for the best, but now she needed to figure out how to convince her father not to haul them all off the continent. "I understand this is scary for you, Da, but we need to be reasonable. Uncle Ian is right, and you know what? I had a brilliant idea. Maybe I should help the twins for a while." It could be her new career. "I'm sure the team needs someone to like take notes and get lattes and stuff. No one would be worried if I was hanging out with that crowd."

She didn't say CIA team because they weren't supposed to use those words. But the idea played around in her head now. Maybe the reason she hadn't found anything she was good at yet was because she hadn't considered espionage.

Uncle Ian had gone a bit pale. "Uh, I don't think we have any openings for interns, Daisy."

Her father looked like he was going to have a stroke. "You are absolutely not working for the bloody Agency."

"Da," she said on a gasp. "We're not supposed to say that."

Her da's jaw tightened. "Listen to me, girl. You are going to get on a plane for London. We'll leave as soon as your mother gets here."

"She has a bodyguard and she's not going to London, so let's stop panicking," a deep voice said. "And Daisy, you're absolutely not going to become a spy. While I'm sure you would be great at it, the world would collapse. And you are not where I left you. That's twenty. Do you want it now or later?"

Devi gasped and put a hand on Daisy's elbow. "Holy crap. That's Nate Carter?"

Nate. It had in fact been Nate. He was standing in the middle of the hallway in front of her Aunt Erin's office with a bandage around his big bicep and a fierce expression on his face.

He towered over everyone. He even had a couple of inches on her Uncle Ian, and Nate was so masculine and perfect it made her heart skip a beat. Beyond that she knew how tender the man could be, but he didn't look tender now. He looked pissed, and his growly persona did something for her, too. But she had to remember he wasn't hers. She wasn't sure why he was talking in an incredibly possessive way. Probably because the events of the morning were still affecting his masculine sensibilities.

"Yes, that's him, Devi, and I appreciate everything he did for me this morning but I think we'll handle it from here." Had he threatened to spank her in front of her father? And uncle and aunt and best friend? And pretty much everyone since they were all watching now. All eyes were on her and the scene starting to play out. She had to bring this under control.

"You're going to dismiss me?" Nate asked the question as though he wasn't worried about her answer, merely curious.

"Yes, she is," her father announced. "Your poor driving nearly got my Daisy killed. I'm going to talk to Tessa about testing your driving skills. This ain't the outback, son."

"No, it's far more dangerous, and I am not your son," Nate replied steadily. "Nor are you my uncle. There's not a bit of blood between us, Liam O'Donnell, and you should remember that."

Also rude. There was a lot of rudeness running around this morning.

Erin sighed and looked at her daughter. "This is way too much testosterone for this time of day. Devi, you know something I don't?"

Devi leaned in and whispered to her mom. Daisy would have tried to stop that, but Nate was staring at her like he was going to spank her here and now if she didn't comply. Which was ridiculous. Or she was letting her romantic dreams run wild the way she sometimes did. She was Daisy, the one with her head in the clouds. Daisy, the one with all the big dreams, the butterfly flitting from job to job with nothing to show for it.

"You listen here," her da began. "I don't know what you think you're doing, Carter, but you're not getting close to my daughter. She's a good girl, and she doesn't have any idea how to handle the likes of you."

"She handles me fine." Nate seemed determined to blow up her whole world.

"What da fuck is that supposed to mean?" Her da practically shouted the question.

Naturally Aunt Charlotte showed up with a bag of microwave popcorn. "Has Liam figured out what's going on between Daisy and Nate?"

How would her aunt know what was going on? Nate didn't even know.

Or did he? She'd said the words out loud, but had he really heard them? They'd probably been lost in all the adrenaline and violence and gunshots.

He'd been shot. Sure it had turned out to be fine, but he could have been killed. He could have died and it would have been her fault. All her fault because she was so dumb.

"Did you know, Dais?" Nate asked, completely ignoring the rapt audience around them.

Her head was reeling. Maybe she wasn't handling the situation as well as she thought she was. Her heart was thudding a little and she was back in the moment when she'd realized someone was shooting at them. "I didn't know they would come after me."

A cartel. She had a cartel after her. As adventures went, it was a shitty one. And she'd lost her job and she would probably lose her home and her da was going to ship her off to Europe where she would very likely start a land war, and she would definitely not see Nate again.

She'd pushed it all down and it was bubbling back up, a torrential storm of anxiety.

"I don't think that's what he meant," Devi whispered.

"He needs to get back downstairs and leave my daughter alone," her da said. "I'll be having a talk with my son about his choice of roommates and who he's letting around his sister. I didn't work this hard to keep the men off her only to lose her to the first Aussie to walk through the door."

Nate completely ignored everyone but her. He walked past her father, staring down at her with a piercing gaze. "Did you know, Daisy? When you approached me last night, did you know who I was?"

"What the hell is he on about," her da started and then batted something away. "Don't throw fucking popcorn my way, Tag. This is serious."

"Did I know the six-foot-seven-inch dude with the Australian accent was Nathan Carter?" The walls were closing in around her. Nate was pushing her and it had been a terrible day, and he seemed ready to make it worse.

"Of course she knew you." Her da was unrelenting. "Do you think she would get into the car with a stranger?"

"I mean she's done it a couple of times." Devi wasn't helping.

She'd had reasons for that.

"I think he means in a biblical way, not an 'I called an Uber' way," Uncle Ian snarked.

Nate moved into her space. "Did you know?"

She had to nod but she suddenly couldn't breathe. He was here and he was staring down at her and he knew. He knew what she'd done. They all would know she'd taken something from him. Something he likely wouldn't have shared had he known it was her. And then she'd gotten him shot. And no one wanted to protect her because she was trouble. But there was only one answer. "Yes."

"Then you've made your choice and you'll have to deal with it," he said in a tone that brooked no disobedience.

Her father said something about not laying a hand on her and her uncle said hands had totally already been lain and her aunt asked if she was okay. She wasn't. The world kind of went fuzzy and she felt a wash of utter defeat come over her system as her knees gave way.

Right before the darkness took her, Nate caught her, and she was in his arms as the world faded to black.

* * * *

Liam O'Donnell was going to be the worst father-in-law imaginable.

"You let my daughter down this minute, Nathan Carter." He followed Nate as he carried Daisy to the conference room.

"I'm not dropping my sub," Nate replied.

"No blood on the carpet, Liam O'Donnell," Charlotte Taggart said, pointing to Li. She moved in beside Nate. "Are you trying to push him over the edge?"

"Nope. I'm only being honest. It's a thing he should try." He was starting to wonder about the real reason none of the Doms at The Hideout would play with Daisy. He had a hunch and it had to do with her father. Maybe Aidan, too, and if he found out Aidan had been warning men off Daisy, they would have a long talk. "Devi, would you get some water for Daisy? Maybe put on a kettle."

"What would I put a kettle on?" Devi asked. "Also, do we have a kettle? And what would I put in it?"

Americans.

"I'll help her," Erin said. "Come on, sweetie. You can fill me in on what's happening and we'll get some tea started."

"We should call an ambulance," Liam declared as Nate walked into the conference room. "It's obvious she's been injured. She's probably got a concussion."

Nate was almost sure she was conscious again. She'd had a bit of a panic attack likely because she was about to have to face the music, and it was obvious she hadn't been forced to deal with consequences before. It would be different between them.

She'd had every chance to save herself. She could have continued to pretend like she wasn't Dee. He'd pushed and prodded her, getting a feel for who this woman really was. Anger hadn't spurred her to make a confession. When he'd told her the night was just okay, he'd seen the hurt on her face. Her own pain hadn't forced her to drop the act.

It had been his pain.

It was me.

Three words that would prove to be fateful for the little brat because he wasn't about to let her go now.

"She doesn't have a concussion." Nate settled himself into one of the big conference chairs. He cuddled her close and couldn't miss the way she curled against him. "She's got a big case of doesn't want to be here-itis."

And her lips quirked up slightly.

She was so much fucking trouble, and his dick did not care.

He was pretty sure his heart didn't either. Falling madly for his friend's sister hadn't been the plan, but he was going with it. He could have walked away if he thought she'd truly only wanted him for sex, but she'd clung to him. She'd wanted him as much for the personal connection they'd formed as the sexual one.

His father had told him sometimes a man's purpose wasn't a job. Sometimes it was keeping one gorgeous bombshell alive and happy.

"Nathan Carter, you're fired. Get your things and get the hell out of my office," her father said.

Daisy went slightly stiff in his arms.

Nate knew how to handle O'Donnell. "No."

Liam got red in the face. "What do you mean no?"

"I think he means he's not leaving." Ian Taggart was a bastard who obviously enjoyed a good show.

Well, he had to admit his baby knew how to play out a beauty of a scene. "I mean, you can fire me, but I'm not leaving Daisy. Tell me something, Liam. Was it you or Aidan who scared all the Doms off her at The Hideout?"

Devi walked in with a pitcher of water, and her eyes went wide. "Scared off the Doms? No one would do that. The club is a place where we can be honest. You don't understand. We have rules, and no one is going to shame anyone or scare them off. Daisy just… She hasn't had any luck."

"Sure, the stunningly gorgeous submissive with an hourglass figure who looks like she'll melt in your fucking mouth can't find a guy to top her for a night," Nate shot back.

Daisy's eyes fluttered open. "You think I'm gorgeous?"

Her father had done her no favors. "Of course you're gorgeous. I thought you were gorgeous with a silly mask on your face. Taking it off didn't make you any less stunning, love."

"What the hell are you on about?" Liam stood, the conference table between them. "Daisy, get up. We're leaving and we won't come back until your uncle gets rid of the dead weight."

"You know now that I think about it, it *is* kind of weird," Devi said. "When we go out to clubs in the city, Daisy is always the one who gets hit on. Like dance clubs or bars."

"My Daisy doesn't go to clubs or bars," her father insisted. "The only reason she goes to The Hideout is to be around her friends. She doesn't play there. Daisy is a good girl."

"And my Devi isn't?" Erin was back, staring at her long-term partner.

Liam froze. "I didn't say that, Erin."

"No, you said Daisy doesn't go to clubs because she's a good girl." Erin's tone had gone cold. "Devi does go to clubs. She dances and parties and has fun because she's young and she gets to do that. So I'll ask again, partner, are you slut shaming my daughter?"

"Mom, I'm not… I mean the word slut is really triggering," Devi said with a frown.

"Devi, darling, you know I adore you." Liam O'Donnell seemed to realize the trap he was in. "Of course you're a good girl. But Daisy is very innocent."

Her father started going over all the ways Daisy was naïve, just a sweet babe out in the woods.

Daisy looked up at him, shifting. "What did you mean I made my choice? Are you mad?"

"I'm not particularly happy you left me sleeping last night," he admitted. Then he looked at Liam, who was still arguing with the Taggart women. Charlotte had joined in. He totally deserved it. "Though I kind of understand. Is he always like this?"

Daisy nodded. "I don't think he likes who I actually am very much. I love him but he doesn't know me. But I want to know what you meant by I made my choice."

He should be plain with her and her father. "I mean you sought me out last night. You knew who I was and you chose me, and now you're stuck with me. You might decide to walk away after you're safe, but from this moment until the second they put the bastard in jail, you're mine. While I'm your bodyguard, you're going to be my sub. So take this time, Daisy. Enjoy it. See if it's something you want on a permanent basis."

She sat up, looking him right in the eyes. "Are you saying you want me?"

"I think I proved how much I want you last night. I know when you walked in the kitchen this morning, you brought the sunshine with you. Maybe it'll all go to hell, but damn, I want the ride either way." He ran a thumb over her plump bottom lip. "Typhoon Daisy."

Big emerald eyes stared at him. Protect me eyes. Love me eyes. "You'll change your mind."

"I don't think so. Never felt this way in my life, and I'm going to trust it. So we know where I stand, and this is about you deciding what you're willing to risk," he replied.

"My father…"

He could put the fear to rest. "O'Donnell, you need to understand something here and now. You can't scare me off. You can't pay me to leave her alone. You can't threaten me. Words won't work and neither will fists. You won't come between me and Daisy and if you try, well, there's a nice place in Australia where we can hide. You'll see her again in a couple of years."

Liam looked like he was about to have a stroke.

"Nathan, that's rude," Daisy said primly.

But he understood her father in a way she didn't. Her father saw him as a threat. When her dad calmed down and realized he would take care of her, they could have a good relationship. Until then, he would have to push the man. Her mum would be an entirely different story. "It's also true. You made your choice when you slept with me last night. You thought you could sneak in my bed and slip back out again. Well, that isn't how it's going to work."

Ian groaned, his head hitting his hand. "Fucking Aussies."

"You listen and you listen good, boyo," Liam began.

"Liam, what is going on?" The only person in the world whose authority Liam O'Donnell listened to walked in. Avery O'Donnell looked like she'd practically run here. She wore yoga pants and a T-shirt, her hair in a messy bun. "Daisy..." She stared at them for a moment. "Daisy, are you all right? Why are you sitting on Nathan's lap?"

"Because he's holding her bloody hostage, that's why," Liam declared. "We need to call Brody and Steph because their boy is running wild, and I won't have him drag our sweet Daisy down."

Avery's eyes were wide. "I didn't even know they talked. What is going on?"

He thought he was going to have to explain when Daisy suddenly draped an arm around his neck and her backside wiggled over his cock as she went all bouncy and bubbly.

His suddenly hard as a bloody rock cock.

"Mom, I went to the masquerade party last night at The Hideout even though Aidan told me I shouldn't, and I met Nate and we had the best sex. I thought he wouldn't know it was me, but apparently a small mask isn't much of a disguise. I will admit by the end of the night, the mask was the only thing I was wearing, and that might have been my mistake. I should have worn a wig or something maybe. Anyway, now he says I'm his sub and I'm super happy, but I think Da is going to be difficult and I don't understand it because he always says I need a keeper and here he is. Also, Nate thinks Da has scared away all the Doms at The Hideout so I didn't have anyone to play with, but Da wouldn't do that to me, right? Also, the cartel person sent someone to kill me but Nate saved me, and then Da pissed off Aunt Erin by saying Devi isn't a good girl but she is. Devi is the best. I think Da needs some time. Oh, and Nate told Da if he tries to come between us he'll kidnap me and take me to Australia, and I thought it was the sexiest thing I've ever heard."

Avery stood there for a moment as though she needed time to process.

"Do you need some tea?" Erin asked.

"I think she needs some therapy," Charlotte quipped. "Or some vodka."

"I am so confused. Perhaps my family should regroup and find a quiet place to have this discussion," Avery said.

Ian stood. "I'm sorry, Avery. That's going to have to wait because our friends are here. Derek, thanks for coming. How bad is it?"

Derek Brighton was a handsome man who'd made his way to the high ranks of the Dallas Police Department. "Well, as I walked in MaeBe told me to let you know she found a bounty on Daisy's head on the Dark Web. She's running it down now. I think we need to talk about witness protection."

Daisy went stiff again.

And Liam O'Donnell finally sat down.

Trouble, it seemed, might just be the thing to bring them all together.

Chapter Eight

Uncle Ian stood, closing his laptop with a long sigh. "So we agree we'll put Daisy up at Sanctum and we'll keep a guard with her twenty-four seven until we can figure this situation out."

The DPD and Dallas district attorney's office representatives had left mere moments before.

It had been a close one, with her father arguing she should go to London and Captain Brighton defending the joys of witness protection. Uncle Ian had managed to work a compromise. She was going to be stuck in Sanctum for the foreseeable future.

So no job. No sweet little house she got to work on. No future.

Nate would see what it meant to be with her now.

It had been easier when she was sitting on Nate's lap, surrounded by his warmth, but she'd moved to the seat next to him when the serious discussions had begun. When her da had been staring at her like he didn't know who she was.

He didn't, but she'd kind of hoped he never had to.

"I think that's acceptable." Her mother seemed determined to be the voice of reason. "It's actually kind of fitting since when Nate was a baby we stashed his mom and dad there."

Daisy looked to her mom. "Really?"

"I've heard the tale many times," Nate agreed.

Her mother nodded. "Oh, yes. You should tell Daisy the story sometime."

"Or we should learn from history and understand what can happen when you don't protect your daughter," her father said, a frown on his face.

"She ends up happily married for over twenty years with two kids she loves?" Nate asked.

Uncle Ian stood, shaking his head. "O'Donnells, this is where I leave you to handle all your family shit. Daisy, please stay close to Nate. Nate, let me know when you need someone to take a shift or two. We'll arrange for some days off."

"Don't need 'em," Nate said. "I won't be leaving her."

Uncle Ian sighed and took Aunt Charlotte's hand. She was giving Daisy a grin.

"I'll let Erin and Devi know what's going on," Aunt Charlotte promised. "And I'll work on finding you something to do while you're there. If you don't mind, you could take the Saturday night kid's club. We're kind of low on subs willing to hang with the kiddos."

"I would love to." It was something she used to adore doing. During high school and college, she'd made a lot of money by handling the kiddos on Friday and Saturday nights. It was probably her favorite job ever.

"I'll see you then, sweetie." Charlotte followed Ian out, and she was left alone with her family.

It might have been the longest three hours of her life, and it looked like it wasn't over. Although maybe she could get out of this. "I think I'm supposed to be taking over the phones this afternoon so the receptionist can have her break."

Her father's brows rose. "You think I'm going to let you sit in the lobby? The whole front of the place is glass, girl. There's a bounty on your head."

"Liam," her mother said.

"He's right in this case." Nate sat back as though settling in. "The glass is bulletproof, but I don't want anyone getting a look at her. I'm considering how I'll get her out of the building in the safest manner possible."

"The safest manner possible would be putting her on a bloody plane with her family," her da muttered.

She'd argued for staying at The Hideout, but there had been so many eyerolls she'd known she was going down in defeat.

At least her father wasn't screaming at Nate anymore. They'd gotten down to growls and dirty looks and some Irish she was grateful Nate didn't speak.

"Liam, we're not going to London. Let it go. Daisy, are you okay?" Her mom stared at her from across the conference table.

Daisy simply nodded and forced a bright smile on her face. "I'm good. I can use some time to myself."

She wasn't about to tell her mom how useless she felt. Fake it until you make it. It was her motto.

"You won't be by yourself," her da complained.

Her mom sighed and stared at her da for a moment. "Are we doing this now?"

The big family talk. The one where everyone cried and said how worried they were about her, and did she know what she was doing? Nope. She didn't want to do that at all. She rather wanted to run to Sanctum and lock herself in with Nate and enjoy what little time she would have with him.

"Nathan, I think you should go back to your desk so I can talk with my family," her da said. "Ian's right. We should get our shit together as a family."

Nate turned her way. "You want me to leave?"

That was an easy question. "No."

Nate turned back to her da and shrugged. "Sorry. If she wants me here, I'm staying. Besides I kind of think she needs someone to protect her."

"From her own da?" Her father was getting red in the face again.

"Nathan, could you go into the break room and grab the sandwiches I sent with Li this morning? Daisy hasn't eaten all day," her mother began. "She's pale."

Nate obviously wasn't used to her mother manipulating situations. Or he didn't notice because he bought her mom's request immediately. "Of course. I'll get something for you, too, Mrs. O'Donnell."

"I don't suppose you're going to call me Aunt Avery," she said wistfully.

"I can't," Nate replied. "I know your husband doesn't believe me, but I'm serious. Do you want some coffee, love?"

The last question had been directed at her. Well, her mother obviously wanted to get her alone, so she might as well get something out of it. "I would rather have a soda. Whatever they have in the vending machines is okay,"

"I'll take a coffee, if you don't mind," her mom said.

Nate looked to her da, but his eyes stayed steady on Daisy.

Nate finally walked out, promising to be back soon.

"Daisy, I know Nathan has convinced you he's interested, but you have to understand no one will protect you the way your family will." Her da barely waited until the door closed.

"He is family, Liam." Her mother looked at a loss for words. "I don't understand what's happening."

"Well I do, and he's not the sweet boy you remember. He's a man, and he's doing what men do to innocent young women," her da said. "Daisy, I know you don't have a lot of experience with men."

Her mother groaned.

"Which is why you have to understand I'm only looking out for you," her da continued.

"But I like Nate."

"You don't know him." Her da stood and paced.

"I do," her mom argued.

A familiar figure raced by. Aidan. He wore green scrubs, and he hadn't bothered to take off his cap. Carys followed after him, stopping when she saw they were in the conference room. She pushed through the door. "Daisy. We just heard what happened. Are you all right?"

Aidan had turned back, following her in. "I'm so sorry. I was in surgery. I came as soon as I could. Da said someone tried to kill you."

At least her brother loved her. Sometimes she worried he viewed her as a burden. "I'm fine. Nate took care of the situation."

Aidan's eyes went hard. "Yeah, I heard about that, too. I'm going to be having a talk with him."

She was about to challenge him when her mother's eyes narrowed.

"Why would you have a talk with him? Beyond saying you hope he treats her well, son?" Her mom didn't usually sound so cold.

"He's going to do what needs to be done." Da stood next to Aidan, putting a hand on his shoulder. "He's going to let Nate know she's not without protection."

"I thought Nate was her protection," Carys said, looking at Daisy and then the men, seeming to understand something was going on beyond a simple assassination attempt.

"Nate is her bodyguard, but it appears he is also her boyfriend," her mother explained. "Why don't you sit down, sweetie? It looks like we're having a family meeting, and this could take a while. Aidan, I'd like to know what your father is talking about when he says you'll do what needs to be done. What needs to be done, son?"

Aidan stopped, seeming to realize he was in a trap of some kind. "Uh, look, Mom, all I know is Da called and told me Daisy's in trouble again. She got freaking shot at and now there's a bounty on her head, and apparently my friend tricked her into bed with him. So yeah, I'm going to talk to him."

Carys looked Daisy's way. "I don't think that's what happened."

Poor Carys. She didn't want to give her up. "Mom and Da know, Carys. They know I spent last night with Nate and he didn't know who I was at the time. Apparently, though, my super-secret disguise didn't work, and he recognized me as Dee this morning."

Aidan frowned. "Wait. Carys knew you were on the dungeon floor last night? And she didn't bother to tell me?"

"Why would it surprise you?" Carys seemed genuinely shocked at his attitude. "She belongs to the club and has since the day it opened. She has every right to play at her home club."

"But she doesn't play," Aidan argued. "She hangs out in the locker room and comes to social parties."

"Because she's not really into all that stuff," her da proclaimed.

"Stuff?" Carys moved around the conference table, taking a place at Daisy's side. "Stuff like the lifestyle we were all pretty much raised in? The one her parents practice and has helped them have a very healthy, happy marriage? Are we talking about that stuff? Or are we simply talking about sex?"

"Maybe we should leave this discussion to Daisy and our parents," Aidan hedged.

"I'm happy to have Carys here," her mother said. "I'm also very glad Carys has apparently been mentoring Daisy at the club. She's right. I would like to know why my daughter stays in the locker room when she has a whole club to play in and Liam"—she pointed a finger Da's way—"don't even start on her being a good girl because I will bring Erin in here. I love you, but I won't let you shame our daughter. She isn't some shrinking virgin."

"Well, she's not anymore, and that's young Nathan's fault," Da shot back.

"No, it's Justin Harper's fault." He'd been her boyfriend, though she wouldn't have called them terribly serious. They'd had a bunch of classes together and they seemed to fit, and not once had she felt for him like she did for Nate.

Probably because he wasn't Nate and never had been even close. She had to acknowledge the fact that she'd been thinking about Nate Carter for years.

"I don't need to hear that," her da said. "I knew we shouldn't have let you go off to college."

"You probably shouldn't have let me out of the house," Daisy said quietly.

"Aidan, I'd like an answer." Her mother stared a hole through her brother. "What does your father mean?"

"I'd like to know, too." Carys crossed her arms over her chest. "I would also like to know why it's perfectly okay for me to play in the club but it's too dirty for Daisy."

"Now, you know what I'm talking about, Carys," her da insisted. "You have a perfectly good fiancé. It's fine for you and Aidan to do whatever you like."

"But I'm alone so I should be a virgin?" This conversation was everything she'd been afraid of.

"I only want you to be safe," he replied, his voice going low. "It's not the same for you as it is for Aidan. We have to protect you, and part of protecting you means having conversations with the men who want to get close to you."

What had Nate said? She hadn't believed him at the time, but now she wondered. "Like you had Aidan talk to guys at The Hideout?"

"What?" Carys's head shook like she didn't even understand the words Daisy was saying.

"Sweetie, why would you think your brother did that?" her mom asked.

She felt tears fill her eyes. "Well, it's not like I haven't tried to play. But when I do, suddenly no one is available." She turned to her brother. "Did you or did you not warn all the Doms at The Hideout not to play with me?"

"Don't you dare lie to her," her mother warned. "Aidan, I've dealt with your father putting Daisy on a pedestal because I thought he didn't know how to handle having a daughter. But you damn well know how to handle a sister. So I need to know if you've been meddling with your sister's relationships."

"I've been protecting her." Aidan sighed and pulled the cap from his head, shoving it into the pocket of his scrubs. "I know those guys, Mom."

Oh, but he didn't. "You barely knew that guy named Grim. And Josh Barnes."

"I knew his name was fucking Grim, and he wasn't getting his hands on my sister," Aidan shot back.

Carys's jaw had dropped. "You warned Doms off her?"

"I did what my father asked me to do," Aidan replied with a frown.

"Yes, he's done a good job, but he took his eyes off her this time," her da replied.

The room went quiet for a moment and her mother stared at her father. "Li, I need to speak with you in private."

She rarely heard her mother talk to anyone in that tone of voice. It was usually directed at her, a sure sign she was in trouble. She almost never heard her mother use a harsh tone when talking to Da or Aidan.

Daisy's gut clenched. She didn't want to be the reason they had this conversation. She hadn't meant to make her mom upset. She loved her mom. Loved them all. Her family was all she had.

Were they going to ask her to give up Nate?

What would she do if they told her she had to choose? Should she choose momentary joy over her lifelong family? When Nate eventually decided she was too much trouble, who would she have?

She'd only spent a single night with the man. The best night. The hours she'd spent with him had made her happier than she'd ever been, made her feel more than she'd thought she could, and it hadn't all been about sex. He'd talked to her, opened up to her, and it had been everything.

But if it hurt her father, did she have any right to momentary pleasure?

"Avery, you don't understand," her da argued.

Her mother stood and started for the door. "Oh, I understand. I understand what you've done to our girl. Daisy, I want you to know how much I love you and how proud I am of you. I'm going to have a discussion with your father and he's going to stay out of your relationship with Nate. I'll send over supper for both of you tonight, and I hope you have a lovely time. You should try the privacy rooms. They're a lot of fun."

"You shouldn't…" her da began but her mom was already walking out of the conference room. Her da followed behind. "Avery, slow down."

The door closed behind them.

"Dais," her brother began.

"So, all those times I worked up the courage to ask someone to play with me, you knew they never would?" It felt like a betrayal.

Her brother's face fell. "It wasn't like that. I wasn't trying to hurt you."

"And yet you did a fabulous job." Carys stared at her fiancé like she didn't know him. "I can't believe you did this."

Aidan leaned her way, an earnest expression on his face. "Why is it wrong to protect my sister?"

"You're protecting her from what, Aidan? From enjoying her life? From having good sex? From finding someone who she can love? You damn straight didn't protect her from feeling like no one wanted her," Carys pointed out.

It was good to know Carys hadn't realized what was happening. Another woman being in on it would have hurt far worse. "So my friends didn't know?"

Carys shook her head. "Absolutely not. I'm shocked no one talked, and now I'm worried the guys are being assholes and have some sort of pact to protect the little women. Are the other guys in on it? TJ? Tristan?"

"TJ doesn't have anything to do with it. Tris is looking out for his sister like I'm looking out for mine. When we started the club, Da was worried," Aidan began.

The door came open and Nate strode in, carrying the bags of sandwiches her mom had sent with Da this morning. Food was her mother's love language, but she didn't feel much like eating now.

"Are your parents okay?" Nate asked, setting the bag down. He also had a green can he handed to her. "You still like lemon lime? It's all you used to drink as a kid."

She loved it. "You remembered?"

His expression softened. "I remember a lot, love."

The way he was looking at her…like she was precious. Like she was the whole world.

"My parents aren't okay." Aidan reminded her he was still here.

"Neither are we," Carys said. "Nate, did he try to warn you off Daisy and Brianna? Any other young virgins who need to be protected at all costs?"

Nate whistled and started unpacking the food. "So, I was right and that's why all the Doms freaked out when they realized it was Daisy." He sat down beside her. "I watched you from the lounge. You should understand there wasn't an eye not on you last night. Every Dom in the club wanted you the minute you stepped out because you were the most gorgeous sub on the floor. It was only after they realized it was you that they started acting like you had an infectious disease or something."

Every word was a balm to her soul. "Well, I'm kind of glad now because I think it worked out for me."

He shook his head and took her hand in both of his. "I would have come after you. I knew what I wanted, and even if you'd started playing with someone else, I would have made a move."

He brought her hand to his lips and kissed it, sending a thrill of arousal through her.

"Is that what you wanted to protect her from?" Carys asked quietly.

Aidan's eyes closed, and he took a long breath. When he opened them again, there was regret in his gaze. "From the moment you were born, Da told me it was up to me to protect you. It's always been my job. I honestly wasn't trying to hurt you. I want the best for you, and I know that's you finding someone who loves you and having a great…sex life, but you're still my kid sister. The one I'm supposed to protect from everything."

"He's going to stop now," Carys promised. "And we're going to have a long talk with Tristan if he ever fucking comes home again."

Carys had enough on her plate. "I'm sorry. I don't mean to cause trouble between the two of you. Aidan, you should know I had already decided to find a new club. You won't have to worry about watching me make any mistakes."

"Daisy, please don't." Aidan slumped down onto the chair across from her. "I was trying to please Da. You know how much he adores you, and he's never been able to see beyond you being the five-year-old girl who wanted nothing more than to be with her father. Can you forgive me? I will talk to every Dom at the club and explain I was wrong."

"Maybe we should play on different nights." It still hurt, but it was easy to see her brother loved her. She wasn't so sure about her da, who seemed to be figuring out she wasn't a little girl. Daisy wasn't sure he would be able to love the woman she'd become.

"Nate and I will work that out," Aidan promised. "Car, do you want to talk?"

Carys sighed and moved around the conference table, sitting next to her fiancé. "Not really. If Daisy is willing to accept your apology, then I say we sit here and have our first double date." She reached for his hand. "Life is too short to be mad."

"Thank you." Aidan leaned over and kissed her and then looked to Daisy. "And I'm so sorry, Dais. I love you. I want you to be happy, and if your version of happiness means you've got a three-hundred-pound Australian tree on top of you most of the time, then I'm glad for you. I will talk to Da."

"I'm not three hundred pounds," Nate said with a frown. "I'm barely two sixty."

"And it's all muscle," Carys said with a wink.

"Hello, fiancé right here." Aidan frowned Carys's way.

"Well, I can look, and I'm going to high-five Dais when you two aren't looking. Now, is there a ham and brown bread? I'm starving, and I have to get back to the hospital for afternoon rounds soon." Carys took the sandwich Daisy gave her.

Aidan stood again. "And I will go get us some sodas since Nate only remembers what Daisy drinks."

"Mate, I didn't even know you were here." Nate had a big smile on his face.

"Well, you should know I'll be anywhere my sister needs me," Aidan vowed. "And I'll check and make sure Da is still breathing."

When the door closed behind him, Carys leaned over. "Thank you for not being too rough on him. The wedding is…well, is coming up way too fast, and it's settling in that Tristan isn't going to be there."

In some ways she understood. Daisy forced a smile on her face. "It's okay. I don't need revenge or anything."

"So I shouldn't have texted the twins and asked them what's going on?" Nate opened his own soda casually, like he hadn't dropped a bomb that was going to explode in her brother's face.

"You did what?" Carys asked, her jaw dropping slightly.

"Oh, I just figured if anyone would be able to tell me if I was right about what was going on, it's the twins." Nate was a gorgeous bastard, and she kind of wanted to jump him right there. "I mean they are in the information business. Kala said she would handle it. I don't know what she means by that."

Carys stood. "I have to go warn Aidan. Are they back? How long do we have?"

She rushed out the door, and Daisy was left alone with the most gorgeous man she'd ever met. The one who would probably break her heart.

"Hey, I didn't actually text the twins. I'm not trying to get your brother killed," Nate explained. "Just uncomfortable."

She grabbed a sandwich and forced herself to relax. "Well, if my brother thinks the twins are coming after him, he might move. Far away. Though they might think about recruiting him because I swear the twins know everything. Big brother did a great job hiding it."

But it was all out in the open now, and she would have to deal with the ramifications.

* * * *

Nate made sure the security system was on and then sent Avery a text letting her know they were safely locked in for the night.

He'd promised his mum's best friend he would protect her daughter with everything he had.

What he didn't tell her was he intended to protect her soul, too.

Something was up with Daisy. Oh, she was smiling and polite, and she'd been incredibly patient. But he saw right through her. Something had happened the night before, something that had shifted his universe into place, and he had zero intention of allowing those stars to unalign.

Daisy was the sun in the sky for him, and it didn't matter that everyone would tell him he hadn't known her long enough. He knew this deep in his bones. He'd spent the night with her and known he wanted all the nights with her.

He stepped out of the security office and jogged up the steps leading to the lounge and beyond, the dungeon floor.

Daisy sat in the lounge, her head down, staring at her phone.

This was what he'd dealt with all afternoon. After the confrontation with her father, she'd shut down. Oh, she would smile when she needed to, and she'd been polite when her father had walked in and told her to be careful, but when he'd hugged her, she'd barely hugged him back.

She'd done everything she'd been asked to do, including make a list of things for Devi to pick up for her and drop off at Sanctum. Devi had gone with her mom, and they'd even stopped at the grocery and stocked the kitchen for them.

"We're locked in for the night," he said, studying her. She was simply stunning. All the awkwardness of her girlhood was gone, and nothing but a glorious sun of a woman was left in her place. Which was precisely why he hated the fact that her glow had dimmed.

He had to find a way to wipe the afternoon out of her head for a little while.

She looked up. "Oh, good. I'll go see what Mom sent for dinner."

"I think we should talk first."

She sighed. "What is there to talk about, Nate? I've done everything that's been asked of me. I'm putting my life on hold so no one has to worry. If you've changed your mind, I can handle that. My family was a lot today."

She didn't understand him at all, but maybe he hadn't made himself clear. "I don't want to talk, Daisy. I want to chase you through this club. I want to rip your clothes off and fuck you on every possible surface."

Her eyes flared. "So we're going to do that thing where we're together in the club?"

"The club is simply where we are right now. If I'd thought for a second you would have been up for it, I would have hauled you into a closet at the office and fucked you there, but you were going through some things," he admitted. "And I don't have an actual office. It's a cubicle, and I'm too big to hide behind those walls. Besides, I want to hear you when you come."

"Nate," she began. "Maybe you should think about this. There's a reason my brother warned his friends off me, and no matter what he said, I have to think it was at least partially about protecting them."

"From how gorgeous you are? From how you could rock their whole fucking worlds?"

She stood, her hands going to her hips. Her fighting stance. "From how much trouble I can be."

He needed her to understand he could handle a fight. But he was also open to negotiations. "How about we make a deal, love? You get into trouble and you call me. When I get shot for you, you owe me some submission time."

Her expression softened, and she moved into his space. "I forgot. Nate, I should look at your arm."

He shook his head. "I don't need a nurse. It's fine. I don't even feel it. It was more like a graze. Now what happened to my truck is another story entirely. I'm going to need quite a bit of time for that. We were lucky to have Alex drive us here. Tomorrow they're going to give me a rental, and it won't be big enough."

She stepped back, putting space between them. "I'm sorry. I certainly didn't intend to wreck your truck. You know I didn't plan any of this. I didn't exactly go into the week thinking *Hey, I'd like to witness a bunch of crimes and lose another job and get shot at*."

At least the hollow look was out of her eyes. How often had she felt weary and no one else saw through her pretty mask? All he'd heard was about how crazy Daisy's life could be. Did anyone think about the toll it might take on her? How it affected her view of herself? "And yet it happened, and in the middle of a firefight, you wanted to make sure your da had breakfast."

"I told you, he's cranky when he doesn't eat." Daisy's arms crossed over those gorgeous breasts. "See, I'm trouble. I also don't behave the way people think I should. And you know what, it wasn't much of a firefight. I could have helped if you'd given me a gun."

The thought damn near gave him a heart attack, so why did the idea of an armed Daisy also get him a little hot? Not that he wasn't hot enough for her already. "If you don't like how I protect you, we can discuss it."

She stopped, her expression going blank again. "I know what you're doing, but it can't work. Nate, I know this whole sex thing is hot, but it wears off."

He didn't like the space between them, but he had to be careful. He moved toward her. "It won't with me. It's more than sex."

Sure enough she stepped back, but her eyes were on him, and he could see the longing plain in her gaze. "You can't know that."

He wasn't even sure she realized he was herding her to the back of the lounge, where there would be nowhere for her to go. He could feel his body heating up. This sensation was completely new for him. He'd certainly wanted sex before, but it had never been this crazed need for one woman. "Is it all about sex for you? Was that the only connection?"

"How would I even know? The truth is it was the best sex I've ever had. If you want me to stroke your ego, I can certainly do that."

His ego wasn't what he wanted her to stroke, but he had a point to make. "It was the best sex of my life, too."

"It's not enough to build something real on."

She was forgetting they had a past. "Daisy, we were friends once. It's not like we don't know each other and this is all coming out of nowhere."

She'd left her phone behind, and all her attention was now where he wanted it. On him. "I was Aidan's sister."

"Then how do I remember what soda you like? How would I know that when you were ten, your greatest ambition in life was to be a teacher? Back then you were afraid of the dark because your cousins once played a prank where they hid in your closet and pretended to be monsters." He wasn't going to let her be afraid of what they felt for each other. Another step and he had her where he wanted her. "Here's what you don't know. Before I came here, I think I was in some kind of depression. Not clinical, but I was definitely at a low place in my life because I was numb. I got out of the military because it wasn't filling my soul the way I thought it would. I thought since my father served, following in his footsteps would be the right thing to do, but I really went in because I didn't have any other plans. Funny thing is, I think I *am* going to follow in his footsteps. My father didn't have some grand career. His job was loving my mum. That was his place in the world, and last night I found mine."

She was backed up against the bar. "Nate, you can't know that."

"I can, and I think you know it, too." He wanted to kiss her and blow past all her walls, but she was in a delicate state. Still, he could feel the heat building between them. "One of the reasons I came here was because most of my favorite memories revolve around you and Aidan. I was going to meet with you, and a part of me hoped you would still be that girl following me around, looking up to me."

"You knew I had a crush on you?" The question came out breathy, as though she was trying to force herself to concentrate.

It was so easy to be honest with this woman. He wasn't the kind of man who prevaricated, but he also didn't open up easily. But with her, being honest was like breathing. "Of course. I hoped you still did because I thought that awkward girl would be perfect for me. I thought she would be a balm to my soul. I even entertained the idea of seeing if there was a spark between us. I needed something in my life to work. Something easy."

Her eyes narrowed. "I'm not easy, Nate."

He reached up and stroked back her hair, giving in to the undeniable need to touch her. "No, you're not. I was looking for an ember to keep me warm and I got the bloody volcano, and I won't go back for anything. If you're scared I'm going to get fed up with the chaos that seems to follow you, I won't. If you're scared I'll back out, let's settle it. We can get married."

"What?" She tried to move away from him, but there was nowhere to go.

It felt good to throw her off. He got the feeling he would be chasing after her for the rest of his life, so he would take these moments when he surprised her. "I can cause some chaos, too, baby. Think about it. It solves the problem with your da. We can tell him we were joking and I took your virginity on our wedding night, and you can be pregnant by the end of the year. I've heard pumping out a few adorable kiddos softens up the mad dads pretty quick."

She ducked under his arm, moving away again. She started to pace, putting one of the luxurious sofas between them. "Nate, that's a crazy idea."

He could pick that sucker up and toss it away if he wanted to. "Yeah, it is. Let's do it."

She stopped, staring at him like he'd gone insane. "We can't."

He shrugged. "Why not? We're young and stupid, and I'm so fucking crazy about you. If it's a mistake, it'll be the best one I ever make."

He moved closer to her.

"You can't be serious." She held her ground, but it was easy to see she was... Not exactly nervous. Aware. She was aware of him.

Beware, little sub.

"I am bloody serious."

She bit her bottom lip. "Nathan, are you stalking me?"

It was good to put it plainly, though he rather thought he'd already done it. "I told you what I want, Dais."

"You want to chase me through the club." Every word was the tiniest bit shaky, like she knew what came next. "You don't want me to make it easy on you. You don't want simple."

At last she understood him. "I want trouble. I want whacked-out, crazy fucking trouble. Can you give it to me? You have a safe word. You should be ready to use it because I'm feeling feral today, love. I'm never feral. I'm perfectly polite. Been that way all my life. I learned how to shove the beast that lives in me way down or I scare folks. But you bring it out. So I'm going to ask you again. Are you going to give me the trouble I'm craving?"

"Just in the club?"

He shook his head. "Nah, love. You made your choice. You get me in and out of this club. I don't want boundaries or walls. If we're in the office and you need my cock, I'll get really fucking creative. This isn't a ploy to get a couple of hours of sex from you. I want it forever. You and the sex and all the trouble I can stand."

Daisy's lips curled up in the sweetest smile, and then she took off running.

Nate's beast growled in the best way as he stalked his prey.

Chapter Nine

Daisy ran, sprinting toward the dungeon floor, dragging air into her lungs and letting the high of adrenaline flood her system.

She wasn't afraid of him. Not in any way.

Well, not physically. Physically all he would do was make her ache before he gave her everything she wanted.

Her heart, though. Damn. Her heart was already his, and she wondered if it hadn't always been. He'd talked about the awkward girl she'd been and how she'd followed him around. She had. When she'd learned he was coming to Dallas, a part of her had wondered if it was their time.

He was here now, and he seemed to want her.

She was trouble, but she never meant for bad things to happen. She'd helped a lot of people with her misadventures. Her mother often talked about the world always trying to find balance. What if the universe had sent her a big Aussie hunk to balance out the bad stuff?

The fight with her family was sitting in her head, but for now she banished it because she was a sweet sub being chased by a brute of a man who was going to inevitably capture her and fuck her senseless. All she had to worry about right now was how many orgasms she would get and how much he would make her pay for each and every one.

As ploys to get her out of her own head went, he'd come up with a winner.

She found her way onto what was obviously the dungeon floor. If they'd been doing this at The Hideout, she would likely have already run out of running space, but Sanctum seemed massive and she was only on the second floor. She sprinted into the shadows. There were some lights on the floor tracing the paths around the scene spaces and stages. The lounge had been lit with low, sexy lighting. She hadn't appreciated it, nor had she truly taken in the surroundings. She'd simply been waiting for Nate to give her the go-ahead to head up to the apartment her uncle had explained he'd had built because some "fucker" always needed a place to stay.

Her uncle had a way with words.

Nate did, too.

I learned how to shove the beast that lives in me way down or I scare folks. But you bring it out.

The words had worked some magic on her. She'd never been the girl a guy was crazy about. Except for the stalker in college her da had talked to and explained Daisy wasn't interested in.

Her father had always been there for her. Would he still be?

And she always wondered what he'd said to Carl since the dude left all his classes to become a ski instructor. She was pretty sure he'd never skied before because he was from Mississippi.

Actually, now that she thought about it, no one heard from Carl again.

"This only ends one way, Daisy."

She needed to get her head into this ridiculously hot game of his. She wasn't thinking about anything but him tonight.

Nate thought they could work. Maybe it could. At least for a while.

Daisy found herself in one of the scene spaces. There was a big desk and some bookcases. Office play. It gave her a place to hide. She ducked under the desk as she felt the hardwoods under her move slightly.

He was so big, she could feel it when he was walking toward her.

Big and safe and gorgeous. And he was stalking her. He was a beast for her.

"You want to know how it ends?"

She was pretty sure it ended in her taking a massive Aussie cock and screaming out his name, and they might not even get around to dinner tonight.

"It ends with me inside you." His voice was low and slightly menacing in the twilight glow from the ground lights. "That's the way it's always going to end, but don't think you're not inside me, too. I think you might have been in there all along."

She stood up, frowning his way. "Well, now I don't want to run from you. You're supposed to be a beast."

The grin he gave her was so feral. "Oh, I'm a beast. And now I have you."

She took off again because she wasn't finished with this game. What had he said? He'd felt numb? Had she felt the same, going through her days with only the hope she'd find a place? She didn't feel numb now. She felt more alive than she'd ever been before. She raced past the main stage. If she could get to the stairs, she was sure she would find the privacy rooms.

A big arm clotheslined her, plucking her right out of the air.

"Got you," he whispered as he held her tight against his chest.

He carried her off like she weighed nothing at all. Her feet were dangling above the floor. "Nathan, let me down now."

She didn't mean it, but the play was beyond exciting. Being picked up by him, manhandled wildly, sent her into arousal like nothing she'd felt before. The night they'd spent together had been amazing but controlled. There was a wildness to him that brought it out in her.

In Saint Daisy. In Ditzy Daisy. In Daisy, the Chaosbringer.

She felt like a new version of herself.

She'd been in scenes before, but nothing like what she did with Nate. With Nate there was fantasy, exploration.

"Not on your life. I told you. You made your choice, and you'll have to live with it. This is part of living with it, Dais." He set her down in the office space. "And you owe me, sub. Do you understand the heart attack you nearly gave me? First you leave our bed…"

He was rewriting history, and she wasn't going to have it. "I didn't know it was our bed. I thought I left the space we had agreed to play in for a brief period of time."

He growled her way. It was the sexiest sound.

"Well, it wasn't like we signed a contract. You should tell the next sub you're claiming her." She knew she was being a brat, but he hadn't even spanked her yet.

The heat in his eyes let her know he was up for it. His hand came out, circling her throat. It would have been menacing coming from anyone else. From anyone else, she would worry. From him she simply allowed herself to be pinned to the wall behind her, to feel how he could circle her whole neck with one hand. She let her body react to this man who somewhere deep down she recognized as her mate.

He was right about one thing. She did know him. They weren't starting from scratch.

Were they simply following fate?

His gorgeous face loomed over her, eyes practically glowing in the dark. "I already claimed you, sub. Do you want to question my rights?"

Her nipples were so tight as his body brushed against hers. "Your rights to what, Sir?"

"My rights to your body. To every inch of you. To your mouth and your breasts. My rights to have your legs wrapped around my waist while I shove my cock into its home. Your pussy, love. I'm definitely claiming rights to that. You should know I'm going to be the one scaring off all the Doms from here on out."

"Because I'm yours." She was. She was his. Maybe she'd always been his, always would be, and this was the magical moment in her life when he was hers, too.

"Because you are fucking mine." His mouth came down on hers, and she felt devoured in the best possible way. His tongue surged inside as he released her neck in favor of pinning her between the wall and his massive, muscular body. "Say it again, Dais."

He was a greedy Dom. He wanted everything she had and wouldn't accept less.

She was supposed to fight him, but her arms found his waist and tugged at the shirt he wore. It needed to go. The need to touch him was a desperate thing. A hunger she couldn't deny.

He pulled back slightly and stared down at her. "You want the shirt?"

She nodded.

Nate took the sides of the neck of the shirt and ripped it off, the sound of fabric tearing sending a thrill through her.

It was dumb because she knew he could have easily pulled it over his head. Instead he dragged it off, and it was a useless thing. Like the shirt wasn't important because she wanted something. She wanted him naked, and he would give it to her no matter the cost.

It made it easy for her to rip open her own blouse, the buttons pinging against the floor as they scattered around the dungeon. She tossed it aside, not caring where the fuck it went.

This was their paradise, and nothing could touch them here.

And she liked this game. Nate was staring at her, and she didn't like how sure he was of himself. So she ran away again.

He caught her in moments and dragged her to the medical playroom, ripping her bra off and throwing it behind him.

"Wrap your legs around me," he ordered as he lifted her up. And up. She'd thought he was planning on taking her lips, but instead he forced her higher so he could suck a nipple into his mouth. He licked her nipple and sucked and then gave her a nip that had her writhing against him before switching to the other breast and torturing it, too.

He let her slide down his body, setting her on her feet. "No more running, Dais."

But she was feeling every bit as savage as he'd claimed to be. "You want me, Nate. Earn me."

She took off again, but he was on her in a second, dragging her to the ground. He pinned her to the floor.

"I'll teach you not to run from me, sub." One hand stayed holding her to the ground while the other ran up her leg, under her skirt. He cupped her ass, giving her a squeeze. "But first, I'm going to make sure you're with me."

"Of course I'm with you." Where did he think she was?

Then she understood because his hand slipped between her legs and under the edge of her panties, one big finger sliding easily over her pussy. A low groan came from his chest. "That's what I want. I want you hot and wet and fucking ready."

She was. The need for sex was driving her. The need for him. "I'm ready. I'm so ready, Nate."

"And yet, you still have a lesson to learn." His voice had gone deliciously dominant as the hand that had softly stroked her withdrew, and she felt cool air on her legs as he shoved the skirt over her waist, exposing her. "These are going to have to go."

He dragged the underwear down, but only to trap her thighs, holding her legs closed as he forced her ass into the air.

There was no question what was about to happen and yet when his big hand came down on her cheeks, she couldn't help but shout out as the pain exploded against her aroused skin, heightening the sensation and giving it depth. She was bent over and contorted as he maneuvered her into the position he wanted, over one knee, his big leg acting like a brace, folding her in two as he slapped her ass without mercy.

She held on to his ankle, letting every smack flow over her, driving her higher and higher to a place she hadn't thought she would be. A place she'd wanted to hide from him.

The physical pain shoved against the events of the day and suddenly she was crying.

She hadn't realized how much she'd bottled up, how much she'd shoved down over the last several days. Weeks. Months. She'd been so fucking alone.

The sobs began, and then she was lifted up into the air. Nate managed to get her skirt and underwear off and cradled her naked body against his chest. She felt warm and safe, and it was okay to cry with him. He wanted her emotions. He wasn't going to tell her she had fucking crazy eyes and she should see a therapist.

He'd wanted her here because he wanted to share the burden of what she'd been through.

Nate carried her through the dungeon, carried her up the stairs. She barely recognized they were moving, she held on to him so tightly.

She'd lost another job, been the one who worried her parents, who couldn't do a simple fucking task, and now she might lose her family over the only good thing that had happened to her in forever. It wasn't fair. It wasn't fucking fair.

Nate kicked open the first door, and she found herself in a large, luxurious bedroom. She barely saw anything as Nate strode to the massive bed. She thought he'd toss her on it, but he wrapped his arms tight around her and sat down, maneuvering her so she was straddling him.

"Tell me," he commanded, his hand tangling in her hair.

She shook her head. "Later. Not now, Nate."

"Then take what you want, sub. Take what you need."

She knew what she wanted. To drown in him. Her ass ached as she slid off his lap, fitting herself between his legs. He hissed above her as she worked the fly of his jeans, easing the zipper down.

"Damn, me," he said as she pulled at the waistband of his boxers and freed his cock.

This was what she needed. He'd given her the emotional release she'd required to be open to him. Now she could show him she was exactly the storm he wanted.

She stared at his gorgeous cock, wrapped her hand around it, and felt his groan in her pussy. She was probably the biggest mess. She was sure her mascara was everywhere, and he was still looking at her like she was the most beautiful thing he'd ever seen.

Daisy stroked his cock, watching as a pearly bead pulsed from the head.

"You're killing me," he whispered. His hand came out to smooth her hair back. "And I'll die happy."

She lowered her head, giving him a lick. They hadn't gotten to this part the first time. He'd been too into tying her up and torturing her. It was time for some sweet payback. She kept her eyes on him as she sucked his cockhead past her lips.

Nate's chest hitched, his head falling forward and then back as he gave over to her.

He tasted so perfect. Salty and masculine, the scent of his arousal filling her senses. She took him deeper, rolling her tongue over his dick. He filled her mouth like he filled her pussy—to overflowing. He was almost too much.

Like she was.

Too much might be just enough to build something real.

"That's right. Fuck, you feel so good, baby," he said, his eyes on her, watching where his cock disappeared into her mouth.

She ran her tongue over and around him, fighting to take as much as she could.

"Daisy, I don't want to come in your mouth. Please, love. I want to look in your eyes this time," he said, his hands on her hair, but he didn't force the issue, merely gave her the choice.

She went back on her knees and watched as he managed to shove his jeans down. There were condoms on the nightstand and she picked one up, a solemn feeling spreading through her because while it had started out as a hot game, she felt so connected to this man. His pull drew her in, and she couldn't help it. A moth to his flame. It didn't matter if she burned. Her path was set.

She eased the condom on and then straddled him again, not even giving him a chance to kick his pants off. He didn't need to. Nathan Carter was right where she wanted him.

"Daisy," he began.

She shook her head and lowered her lips to his even as she felt his cock at her pussy. Pure pleasure threatened to drown her as she slid onto his cock. Her tongue tangled with his, arms wrapping around each other until she wasn't sure where she ended and he began. She tilted her hips, taking him inside. She loved how fucking big he was, stretching her, but she could handle him.

She worked her way down his cock in little passes until she finally had the whole of him filling her up.

"Fuck. You feel so good, and it's not just about how perfect you fit me." Nate's hands gripped her hips.

It was more than sex. It scared her but maybe that was a good thing.

She started to move, her eyes held by his as he shifted with her. She found the perfect spot and worked his cock over and over until she couldn't stand it a second more and then held herself tight against him, riding the wave of her orgasm. The second she was limp against him, he rolled them over on the bed, bringing his weight down on her.

She loved the way he pressed her into the mattress, adored how he didn't pretend she was fragile and he was worried he would break her. He simply took her because she was his and he was hers and this was natural.

She wrapped her legs around him, watching his gorgeous face as he thrust in over and over. Then he stiffened, and his eyes were on her as he went over the edge.

Pure satisfaction filled her soul as Nate fell to the bed beside her, and for a moment, everything felt right with Daisy's world.

* * * *

Nate stretched on the big bed and watched as Daisy walked out of the bathroom, her hair wrapped in a towel and an oversized robe around her body. He'd taken a shower with her, slowly making love to her again. He'd pressed her against the tile and filled her with him.

Fuck, she was beautiful. And he'd meant what he'd said. She was his. Oh, he was absolutely certain she was thinking this was all play, but it wasn't. If this was a game, it was the most important one of his life, and he intended to win.

"You don't need the robe."

A brow arched over her emerald eyes. "What if I'm cold?"

He pulled the covers down. "Then I'll keep you warm. I've been told I'm a furnace. It's sad for you, but you'll get used to it."

She wrinkled her nose, an expression he was learning meant she was going along with something but she wasn't totally sold on an idea. The robe came off, and she crawled into bed with him. "What do you think that's about?"

He glanced over and frowned. How the hell had he missed the floor-to-ceiling, velvet painted rock-star portrait? Well, his mind had been full of her, but it was a detail he was certain would have registered at any other time. "Someone really likes old music. I'm not sure. He looks familiar, but in a classic rock way. Though I'm not supposed to call it classic rock because my father then does some math and bemoans his age."

Daisy sat next to him, her back against the headboard. He noticed she didn't pull the covers up, preferring to leave her gorgeous body on display. Yeah, that was why the blond dude in the bandana hadn't made an impression. "I have never actually been in the club part of this building. There's a daycare in the building next door. I spent a lot of time there, but I never came in here. I finally get why Uncle Ian calls The Hideout a dump. We don't have anything like this. It kind of makes me wonder how much all this cost. Da complains about the price of raspberries. I wonder how much the obviously custom-built spanking bench cost. I bet it's a lot of raspberries."

"Well, from what I understand, this place started out a lot like The Hideout." He shifted so he was facing her. So it was easy to lean over and brush his lips against her shoulder.

Her family had put a wall up between them, and he had to find a way to break it down. He'd been certain crying would help shake those walls, but he worried she'd rebuilt them.

"Well, it's beautiful now. I suppose that's what matters," she said. "It's just weird to be here. Like something forbidden."

"I've been to this club, though I don't remember it."

She looked his way finally, curiosity in her green eyes. "I didn't know you spent much time in Dallas. I mean I know you came to visit over the years, but we mostly visited you."

He'd been told the story, though it wasn't one he shared often. It felt right to share it with her. He eased down so he could lay his head on her lap, feel her soft skin against his cheek. "My mum got into a spot of trouble. A bit like you have. She was trying to help someone and it caught the attention of some very bad blokes. I was only a few months old. Mum went on the run and came to the place where she felt safest."

Her hand came to his head, fingers starting to play in his hair as though she couldn't stop herself from touching him. "She went to my mom."

"She did," Nate replied. "She came to Dallas looking for help, and a day or two later my father showed up. He was standing in the daycare room at the McKay-Taggart building when he found out I existed."

"Really?" The hand on his head moved in soothing strokes. "He didn't know? He wasn't there when you were born?"

He felt like a big tiger being utterly tamed by a kitten. "Nope. He'd been a dumb arse who decided he wasn't good enough for my mum, and so they had a one-night stand and he left. She tried to contact him, but he wouldn't take her calls," Nate explained. "So, yeah, he wasn't there when I was born. He didn't know I existed until he walked into the McKay-Taggart building and I was in the daycare. Adam Miles still complains about his back because my tough old dad fainted dead away at the sight of me."

A chuckle came from her. "Oh, now I understand what Uncle Adam means when he says Australia fell on him. I always thought it was some weird metaphor. So let me guess. They decided to stash your mom here."

"Bingo."

She leaned over, looking down into his eyes. "Did they fall in love all over again right here?"

"I don't think so. I don't think it was easy. My mum… You know her history, right?"

Daisy's expression fell. "Yes. I know. I know your mom was in an accident with mine when they were young, and that's how my sister died along with Mom's first husband."

"And your mum found a way to forgive her and saved her life. I'm here today because of Avery O'Donnell's boundless love. But her love couldn't fix my mum's guilt. It took something else to do that. She was ready to reject my father's love because she didn't think she was worthy of it. She was ready to let me go live with him. And then your da got stung by a bee."

At the mention of her father, her hand retreated, and she went slightly stiff. "My da is very allergic to bees. Everyone jokes with him, but Mom saw it once and still shudders when she thinks about it."

He was glad she didn't remember that day. "My mom saved him, and what she realized was she wouldn't have been there to save him if she hadn't been on the road that night. She wouldn't have learned what she needed to know, wouldn't have had the skills to save him. Daisy, do you know why I'm telling you this?"

She shook her head.

He sat up. This was a conversation where they had to be face to face. "Because I'm not my dad. I need you to understand I don't question fate. I don't sit around and wonder if I'm good enough. I will make myself good enough for you."

"Nate," she began.

"No, don't Nate me. I told you. You made your choice. If I thought for a second you pulling away from me had anything to do with your heart, I would step back. But this isn't about your heart. You were perfectly happy before your father made an arse of himself. This is about you being worried he's going to see you differently. He will, and it's about bloody time, Dais."

She sniffled. "You don't understand."

His heart ached, but he wasn't going to let her continue down this road. "Don't understand what? Being the kid in the family who doesn't seem to have some awesome destiny? Who isn't clearly talented? I do understand that. Since the day Elodie started to dance, I knew she was more talented, more driven than me, and therefore had a whole lot of our parents' attention. That's what it's like to be the sibling who isn't gifted."

"I don't resent my brother," she replied quietly. "Not even after what I learned today. I'm happy for him."

He believed her. "And I'm thrilled for my sister. I love watching her dance. She's happy and she makes other people happy. They have their path, and we have ours."

"Ours is apparently getting stuck in this club."

He shrugged. "Maybe that's fate, too. Maybe it wouldn't work if you had too much time to think. If there was space between us, your father might decide I'm not worthy of his sweet daughter and he would get a chance to convince you. But that's not what happened, and we're here for a while. I meant what I said. I'm not leaving you. If you're stuck here, then so am I. If it gets to be too much, we can go to Australia. My parents' station hasn't sold yet. We can stay there for a bit and then move to The Garden. Traveling might be good for us."

Daisy sighed. "Somehow I don't see Uncle Ian paying you to go on vacation with me."

"I think you'll find everyone wants you safe. They might fight me on travel, but it's a fight I can win. If for some crazy reason he fires me, well, I've got a bit of cash saved. I can take care of us until you're safe. I'll find another job, and we'll figure out where we want to be."

Tears filled her eyes. "You are too good to be true."

"I assure you, love, I'm not."

"I want to believe you," Daisy whispered. "I want to believe in this. You don't even understand how weird this is for me."

"I do," he argued. He knew her better than she thought he did. "You're the girl who throws herself into everything. When you decide to do something, you give it one hundred percent of yourself. You take it with both hands and try everything you can to make it work."

"Nothing works, Nate."

She'd had the roughest of days, and he needed to find a way to bring back her natural resiliency. "Sure it does. You have friends who adore you, a family who does everything they can to protect you."

"Yeah, up to and including ruining any chance I had at finding a boyfriend."

He was upset for her about what her father had done, but he rather thought it had proved a point. "Baby, if a man is too afraid to date you because your father and brother threaten him, he doesn't want you enough. I need you to understand absolutely no one in this world can keep me away from you except you. If you don't want me, I'll walk away, but you're the only one who can make me. There's no threat, no incentive, nothing can control me with the exception of you."

"How can you know you want me?"

"Do you want me?"

Tears dripped from her eyes. "So much it hurts."

He pulled her close. "And how can you know?"

"Because I always have," she whispered. "Because I knew what I was doing when I put on Kenzie's mask. I was going to steal a night from you."

He chuckled, a warm feeling invading his bones. This was so much more than lust. This was the reason his dad lit up when his mum walked in a room. He couldn't imagine the demons his father must have fought, the ones that made him walk away from this feeling. He wasn't making the same mistake. He cuddled her against his chest. "Sorry, love. Your plan is not going to work out."

She seemed to give in, relaxing against him. "You better be sure, Carter, because you're right. When I'm in, I'm in. And when the whole stupid assassins are after me thing is over, I'm going to find a job I love and you can move into my house and… I still don't know what to do about my da."

"Your da is being an idiot." Of this he had zero worries. Liam O'Donnell was scared of losing his daughter. He would figure this out. "And he'll come around. He's a smart man. Your mum is already cool with this."

"My mum loves you," she said quietly.

"I know it doesn't seem like it, but your da does, too. Liam has been a solid figure in my life since I was a baby. His world is getting rocked right now, but he'll see this is for the best in the end." He breathed her in. There was such peace here. Daisy was a storm, but like a storm she was necessary, and the world felt fresh and new. "I promise you, this won't last. He adores you, but change is hard. Aidan's already on board. There's no way your father doesn't see this relationship is good for both of us. Until then, we should enjoy being alone. How many new couples get this kind of time together?"

She turned her head up, her lips curling in a sexy smile. "So what you're saying is me getting on an assassin's hit list is actually a good thing."

His girl could turn a frown upside down. "My dick thinks so."

That smile turned brilliant. "So you're all in?"

In the end it was the easiest decision he'd ever made. "I'm all in, love."

"And you're okay with what it means for me to be all in."

Oh, she could bring it on. Being with Daisy would mean danger at every corner. Or at least mischief. But then he'd complained about life being boring. "I told you. I love your winds, Typhoon. I guess I should call you a hurricane since I'm here now."

She sat up, throwing a leg over his waist and sliding her core right over his cock. "Then you should know, I have some making up to do. Saint Daisy needs to get a little dirty, baby."

He held on as the storm started all over again.

Chapter Ten

Nate woke the second his phone buzzed. He'd connected it to the security system the night before. Any disruption would send an alert.

Someone had turned off the alarm and then reset the sucker in under thirty seconds.

He'd been plain. Anyone coming in or out of Sanctum when the club wasn't open was supposed to send him notification. There had been no notifications.

So either the elders were testing him or they had an assassin who happened to know the ever-changing code to the security system at Sanctum. One of those was hard to believe, and the other not at all surprising.

He should have expected it. He'd heard rumors about all the bodyguards getting wild tests of their skills when they signed on at McKay-Taggart. He was literally guarding one of the founder's beloved daughters. There was zero chance they wouldn't try to fuck with him and prove he couldn't do it.

Daisy shifted in bed when he moved away from her, like she was a heat-seeking missile. It was dark without the light from his phone, but the illumination coming from the jukebox gave everything a low glow. Yeah, there was an old-school jukebox. He hadn't played anything off of it because it was all old stuff, but it had been exactly the right height to fuck Daisy against.

"Wake up, love. We've got incoming."

She shot up in bed, her hair wild around her shoulders. "Holy shit. You think the bad guys are here?"

Damn, but she looked good enough to eat. He eased out of bed, reaching for his boxers. If he knew Taggart and the crew, they would move quickly in the hopes of catching him in bed. Unfortunately, catching him in bed meant catching Daisy, and he didn't want her embarrassed. "Nah." He grabbed his SIG. "I think this is more about me than you. Your da is testing me. Lock yourself in the bathroom just in case, and call the MT building. Let them know someone used the security code to enter Sanctum unauthorized."

Daisy moved swiftly, dragging the sheet around her. "You're sure it's Da?"

"Whoever it was, they knew the alarm code," he replied. "It runs on a constantly shifting algorithm Hutch created. As it can only be accessed by a few phones, I doubt it's our bad guys. Now hurry because they'll try the apartment first, but they'll figure out quickly we're not there. If they catch me, your da will try to get me replaced."

She held the sheet around her with one hand and her phone in the other. "Just remember he has a bad back. They all do, and they all think they're still twenty-five and in perfect military condition. Be nice."

She kissed him and moved to the bathroom, already on the phone. "Hey, I needed to let you guys know we're apparently being invaded by cartel members down at Sanctum. It's okay. Nate is taking care of them. I'm pretty sure he's already taken most of them out. It was a lot of blood. I was hoping Aunt Charlotte would give me some cleaning tips."

He loved her.

Damn, he loved her. There was no real time to deal with the revelation because if he got caught, there would be all kinds of hell to pay.

Or he could be dealing with a very well-prepared assassin.

The minute he eased out of the privacy room, he realized he was definitely dealing with the big bosses, and they didn't even respect him.

"How long should we wait?" Devi Taggart was in the lounge below, standing with Brianna Dean-Miles and... Damn, they'd brought Avery with them.

"I don't know," Avery said quietly. "I don't like this. He was in Aussie Special Forces. How much should he have to prove?"

"I think it's kind of exciting." Brianna had a water bottle in her hand and looked like she'd come from a yoga class. Or was going to one. She stood beside one of the tables which was covered in bags, some luggage-like and others from a local grocery store. "Also, do you think they'll drag him out here naked?" Bri gasped as Devi punched her arm. "Sorry. I can look, right? I mean the dude is hot. Do you think Daisy's sleeping with him?"

"From what I can see, there's probably not a lot of sleeping," Avery said with a sigh. "I'm pretty sure that's Daisy's skirt on the dungeon floor.

I wish they'd picked up after themselves."

Well, he'd meant to tidy up this morning.

"Good for Dais because Bri's right. I got a closeup look at him and he's hot," Devi announced.

He moved down the stairs. It was good to know he still had it. They weren't looking his way, so it was easy to maneuver around them. The apartment was on the other side of the building, over the locker rooms and the security office. It was where they would look because they were supposed to stay in those apartments. Like the good boy and girl they were. In two separate rooms.

It was exactly what he would have done had the client been anyone but Daisy O'Donnell. He could be attracted to a woman and stay professional. Hell, he'd worked with women he would have been more than happy to sleep with and never once made a move on one.

He couldn't keep his hands off that gorgeous ball of trouble. Not for anything.

He caught sight of a big guy slipping down the stairs, moving toward the first floor. It was obvious he'd already checked the dungeon and was moving through a predetermined sweep.

"What do you mean the apartment is empty?" the man questioned quietly over the comm he was using. They'd brought in actual comms. Like this was a real op. Nate wasn't sure if he was flattered or offended. It wasn't like these men hadn't known him his whole bloody life. "No. I don't know where the fuck they are. Well, I know where they've been. There's a trail of clothes all over the dungeon. Li's going to lose his shit. I told you this was a bad idea."

Alex McKay was almost to the stairs. Nate put his back to the wall and shuffled against it, keeping to the shadows. Fuckers had turned on some of the lights. Guess night vision degraded with age. The club didn't have windows for obvious reasons, so the fact that it was morning didn't change the situation. It stayed pretty dark, with only ambient lighting on.

"I don't know. They're young and clearly into each other. You put them in a freaking sex club and you're surprised they played?" Alex asked. "I'm checking downstairs. Someone go check the privacy rooms, but I have to assume he's asleep. Probably because he was awake most of the night. And no, I'm not telling Liam. I'll contact you when I get down to security."

Nate rounded the corner and put his SIG to the back of Alex's head. "Or I'm awake because I'm also on a job. Do I need to incapacitate you or is it enough that I could have killed you?"

"Fuck." Alex's hands came up. "Nope. I'm out. I'll go join the ladies if you'll let me. And no, I won't be informing anyone. I'd like to see how you handle them."

Hopefully the same way he'd handled Alex. "Yeah, I'll take the comm unit. You go tell Avery that Daisy is perfectly safe but her husband might not be."

Alex handed over the comm unit. "Good luck, man. And dude, couldn't you have put on some clothes?"

He would have if they'd given him time, but this was exactly what they'd wanted. Him with his pants down. So they could deal with his dick barely encased in his boxers. Nate settled the comm unit into his left ear.

"Alex, I asked you a question." Ian's voice came over the line.

Nate kept quiet. He glanced up. He'd made a pretty thorough inspection of the place when they'd first gotten here. The apartment could be accessed only by the stairs at the west side of the dungeon floor. Luckily that part was still pretty dark and there was only one sniper position, and he'd just come from it. He moved through the shadows to the edge of the stairs, kneeling down.

"Fuck, Li. Alex isn't answering which means Nate got him. Can we call this off now? I told you he's solid, and I hope he didn't think we were actually here to kill his sweetheart." Ian sounded irritated as hell.

"Solid? The fucker apparently spent the whole night ripping off my poor Daisy's clothes." Liam sounded way more irritated.

The ripping off portion had been a small part of the night, and she'd done her fair share of damage, too. He was pretty sure he had some nail marks on his back. His baby could get wild.

Wild was exactly how he liked her.

Ian jogged down the steps and moved right where Nate needed him to be.

"Hold on. Charlie's calling." Ian put his cell to his ears. "Hey, baby...wait...what? No. No one is dead. Don't call the police. Don't..."

His baby had given him the chaos he needed. He put the SIG to the back of Ian's head.

"Fuck me," Ian said, dropping his cell and holding his hands up. "Nate, this was not my idea."

"No, it was mine," Liam said.

And that was when he realized Li was behind him. Damn it. "Ian, I need some advice."

A low chuckle came from the big boss. "Well, Nate, my advice is to not shoot me in the back of the head. Are we in some weird standoff? I can't see, and honestly, I'm too old for this shit. Are you sure you don't want one of the twins? I'll hand either one off no problem. I'll even throw in a new truck. Don't discount that. One of the reasons we're here is I picked up your rental. It's a Fiat. I had to get Bri and Devi to drive it over because none of the rest of us fit."

"I suggest you put the gun down now, Nathan," Liam threatened.

Nate hadn't gotten the advice he so needed. "Do I take him out or let him shoot me? Because I'm torn. Daisy told me he's got a bad back."

"A bad back my arse," Li bit out.

"She didn't say anything about your arse," Nate allowed. "Just your back. I'm supposed to be nice to you."

Ian snorted. "Take the old guy down. It's the only language he'll understand."

"As if he…" Liam began.

Nate turned, his arm coming out to knock the gun away, and then he shifted, one leg sweeping under Liam's and putting him on the ground. Nate was on one knee, his hand around his future father-in-law's throat before Li could take another breath.

He could suddenly see exactly how amped Daisy's father was.

"Charlie, baby, I'll call you back. No. I'm going to assume Daisy wanted to give Nate some cover so she called in and told a whopper of a story and it worked," Ian was saying. "However, Nate's trying to decide if he's going to kill Li. I know. I already offered him one of the twins. He seems intent on Daisy."

"Nate, what are you doing to my da?" Daisy was out on the stairs leading from the privacy rooms down to the lounge, still dressed in the sheet she'd taken from the bed. "I told you about his back."

Nate stood, holding his hands up. "He put a gun to the back of my head."

"Yes, and I could have killed you if I wanted to. Well, if I'd thought I could get away with it." Liam sat up and groaned when he looked over at his daughter. "Girl, where the hell are your clothes?"

Avery rushed over. "Liam, are you all right? Did you hurt your back?"

Liam stopped looking angry long enough to reach for his wife's hand. "I'm fine, my darlin." The frown was back when he looked at Daisy, who'd made her way down the stairs and was joined by her friends. "I'm still wondering where our daughter's clothes got to. Did they run away from you, girl?"

Daisy shrugged. "They're kind of all over. Nate chased me through the dungeon and then we ended up in this weird room with Elvis, I think."

Ian turned her way, his jaw dropping. "You slept in my personal privacy room? And that is not Elvis. Li, you have ruined that girl. Fucking Elvis. That is Axl Rose, you infant."

"Who?" Daisy asked, her eyes wide.

Axl Rose. That's who the dude was. Now he remembered. "Babe, I think he was like a singer in the olden days."

"Don't matter who he was. The fact is this man is taking advantage of my daughter." Liam managed to get off the floor. "And where the hell are your clothes, Nathan? Do you think you're in the bloody Garden of Eden? You are supposed to be a bodyguard not some gigolo."

"Is that an old-time singer, too?" Daisy asked.

It was good to know she wasn't up on all the ways a man could be called a sex worker. He was going to ignore it. He definitely wasn't going to tell Liam he would fulfill his daughter's sexual needs for absolutely no money at all.

"Well, I thought someone might be trying to kill us so I locked Daisy in and came out to save us," Nate explained with a long sigh. "Then I realized it was just the old guard trying to test the new."

"Old guard, my arse," Liam began and put a hand to his lower back.

"Li, are you okay?" Avery stared at her husband. "I told you this was a bad idea. Nate, I'm sorry. He wanted to make sure you were taking the job seriously. I told him you were."

"I was right. Look at him. He's not even dressed," Liam complained. "And I easily got him."

Alex frowned. "I told you where he was because I thought it would be funny to watch him take Ian down. You had no idea where he was, and I only did because he let me go. What the hell, man? Nate, you did a good job. I thought we would catch you sleeping. The alarm didn't go off."

"The uncles made us run through really fast. They were yelling like we were in the Army," Brianna complained.

Liam shook his head. "Well, young lady, you were taking your sweet time."

"She was trying to bring her friend some coffee." It was obvious Avery was not happy.

Damn. This would set Daisy back.

"There's coffee?" Daisy came running in. Not running, exactly. She looked like a princess skipping through some meadow. Except she had crazy sex hair. "Please tell me you got…"

Brianna held out a covered cup. "White mocha nonfat with extra foam. And I got Nate a regular old coffee because I didn't know how he took it. There's also a flat white if you prefer, and I brought a bunch of ham and cheese croissants because I figured the big guy could eat. I asked Mrs. Ward to give us whatever she thought her husband would eat. It was a lot." She gave him a smile. "Hi. You look way different than when you were fifteen, and I kind of thought you were hot then."

"Bri," Devi said.

Daisy waved her off. "No, it's okay. He's a work of art. Look all you like. I can share."

Nate raised a brow.

Daisy blushed. "Not like that. You're pretty and stuff. I don't want you to dim your glow because I might get jealous. We're not going to be like that. Now I told you not to hurt Da. He's delicate."

"I'm not delicate." Liam closed his eyes. "Except when it comes to this. For the sake of all the heavens, girl, put some clothes on."

"She is perfectly covered for a young woman who had her sleep horribly interrupted," Avery argued.

"Well, she needs to get dressed because we're finding another bodyguard. One who doesn't take advantage of her," Liam shot back.

"That room is sacred," Ian said with a shake of his head. "It is a temple to my marriage."

"Then you should have locked it up." Nate didn't see the problem.

"And from what the twins have told me, we suitably honored your marriage, Uncle Ian," Daisy said with a sparkle in her eyes. She'd secured the sheet, and it honestly looked like any number of formal gowns he'd seen. It draped over her gorgeous body. Of course most of those gowns wouldn't smell like sex.

Damn, he wanted her again, and they were standing in a room full of her relatives. His brain was all Daisy all the time.

"The twins have told us many tales," Devi said, her nose wrinkling. "Like whenever they hear that old band playing, they know their parents are going at it. It's horrifying."

Ian's eyes narrowed. "I've got two words for you, niece. Taylor Swift."

Devi gasped. "No. That's just because Dad likes her. It's not...ewww. It ruins so much music for me."

"Ian, everyone's used the jukebox room," Alex pointed out.

"I'm not getting another bodyguard." Daisy got in the middle of her parents. "Nate did a great job. He made me hide, and then I thought it might help him if I called Aunt Charlotte and told her Uncle Ian was about to get sniped. I knew Uncle Ian would be here because he is always in the middle of drama. I was going to call the cops. Bringing in the authorities would have caused more chaos, but Aunt Charlotte begged me to give her a couple of minutes. And then I went to check and I saw that Da was being an asshole."

"Daisy, language," her father admonished.

Daisy shrugged. "Well, you're already mad at me for having a sex life. I don't have to pretend to be some perfect princess so you'll still love me. I can be me. I can be honest. Nate did an excellent job."

There was one problem with what she was saying. He appreciated the support, but she'd disobeyed. "Which you shouldn't have seen because you are supposed to be locked in the bathroom waiting for me to give you the all clear."

"Well, I couldn't hear anything. I think those rooms are like noise canceling or something," Daisy complained. "We should get whatever it is at The Hideout. Sometimes the privacy rooms get real loud, if you know what I mean. Also, do you think we could ask the board to get a room with a jukebox? Because it's the exact right height."

Ian put a hand to his heart. "Not my jukebox."

Alex snorted.

"Right height?" Her father had gone pale. "You shouldn't have been in dat room at all. You were supposed to stay in the apartment, which has two bedrooms."

"I mean, if you think about it, he can probably protect her better if they stay in the same room," Brianna offered. "A lot of my mom's books fall into the only one bed trope."

"I assure you there are plenty of beds in this place, and this ain't one of Serena's romance novels," Liam shot back.

"I don't know. Let's see. Childhood friends take one look at each other after a decade apart and fall madly in love," Avery began. "Sounds like a romance to me."

Liam wasn't finished. "How about this scenario? Asshole can't handle the military and comes to America to find an easier life and takes one look at an innocent girl and sees a meal ticket."

Ian groaned and looked to his best friend. "We can't save him. You want to break into the Scotch? It's going to be a long day. The twins finally dug Zach out of the rubble and they're on their way back, so I have to sit in on them complaining all afternoon. Have you ever listened to a whiny captain yell about how a bomb exploded and he got caught for days in the inevitable landslide it caused? It's a lot, man. And it's not like Lou didn't invent an extremely long straw to keep the fucker hydrated. Kids are soft these days."

Alex slapped Ian's shoulder. "Yeah, Scotch sounds like a good idea. I've never been so happy Coop is mostly transportation."

"Your boy was the smart one," Ian agreed.

"Meal ticket?" Daisy asked, her voice going low.

"Oh, shit," Devi said under her breath. "Dais, you should think about this. You're kind of half naked in front of your parents, and you have that look in your eyes."

Brianna shook her head. "There's no stopping her now. We should go with the uncles."

"This is going to get bad," Devi whispered. "Daisy is super sweet until she gets angry and then… Well, it's bad. But she never does this around her parents."

Avery sighed. "No, she never does this around her father. I assure you I've seen my daughter get really angry. It's odd. Almost like she got it from somewhere. From like DNA or something. I wonder from who."

Daisy's eyes had narrowed. "Nathan, I'm going to need you to hold my coffee. Maybe you should go pour some Bailey's in it. Or whiskey. I'm feeling like whiskey this morning." Her accent changed, and she sounded as Irish as her father. "*Táim chun labhairt le m'athair.*"

Devi held Bri's hand and started to back away. "She's gone Irish."

Nate took her coffee. "Daisy, it's okay. I told you I don't care what he thinks about me."

Daisy ignored him. "What meal ticket do you think I am, Da? *Minigh seo dom.*"

"I don't have to explain anything to you, *iníon*," her father replied. "I have obviously been too lenient, and that stops now."

"Liam, please," Avery begged.

He shook his head. "No. Avery, you know I love you. You're my world. But she's my responsibility, and I've failed."

He watched Daisy's skin go pale as her father's words hit her.

"I'm a failure?" Daisy asked.

Damn it. "He doesn't mean it."

"I didn't say you failed," Liam replied, a shocked expression hitting his face. Like he hadn't thought those words through. "I said I did. I should never have let you go off to college. I should have known you would run wild."

"Oh, Da." She shook her head. "I started running wild so long before college." She'd gone a bit cold. "You want to know all the reasons why I'm a failure? Let's talk about who stole your whiskey when I was fifteen. You were so sure it was Aidan. It was me. And then when you locked it up, I still got into it. I replaced it with the big jug of iced tea I always made Mom get from the store. The one I kept in my room and everyone wondered how I could drink it without ice. You told me a proper Irish girl wouldn't drink it at all. Well, that's because this proper Irish girl was drinking your whiskey."

Devi held up a hand. "Okay, could we maybe not mention this particular part to my parents?"

Liam pointed a finger his daughter's way. "I knew it wasn't whiskey. I convinced myself it had gone bad."

"It was delicious," Daisy replied, a dark gleam in her eyes. "And the time the school let out because the fire alarms went off? I made good use of the free time, Da."

"Yes, you went to the library."

"I went to the lake with Leo Hall, and you do not want to know what we did in the back of his truck," Daisy taunted.

Liam went pale. "No. You wouldn't."

Avery threw up her hands. "Of course, she would. She is your daughter, Liam. You know I love you, but you have blinders on when it comes to her, and it's not doing either of you any good. She feels like she's forced to lie because you won't love her if you see the truth, and you're trying so hard to not notice she's your mirror image except she's got boobs, and that makes her even better at getting what she wants than you were. And I swear if you wreck her shot at happiness with Nate, we're going to have serious problems."

"I did a spot of underaged drinking myself," Nate admitted. "And there's this billabong on the station. I actually lost my virginity in it. Damn lucky it wasn't full of crocs."

"Oh, I can do so much worse, Nate," Daisy promised.

"She can," Bri agreed. "She probably shouldn't, though. Hey, bestie, remember all those 'we're never telling anyone about this' vows we made?"

"I don't need to hear it." Liam stepped back. "I've got work to do." He pointed Nate's way. "If you get my daughter killed, I swear on my soul I'll take yours. And I'm leaving my wife here, too. I'm going to go fix this for Daisy. Avery…"

Avery's eyes narrowed. "If this is anything beyond a polite 'will you please stay here while I run off to do something dangerous that will save our beloved daughter,' you should rethink."

Liam sighed. "Avery, would you please stay here for a few days while I take care of this situation for our beloved daughter?"

"I will," Avery promised.

"Daisy?" Liam's voice had gone soft.

Daisy was stubbornly silent.

"I love you, girl. No matter what." He glanced down at his phone. "They're here."

"Who's here?" Nate's morning had gone to complete crap, and now he was probably going to have to deal with more bodyguards. Bodyguards who would question him.

The door opened, and Nate realized it was much worse because Erin Taggart walked in, and she wasn't alone.

"Nate?" His mother rushed into the room. "Are you okay? Sweetie? What happened to your pants."

"Well, hell," his father said, looking at him first and then Daisy. "I suppose that was inevitable."

"Ain't nothing inevitable about it. Come on, Brody," Liam said. "We're going to El Salvador."

"We're what?" His father looked deeply confused.

"You're not taking my jet." Ian was suddenly at the railing of the lounge, a glass in his hand.

"Already pinched it, mate," Liam said, walking out.

His father looked to his mother.

"You should follow him." His mom had her worried mask on. "It's obvious something's going on, and we don't understand. Avery, is everything okay? Li called and said Nate was in trouble and we had to get here as soon as possible."

Avery pulled his mom in for a hug. "I'm so happy to see you, old friend. Come on. Let's join Ian and Alex, and I'll fill you in. By the way, the kids are together now. In a biblical sense."

His mom smiled. "He always had a thing for Daisy."

"I did not. I mean I thought she was sweet and everything," Nate argued and then realized he wasn't this dumb. "I mean. I did. Always."

Daisy's eyes were on the door her father had walked through.

"You did," his mother said. "You just didn't understand at the time, but I knew." His mum moved over to Daisy. "Sweet girl, are you all right?"

Daisy burst into tears, and all the women surrounded her.

His heart ached, and he hoped they could make it through this particular storm.

* * * *

Daisy sat outside on the rooftop section of Sanctum. It was pretty and had a great view, and she hadn't known it existed until today.

They definitely needed something like this at The Hideout. If she was allowed back at The Hideout.

The morning had been perfectly horrible, and she wondered if her father would ever speak to her again. Oh, he'd said he loved her, but that might be habit.

Bri and Devi had brought more of her things. And she'd definitely noticed someone had slipped a box of extra-large condoms in. It was either her friends being cheeky or Uncle Ian being true to form. Her friends had been sending her texts all day, checking in on her. And she'd gotten a surprising amount of texts from the guys at The Hideout asking if she was coming in next weekend. What was up with that?

What she hadn't gotten was an update from her da, who was apparently on his way to Central America.

"Hey, I made you some tea," Nate said as he walked out onto the balcony. The sun was starting to move to the west, and this particular part of the rooftop space faced east. He had a tray in his hands. "I added some pastries Bri and Devi brought. Remind me to thank them for breakfast. Mum is making us a late lunch, but I thought you might be hungry. The moms are taking the apartment, by the way. Do you want to stay in the jukebox room?"

She forced herself to look up at him. "Do you want to stay with me at all?"

Nate had been with Ian and Alex most of the day, or helping his mother get comfortable. They hadn't talked much after he'd held her while she cried. She'd wanted some time alone. Was reality hitting him hard?

He frowned. "Why wouldn't I? Is this about the mess with your father? Love, I never once thought you were some saint. Or a virgin who'd saved herself for her one true love. Though you should know I do intend to be your one true love, and I'll keep you so satisfied you won't look at another man."

She wanted to believe him. "Nate, I wasn't lying to my father. Not this morning. I got into a lot of trouble as a kid. Or rather I didn't. I was good at covering my tracks. I drank and I had sex probably way before I was truly ready. And I can't blame them because they were great parents."

"There's no blame, Dais. You were a kid and you experimented. I was sixteen." He sat across from her. "I shouldn't have done it in the billabong. There was probably bacteria and stuff, but she was seventeen and I was willing to risk a lot."

Daisy couldn't help but smile. And realize there was zero jealousy because this was his past and she wanted his future. "I was nineteen. Though I'd done a lot of sexy stuff before that, it was my first penetrative sex. It wasn't great, but I knew I was just missing something. I've read a lot of romance novels. I know I should say I never had decent sex until I met the man of my dreams."

There was a dimple in his chin when he smirked that made her heart beat faster. "Well, you met me practically at birth."

She was so crazy about this guy, but she had to give him every out. "I'm trying to be honest with you."

"No, you're letting guilt seep in, and it could ruin everything. There's no reason to feel guilty about having good sex. I had some good sex, and I hope it was good for the women I was with. Now I'm only going to have sex with you, and it's going to be the best," he said. "I love your past because it made you who you are."

She sniffled and stood up, moving into his arms. "Thank you, Nate. I wish my father felt the same."

She moved back and looked down at what he'd brought her. A tea setup with a couple of mini sandwiches and some cookies. She poured the tea into one of the cups.

"He'll come around. I assure you my father's working on him," Nate said, standing over her. "What do you think your father meant about saving you?"

She was sure her da was doing something ruthless. Her father was incredibly smart, and he could handle things when the going got rough. She'd been thinking about this all afternoon. "He'll probably figure out a way to start a war between cartels so the guy who wants me dead gets killed in prison. It's what I'd do."

Nate huffed, but he leaned over and kissed her forehead. "Now I understand what your mum meant. You think a lot like him."

Daisy pointed to the second cup. "Do you want me to pour you one?"

He shook his head. "Can't. I'm hopping on a call with my boss. I'm supposed to report in. It shouldn't take too long. Then I'll check on Mum and come back and hang out with you. Besides, you have other company." He nodded as her mother stepped outside. "Avery, you should try the lemonade. The tea is... Well, it's for my proper Irish girl."

"Oh, then I'll definitely have some of that. It's been a day." Her mother sank down on the sofa opposite her. "Thanks for this, Nathan."

Nate tipped his head and strode for the door. "Anything for the O'Donnell ladies. I'll see you in a little while, love. Listen to your mum."

So this was going to be a lecture. She took a sip of the "tea" that was really whiskey. And then another. "This is so much better than what Da used to keep."

Her mother smiled wryly. "Well, your uncle has far more elevated tastes than your father." She poured herself a cup and took a sip. "I'm afraid in so many ways your father is still the poor Irish kid who had to find a way to put food in his brother's mouth when his mum was off doing her important work."

"You mean trying to drive the English out of Belfast?" She knew her family history.

"That's what I mean." Her mother took one of the sandwiches. "Your father had a rough life. Unlike me. Or you. I need for you to think about that while he's gone and think about forgiving him for acting like an ass. He loves you."

Daisy wasn't sure. "He loves the idea of me."

Her mother's head shook. "No. He loves you. He loves the Daisy O'Donnell who's always been a walking ball of chaos. And who's also always been kind and loyal to her friends. Who's been a good daughter, despite the experiments with teenaged drinking."

"Aidan always covered for me," Daisy admitted. "And he would mostly be there. He and Tris would hang out with us, but we knew what they were really doing. Supervising."

"Yes, and he never said a word to me or your da. So you should think about forgiving him, too."

"I already did, though it was mean. He came very close to ruining my positive self-image. I thought maybe I was losing my mojo or I wasn't attractive to Doms, which was sad because I like a top."

Her mother took a long swig. "See, I think this is what your father has been avoiding."

"Knowing I like sex?"

"Knowing how much like him you are," her mother pointed out.

"Well, I would say I would hope I'm like you, too. I know all my friends get the icks when their parents get affectionate, but you should be having great sex. I want to have great sex when I'm your age. You and Da love each other. That love is physical, too."

"My darling, I am talking about who your father was before he met me," her mother said.

Daisy suddenly wasn't sure she was ready for this conversation. "He was Da. Just without you. So I bet he was sad. A little lonely."

"Oh, loneliness was not his problem, child." Her mother sighed like she was remembering something.

Daisy was now certain she didn't want to know. And yet she asked the question. "What do you mean? Like he had friends?"

A wry smile crossed her mother's face. "My darling, he was friends with every waitress in the hot wings business. I'm not sure why hot wings in particular, but it was his thing. And I mean it. I'm pretty sure it was all of them. Like he was a rite of passage."

"My daddy was a ho?" Her brain couldn't grasp the concept. Her father was attractive, of course. But he…he was Da.

Her mother laughed. "I don't think we're supposed to use that word."

Daisy waved her off. "We all have a phase. I mean now we do. I didn't think like you did."

Her mom's head shook. "Oh, I didn't. I had a teen pregnancy phase and then a mourning phase and then I was in the hospital for a long time. Then I met your dad, who changed everything for me. But he did have a phase. A very long and storied one sweeping across two continents. I know you think you're a bad girl, Dais, but you got nothing on your da. And guess what—he turned out fine. Well, until today."

Guilt swamped her. "I'm sorry. I didn't mean to come between the two of you."

Her mother's head shook. "I think we've been moving toward this moment for a long time. It was different when you were in college. Your father could keep fooling himself then."

"That I wasn't a…"

Her mother's eyes narrowed. "Don't you dare use that word. It's kind of funny when it's him. But he would never think that word about a woman. He could pretend you weren't as active as you were."

And there was the shame. It wasn't something she normally felt. Her sex life felt normal to her. She'd gone a little crazy in college, but she'd settled a lot since then. "I'm sorry I couldn't stay pure."

Her mother sighed. "Daisy, this is a hard conversation."

"I don't understand why. If it had been Aidan having a good time, I doubt Da or you would be upset."

"I'm not upset at all, baby," her mother explained. "Please don't take my frustration with your father to mean I'm angry with you. I'm not. I'm so happy for you because I think you and Nate are going to be good together. And I don't care what you did in college as long as you were safe, and you seem to have been. I'm frustrated because your father can't look past his own issues to see it."

A sense of her own weariness hit. Nate liked her now, but what if he turned out to think like her father? "I like him. But I'm sure it won't last…"

"Why wouldn't it last?" her mom asked.

"Because it's me, Mom. Some guys might think I'm attractive for a while, but they usually go away. They think I'm high maintenance or something. I don't know. I've kind of gotten used to the idea I won't find anyone. Why do you think I want a career so badly? I'm pretty sure I'm not going to have a family." She didn't like to wallow, but she was feeling raw right now. "I mean, I'll be a great aunt to Aidan's kids and to my friends' kids. So I know it won't last because no guy wants to put up with me."

Her mother's face fell. "Baby, what made you think that? Daisy, you're a beautiful, smart, funny young woman. Everyone adores you."

"Really?" Daisy could hear the disbelief in her own tone. "It feels like they tolerate me most of the time. I'm merely Aidan's kid sister. Da has always been the one who supported me no matter what, and I know that's because I hid a lot from him. But now he's starting to see who I truly am, and he's got a problem with me. Nate will, too."

"Your father has some blinders on when it comes to you, sweetie. Like I said, it was inevitable they would come off at some point. The way he treats you has a lot to do with his past." Her mom sat back, considering her. "Your father's family was complicated. His mother, from what I can tell, was a hard woman. He didn't have a sister growing up. He only had a brother and a mom. His mother was bitter, to say the least, and so he took care of his brother."

"The one we don't talk about?" She'd always thought it odd since there were pictures of her mother's family—including her first husband and Daisy's half-sister, Madison. They were all gone now, but there was a place for Mom's family in their home. But nothing for her da's family. He'd taken them to Ireland, shown them around Dublin, and every now and then he would mention his brother. He would show them a building and say this was where he and Rory used to hide when the bullies would come for them. Or that's the church where his mum took them every single Sunday. But no real information beyond what they'd passed, and that was that.

Her mom nodded. "Because he betrayed your father in the worst way. Your dad put a lot of his soul into Rory, and it turned out so badly. He watched him die, would have been the one to pull the trigger if he'd been given the chance. He was trying to save me at the time."

Daisy felt her eyes go wide. Her parents seemed to have perfect lives. "Da's brother tried to hurt you?"

"Yes," her mother agreed. "You know your father and I met during an investigation, but what we don't talk about is the mission itself. He was investigating a man who turned out to be his own brother. It's a very long story. Serena did a good job with it. *A Soldier is Forever.*"

Now she felt her jaw drop. "The one where Amy works for the dude who stole a billionaire philanthropist's identity, and Leo has to romance her to get close only to discover it's his long-lost brother who is using the charity as a front for an arms dealership?"

Her mom winced. "Yup."

Daisy felt her stomach roll because she'd read the book. Several times. And not merely for the plot. "But that's the kinkiest one."

She'd never seen that shit-eating grin on her mother's face before. "Like I said, she did an excellent job with it."

"I know I said I thought it was awesome you and Da still do those things, but I'm a little disturbed right now."

Her mother pointed her way like Daisy had made her point. "Exactly how your father is feeling. All I'm trying to say is that your father loves you, and he's doing the best he can."

"My father doesn't know me, and I'm not sure he wants to." Daisy sat back. "I'm very tired of pretending to be something I'm not. I hide a lot of myself because I know I can never compete with Aidan."

Her mother leaned in. "You don't have to compete with your brother. There's no competition. This is a family not a race. I need you to understand I see you, Daisy. I see who you are, and I'm very proud of the young woman you've become. You don't have to be a doctor to be a good person. And I'm happy you've explored the world. Your father is worried the world will hurt you. I happen to know it will happen whether we protect you or not. That's the way life is, my baby. It's how we react to the hurt that matters, and you get up every single time. That's what your dad isn't taking into account. He's so busy trying to pretend you're perfect he doesn't see how gloriously beautiful your imperfections are. Perfect is boring and it's not real. I'm going to tell you something I won't admit to anyone else. I'm worried about Aidan. I'm worried if this thing with

Tristan doesn't work out it will break him because he's never had a damn doubt in his life. But you, my sweet girl, have had all of them, and you keep going. Don't ever let anyone tell you you're not the strong one. You're more than strong. You sway. It's the most important thing you can learn to do. To not let the bad times break you. You bend in the storm and you survive, and when the sun shines again, you are stronger than you were before." Her mother reached out and put a hand over hers. "I don't worry about you because you are a tree that sways. One day when you have children those magnificent branches you're growing will protect them from the worst of the storms until they've learned how to be like their mother."

Like she had.

Tears pierced her eyes because the words were a balm to her soul. "You're really okay with me trying this thing with Nate?"

"Of course I'm okay with it. You fell for a boy. Baby, I did that, too, and it was the best decision of my life. And no matter what your da says, it was fast and furious, and I was scared out of my mind," her mother said. "This is when you need to be Daisy O'Donnell. Toss the fear out and do what you need to do."

She wanted to do nothing more. "And if it all goes wrong?"

A smile crossed her mother's face. "Then you'll get up off the floor, dust yourself off, and do what you do magnificently. You'll try again. You'll do it with a whole heart because nothing can break you. I'll handle your father."

"I think it's going to be harder than it sounds." Nate stood in the doorway, another tray in his hands. "Sorry to interrupt but Mum is cooking up a storm, and she asked me to bring these out to you. I think Liam doesn't want anyone around his daughter, but he has to see she needs someone. I'm not going to apologize for what happened between me and Daisy, but I will tell you I'm sorry it's caused a riff."

"Nathan." Her mother stood and held her arms open. "I'm happy you're here. I'm sorry I didn't tell you earlier. I was distracted. Of course that's not entirely my fault. You didn't come by the house when you got into town."

He shrugged. "Well, if I had, things might not have gone the way they did."

"Oh, do you mean I wouldn't have tried to seduce you?" Somehow the minute he was in her presence she felt less guilty, less worried. Being around Nate made her feel more like herself. He centered her and allowed her to be who she truly was. "Because I still would have. I just might have put on a better disguise."

Her mother chuckled, but her cheeks were stained pink. "I don't know if a disguise would work, sweetie. I'm afraid the kink version of a masquerade is like everything else—just play. I'm glad you had fun. I know it's been frustrating for you."

Beyond frustrating, but mostly because she'd been looking for something real.

Nate set the tray on the table. There were two beers on the tray along with cookies and more sandwiches. "Mum hasn't been able to get in touch with Dad. Any idea what Liam's planning?"

"My husband is planning on saving his daughter," her mother explained. "I believe he's going to try to find a way to get rid of the head of the cartel by starting a war. Yeah. I wish I still didn't find that sexy."

"Mum is worried," Nate said.

"Am not." Steph Carter stepped out with a bowl of what looked like fruit salad. "I would like updates, but I think this could be good for Brody. He's been missing his old job."

"Well, I'm glad Liam's not alone. He'll be a good influence on Li. Brody is excellent at talking an unreasonable person down," Avery said as she looked over the now expansive spread on the table. "You have made enough to feed a small army."

Steph shook her head. "Nope. I'm hoping I made enough. My boy can eat."

Daisy looked over, and Nate already had a plate piled high with food. Like more food than she could have imagined.

He flushed and started to put his plate down.

Nothing had changed. She was still all in with this man. And her mother was right. If the cat was out of the bag, then she was going to be herself. She picked up a cookie and moved over, placing herself right on his lap, her arm going around his shoulders.

Nate's lips curled up as she put the cookie to them, and he ate it up in one bite, gently nipping at her fingers. She lowered her mouth to his.

"Oh, I... Well, we should probably get used to it since we're stuck here for a couple of days," Steph said.

Her mother chuckled. "It's kind of nice to be around young love." There was a pause. "Daisy, we are still here. We do not need to see that."

It was just a little tongue. "We're in a club, Mom."

"A club that is not open," her mother replied primly.

Her cell went off again. Another text. This one from Hunter McKay.

Hey, Dais, hope to see you at play night next weekend.

Maybe her da could fix all of this before next weekend. It would be fun to show off her gorgeous Dom. It would be awesome to try to find some normalcy.

"How about we have a nice tea?" Steph said. "Daisy, tell me all about what you've been doing lately. It's been so long."

Well, mostly the last few days she'd been doing her son. But she probably shouldn't say that.

Nate snorted and kissed her cheek, like he knew what she'd been thinking. "Be a good girl, love," he whispered as she moved off his lap.

She could be his good girl. And his bad girl. As long as she was his girl. "Well, I've been thinking about my future career. I'm still not sure I gave private investigation a real chance."

Her mother groaned and so did Nate. But they were both smiling.

Daisy let herself smile, too. She could win her da back. She just knew she could.

Chapter Eleven

By the time Saturday night rolled around again, Daisy wasn't so sure.

"You haven't heard from Uncle Li at all?" Devi asked, sitting back and watching the kids as they ran around the big playroom like the whirling dervishes of complete chaos they were.

Daisy always felt way more comfortable around them. Six-year-olds were her peak people. She could spend all day with a bunch of kids and come out of it feeling energized. So it was good she was on kid-care duty this evening since she was worried about her father. He'd been gone for a solid week. "Nope. Brody's kept in touch with Nate and Steph, and I'm pretty sure Da's been calling Mom, but she's trying to keep it from me. Probably so I don't feel bad. Have you heard anything?"

If her da needed backup, he would call the Taggarts, especially Erin Taggart.

"Mom's talked to him a couple of times, but I think she's mostly helping with research," Devi admitted. "She asked if he needed her but he says he and Brody have it handled. If it helps at all, I know he told her he's been rethinking his position."

"About me? Yeah, I got that."

Devi's red hair shook. "I think he meant about Nate."

Brianna walked in from the quiet room where the babies were sleeping. "I finally got Lily down. I checked the sleeping bags for when we're brave enough to try to get the big kids to sleep. I swear, give me infants any day of the week."

"Nah, infants don't do all the weird things kids do." Daisy genuinely enjoyed working with kids. Babies were cute, but they had nothing on a truly weird six- to ten-year-old. Though she had to admit Michael and Vanessa Malone's daughter, Lily, was adorable. "They mostly sleep and eat. I find it far more interesting to watch Rand and Slater try to build a fort out of random objects they find. The girls are too smart to go in because they understand physics and stuff. But I admire the boys for their optimism."

Rand Hawthorne and Slater Murphy were constantly pushing the envelope when it came to their architectural endeavors.

All in all, tonight they had nine kids they were watching, though it was getting late and the babies and toddlers were all in bed. Wrangling the older kids was always a fun time.

She wondered what Nate was thinking about. She also wondered if he wanted kids. It was pretty early in the relationship to even consider a family with him, but this was a part of being all in.

Was her sex drive starting to annoy him? He looked tired this afternoon, and she'd caught him yawning. Was she asking too much of him?

Devi frowned. "Maybe I should go check on them."

Daisy shrugged. "If it's dangerous, Rani will come and get us. Or she'll fix it herself and pretend like the boys are doing a good job."

"See, I tried to explain to her that's she's propping up the patriarchy when she lets the boys think they're smarter than they are but then she smiles and starts talking about math and my brain goes fuzzy. Then I wonder if I'm the one propping up the patriarchy," Brianna admitted. "Weird kid."

Rani was on the weird side but she was also pretty much a genius. Rani was part of the Murphy clan, which consisted of two chaotic boys and Rani, who was seven going on forty-year-old college professor.

Of course the actual college professor's kid was currently sleeping beside his cousin. Tate Hawthorne was four, and he wasn't hard to get down at all. He was a sweet kid who wanted a bedtime story. Luckily stories worked on Diana Hawthorne, too.

Diana's brother, however, was one of what Daisy liked to call the wild boys, two of whom were approaching.

"Hey, Daisy, could you tell Slater our parents are at a game night?" Rand was eight, the same age as his best friend. He was an adorable moppet of a kid, with his mom's eyes and dad's jawline.

"Uh, we're allowed at game night." Slater Murphy looked like a carbon copy of his dad.

Devi grimaced, and her voice went low. "This is what I always fear when we work here. How did the others handle it when we asked?"

The talk. The moment when they stopped simply being thrilled they're at a fun night with their friends and wondered what the hell their parents were doing.

And then they figure it out and the world becomes kind of gross but also wonderful because hey, your parents are regular old people who love you and make you grilled cheeses and also, one might like to tie the other one up and spank her until she can't see straight. It was actually beautiful when she thought about it.

"Uh, it's kind of a special game night," Brianna began.

Daisy didn't think it would work with these two. They needed a more interesting explanation to glom on to.

Rand's eyes narrowed as his young brain started working through the problem. "Slater's right. I would be allowed at a special game night," Rand insisted. "My parents let me play all the games. Even the hard ones."

"I told you what they're doing," Slater said in a whisper that wasn't all that quiet. But the kid was trying.

Unlike her besties, she knew this conversation was an inevitability and one they could run with. She'd be more worried they'd figured it out if she was dealing with the girls. What she'd learned was boys had spectacular imaginations at this age. There were days when she thanked the universe the twins hadn't procreated yet. She'd learned the truth far too early because Kala Taggart couldn't let it all be a mystery. No. She had to figure out how to get into the air ducts. There had been pictures Daisy couldn't unsee. She was pretty sure Slater hadn't done anything close. "Oooo, what are they doing, Slate?"

Slater looked around and then leaned in. "I think our parents are in a secret society."

Actually, he was pretty close. Daisy nodded. It was time for a misdirect. She wished someone had misdirected her. "I think you're right. Now the question is are they good or evil."

Rand gasped. "They would be good, of course."

Daisy shrugged. "I don't know. It could be fun to have supervillains for parents."

Supervillains at this age would be way easier for them to deal with than normal, actual sexually active parents.

Rand seemed to think through the problem. "My mom does a lot of stuff with a computer my dad says is ambiguous morally. I don't know what that means, but it could be supervillain stuff. Also, my dad's watched *The Joker* like fifty times."

It meant Kyle Hawthorne needed to watch more movies, and MaeBe Hawthorne was a badass hacker, though her talents were used for good. However, the goal this evening was to stave off the inevitable moment when these kids figured out their parents were total pervs. "See. There you go. Tonight is secret society business. One day you'll be a part of it, too. You should probably get some rest. After all, there will be missions involved."

Rand's eyes lit up. "That's so cool."

Slater grinned. "We should practice. Let's get the guys together."

The boys ran off.

Devi shook her head. "Great. Now they think their parents are supervillains."

Brianna sighed and sat down. "Well, it's better than knowing. I found out way too early what was going on. Of course I also kind of grew up surrounded by sex positive stuff. That's what happens when your mom's known for a series called Soldiers and Doms. I'm thinking about writing Amish romance. It could be my rebellion."

"Nope. Your mom would simply read it and tell you how proud she is of you," Daisy said with a sigh. The Dean-Miles clan wasn't big on shame of any kind. "And my da would say *why can't you be more like Brianna. Look, she's writing books about love without a penis in sight. Just a man and a woman and a cornfield like God intended.*"

"Well, the rest of us have spent all our lives hearing Uncle Li say"—Devi went into a fairly serviceable Irish accent—"*Thank the heavens my Daisy would never do that.*"

Daisy frowned. "It wasn't like I encouraged him."

"You didn't exactly fess up either because let me tell you every time he said it, you had done it," Brianna countered. "So now you have to deal with the fact that your father knows you're as imperfect as the rest of us. The question is, was it worth it."

"Was he worth it?" Devi countered. "That's the real heart of the matter. You've been with Nate for over a week now. Are you getting bored? Because you get bored easily."

Bored? With the hottest man she'd ever met? With the sweetest guy in the world? It was more like she was obsessed with the man. She thought about him all day and dreamed about him at night. It was weirdly exciting to do normal things with Nate. And having the moms around wasn't as awkward as she'd thought it would be. They had meals together and watched movies, and the moms pretended they didn't notice how often she dragged Nate into a privacy room. The things they'd done in the princess castle… "No. I'm not bored. We've been together pretty much twenty-four seven for over a week and I miss him. I wonder what he's doing."

"He's sitting in the other room watching a bank of security cameras," Brianna pointed out.

"Yes. He's too far away." She knew the fire would fade. They'd pretty much gone at it three times a day. The sex was phenomenal, but it was the soft times in between that made her know she was in love with him. Real love. Real, never-look-at-another-man-again love.

"I never thought I would see the day when Daisy O'Donnell got that look on her face for a man," Devi said with wonder.

"I knew it would happen eventually." Brianna stretched and hid a yawn. "I like him. He's nice to her and her friends. I wholeheartedly approve and look forward to your wedding if we all survive."

"Why wouldn't we?" Daisy asked. Everyone was treating this like some horrific, dangerous thing. Like a ball of violence rolling inevitably her way. It was one dude who deserved every bit of prison time the law could throw at him. "Da is handling it."

She had all the faith in the world when it came to her father saving her. He would never allow anything bad to happen if he could fix it. It was what her da did. He fixed things.

"Yeah, well, my father is worried your father is currently starting a cartel war, and we might all get caught in the middle of it," Brianna confessed.

"Da will be very careful." Of that Daisy was sure. Uncle Adam was on the dramatic side. It was why her short stint at Miles-Dean, Weston, and Murdoch hadn't worked out. A girl hit one little delete button and it was like the world ended. It hadn't been the world. It had been a kind of mean-girl AI assistant, and Aunt Chelsea had sent her a cookie bouquet. Not that it had saved her job.

"I'm not so sure about that. You are your father's precious baby girl. He's got to be panicking," Brianna said. "He'll do a lot to protect you. I mean he and your brother apparently scared off all the Doms at The Hideout for years. I can't believe we didn't catch that."

"I knew something was up. I mean when we walk into a bar all eyes go straight to Daisy's chest, and that's the women, too." Devi cupped her own boobs, looking down at them. "I wish you'd grown more. Damn my athletic build. I have my mom's boobs."

"You have fashion model boobs," Bri countered. "You can actually wear the clothes you design."

Daisy was confident in her boobs. Nate liked her boobs. He talked about them all the time.

"I don't design for skinny chicks. I design for all of womankind,"

Devi explained. "Wait until you see the bridesmaids dresses I made for Carys's wedding. They're beautiful, but the twins and Tash are in the bridal party, so there is definite cleavage. Daisy, tell her. You look gorgeous in yours."

Would she be allowed out for Carys's wedding? "They're stunning and very boob forward." She loved it when Nate laid his head on her chest and snuggled. Was he thinking about weddings? They could go to Vegas and spend all the money they would have spent on a wedding on an amazing suite. Or she could use it to fix up her house so they had somewhere lovely to live. A vision of Nate helping her paint and hang curtains floated through her head. She wanted to go grocery shopping with him. "I think I'm in love."

Brianna's eyes rolled. "Of course you are. You've been half in love with him since you were a kid. I knew what would happen the minute you said he was coming to Dallas. I knew you would see him again and it would be over."

"Over?" It didn't feel over. It felt like life was just beginning.

"The flirting. The crazy nights," Bri said, a little wistful. "I miss our crazy nights, but I also know you two are moving on with your lives. You're going into another stage."

"I'm not moving on," Devi replied with a shake of her head. "I don't know if you've noticed, but I'm completely single over here. I'm still one of the nuns of The Hideout."

"But you are," Brianna insisted. "You're completely into a guy. It doesn't matter if he can't love you back. You feel something for him. Something I haven't ever felt. I grew up around this amazing love, and it wasn't only about my parents. I watched my brother. Tristan's loved Carys all of his life. I don't know what he's doing, but I know he still loves Carys and he still wants to share her with Aidan. I've never wanted anyone like that. Like Daisy wants Nate. Like you want Zach."

Zach Reed. From what Daisy had put together, he was the military liaison for the CIA team. She was fairly certain someone had explained it to her, but it was a lot of acronyms. He'd come to The Hideout with Cooper for the first time a year and a half before, and Devi had very quietly lost her mind over the handsome captain.

Not that she'd told him. She'd made Daisy and Bri promise not to say a word. They were a sisterhood within a sisterhood, and neither she nor Bri would ever break a confidence.

"I can want Zach all day, but we know who he wants," Devi said.

"She's engaged." Daisy knew what Devi thought. She'd watched

Zach, and his eyes always followed Tasha Taggart. A month before they'd overheard Kenz and Kala talking about how Zach had admitted he was in love with their sister. "Tash is happy with Dare. Zach is a single man."

"And Tasha is his type. Not me," Devi replied. "So while I might have these feelings, I'm not going to act on them. I'm not going to make a fool of myself."

"Did I?" Daisy mused. She thought her friend was missing the point.

Devi neatly ducked as a pillow was thrown her way. A *sorry* was yelled out, and one of the boys ran to reclaim it. "I didn't say you were a fool. It obviously worked out for you and Nate."

"I wouldn't have known if I hadn't tried. I think it might be more foolish to have these feelings and never give them a shot. Even if he doesn't want you. At least you know. And if you're too scared to be forthright, there's always masquerade night. But you should probably wear a better disguise. Apparently mine wasn't great." She reached out to her friend. "I know how it feels to want someone you think you can't have. I also know what Bri is saying. When we were in college we were an unstoppable party, wreaking havoc and fun everywhere we went. Now we have degrees and we spend our weekends sitting in the locker room at a sex club trying to figure out what to do with our lives."

"I think you know what you want to do with yours," Devi chided.

She was wrong about that. "I know who I want to spend it with. I'm not sure what I want to do. A psych degree sounded like a real thing at the time. Turns out there's not a lot of call for it. Maybe I should give real estate another shot."

Bri groaned. "Or you should go back and get your master's and become a therapist for children. Just don't tell them about the supervillain thing you so recently convinced poor Rand of."

"I thought we were going to let her come to that conclusion on her own," Devi pointed out.

The idea played around in her head. She did spend a lot of her time talking to kids, and most of it was helping them with their problems. When she thought about it… It was…brilliant. "I would be good at that. I would enjoy it."

"Yes, you would. And you're welcome." Bri smiled. "Devi's got a real shot at becoming a designer. I was with her in New York a couple of weeks ago and they loved her work."

"But they haven't called me back." Devi stood.

"There's still time." Brianna was always an optimist.

"Sure. I'm going to go check on the babies. I'll be in there if anyone needs me." Devi turned when she got to the hallway that would lead her to the nursery. "And Daisy, I'm happy for you. If your dad can't be… Well, then he isn't the Uncle Li I know. He'll figure this out and then he'll be all team Daisy again. He'll go from *my daughter is a saint of a girl* to *my daughter can drink you all under the table*. Now, if you love me, you'll remind us all Bri has written three books and never lets anyone read them."

Brianna gasped. "She already knows that." Bri looked her way. "You know that."

"Yes," Daisy agreed. "I know, and I think what Devi is pointing out is time works the same way for all of us. It's going by, and you need to figure your shit out, sister. Be brave. Let us read them. Then let your mom read them."

Bri went a pasty white. "Absolutely not. Maybe someday. When she's old and can't see. Hey, Hunter." Bri smiled, her weird *thank god something is saving me* smile. "Daisy, Hunter is here."

He was. And he wasn't alone. Gabriel Lodge was with him, and they'd brought Lucas Taggart along. Gabe and Lucas were both a bit older than her crew. They'd been a couple of years ahead of Daisy, but Hunter had always hung around them.

"I thought y'all would be at The Hideout. Also, I thought we were locked in." They hadn't even given her the security code. Which was probably good because she wasn't great at remembering random numbers. Nate had let them in, and he'd watched as she'd greeted all the kids. When Michael and Vanessa Malone had brought in way too much stuff for their infant, Nate had held the tiny girl while Daisy had helped them set up. He'd looked so hot. A big muscular man rocking this tiny infant. He'd even hummed. He hadn't looked freaked out or anything.

Because he was a man who could handle some chaos.

Lucas winked her way. He was a gorgeous man in his mid-twenties, but he couldn't hold a candle to her Nate. She'd seen him holding a baby, and he'd just frowned the whole time. Admittedly the baby was his cousin, and he'd needed a diaper change. She rather thought Nate would have simply done it.

"My dad kind of owns the building," Lucas pointed out.

"He doesn't," Bri countered. "Your dad and Uncle Ian donated the money for the building, but Kai owns it. Have you thought about coming in for a session or two?"

Bri was kind of being a bitch, and Daisy supported her. Lucas could be a heartbreaker, and he was a little full of himself. The Ferguson Clinic was housed in the building next to Sanctum. They'd grown over the years from it being run by Kai Ferguson and specializing in PTSD issues to having family therapists and specialists in domestic violence and marriage counseling. What they didn't have was a child psychologist.

"He knows the code because he caters the group sessions they have sometimes," Bri continued. "Why are you acting like…like you? You do remember who we are, right?"

Lucas gave them both a big smile. "Yeah, you're my little cousin and Daisy is… Well, we're not related, Daisy and I."

"Actually, neither are we. Like no blood between us." Bri gasped when she looked over at the indoor playground. "AJ, you cannot hit him with a chair. This is not wrestling."

She ran off to save Wyatt Murphy from Armie Hutchins, who apparently had been watching wrestling with his dad. Or maybe his grandpa had been in town. She looked back at the guys who'd invaded her space. "What do you need? Did you leave something behind? The kitchen's in the back."

Gabriel Lodge wore jeans and a button-down that he'd buttoned down to show off a good portion of his cut chest. He had longish jet-black hair he normally pulled back in a queue, but tonight he'd left it down. "We just wanted to come by and see if you needed some company."

Hunter grinned. "Yeah, The Hideout feels boring without you, Dais."

She wasn't sure why. "I almost never play in the dungeon because I can't find a play partner. Actually, the last time I was in the dungeon you told me I should leave."

The last bit was said to Gabriel, who held up a hand.

"Hey, baby, I did not put it in those words. I asked if your brother knew where you were," Gabe corrected. "You have to understand, your father is extremely scary. I'm not sure the man is well half the time. When he gathered the tops and told us he would murder anyone who tried to tempt you, I believed him."

"Aidan was pretty clear, too," Lucas admitted. "But he has rescinded his order."

Daisy felt her jaw drop. "I'm sorry. You're here because you think now that my brother has stopped pretending I'm a virgin in need of protection, you can… What? What do you think is going to happen tonight?"

Hunter squared his shoulders like he was going into battle. "Look, Daisy, we think you should pick. You're a sub and we're all tops, and the three of us are all open to exploring a D/s relationship with you."

"You are?" She wasn't going to laugh at them. Nope. They had tender male feelings, and she would have to check the part of her that really wanted to guffaw.

"You're gorgeous," Gabe said with a sigh. "I mean, stunning. I know you grew up with these two, but we didn't meet until later, which means you can see me as a man and not a boy."

"I assure you, I don't see you as a little girl," Lucas proclaimed.

"No, you see me as another notch on your overly crowded belt." This was kind of fun. "I should know because I have a belt of my own. A player can see right through another player, Lucas. So I'll have to say flattered but no. Hunter, you're like a brother to me. Eww."

Hunter's face fell. "Well, that's rude."

"You know what's rude? Treating a woman like she's a child in need of guidance, especially when she's been through way more shit than you," Daisy pointed out. "I'd like to see you handle some of the things I've been through. And Gabe…"

His lips curled up like he thought he'd won. "Yeah?"

"If you had wanted me, you would have been man enough to stand up to my father and my brother. I suspect one day you'll meet the woman who inspires that kind of courage in you, and I'll wish you both well. Now, I have a Dom, and we'll be playing at The Hideout as soon as my da gets the drug cartel off my ass. You'll be able to watch me and wonder what could have been because my player stage is done, boys. I found a man, and I'm sticking with him."

A slow clap came from Daisy's right, and she glanced over.

Her da was standing there with Nate and Nate's dad. They took up so much space. She was going to have the biggest babies ever.

Lucas winced. "Hey, Uncle Li. Uhm, how's it going?"

"Well, I'm thinking about how you're going to cook with broken hands, son," her da said with a chuckle. "Oh, don't you worry. It won't be me. My Daisy's found a keeper. Do you need an introduction?"

Nate moved in beside her. "We've met. But perhaps I should make myself plain. She's mine, and before someone asks how it's different, I'll explain it to you. Her da and brother were wrong to treat her like she couldn't make a decision."

"Well, in my defense, I did have to save her from a cult once," her da said, but his eyes were warm on her.

"I thought it was a self-help group, but it turned out to be a sex cult," Daisy admitted. "There's a Netflix documentary coming out. I look good in it."

"You do, me darling girl." Her father nodded Nate's way. "Continue, Nathan. You should explain what you'll do to anyone who even looks your girl's way."

A big arm caught her around her waist and hauled her back against Nate's chest. She felt him kiss the top of her head.

"They can look all they like," Nate began.

She glanced her father's way. "Da, Nate's about to say sexy things."

Her father winced and covered his ears. "Tell me when it's over, Brody. Or at least when he gets to the threats of violence."

Nate's dad snorted. "I'll be sure to let you know."

If Nate was thrown off by the banter, he didn't show it. "Like I said, I'll show my gorgeous sub off in the club. I won't get pissed if some guy does a double take as she walks by because she's so beautiful, how could they help themselves? But I will take apart anyone who thinks to touch her. She's mine. I'm giving her everything she needs, and honestly, I don't think the three of you put together could handle her. Stamina. A man needs serious stamina to keep up with Daisy O'Donnell."

Her father started to hum.

"You missed your shot with her and now she's with me, and I'm not letting her go," Nate explained, and his arm tightened around her. "So if you don't like your insides on the outside, you'll heed the one and only warning I'm going to give you. Otherwise, you'll be a science project for these kiddos."

"Like anatomy?" Rani asked, her eyes wide.

When had she snuck up? Daisy gently disentangled herself and got to one knee. "The guys are just playing around, sweetie."

Rani shook her head. "No, I think your boyfriend is having a come to Jesus with the other guys who want to be your boyfriend. That's what my mom would call it. She's going to think this is funny."

Gabe reached out a hand to Nate. "Message received, man."

Nate shook it. "Just respect my rights and we'll be fine."

Daisy picked up Rani, who was starting to yawn. It was almost eleven o'clock, and it was definitely time to start getting these kiddos to bed.

Her da was here, and he wasn't looking at her like he was ashamed.

"You can listen in now, Da. He's threatened them all with evisceration," she said.

Her da frowned and brought his hands down. "I wanted to hear that part."

Lucas let out a long sigh. "Well, it was very threatening."

"What's evisceration?" AJ asked.

Bri winced. "Sorry, he got away from me. I'll go grab Devi and we'll start bedtime rituals."

"It means Daisy's boyfriend is going to remove Lucas's bowels," Rani explained.

Daisy winced.

"I think he probably needs those," AJ countered. "But it would also be cool."

"Hey, I'm not the only one." Lucas seemed to realize all the kids were now looking at him.

"My mom says you're a walking venral disease," Rand proclaimed. "What does that mean?"

Gabe snorted. "It's venereal, and it's accurate."

"Dude, you could show some support." Lucas sent his friend a "what the hell, man" look.

Hunter was chuckling. "Hey, Dais, hope I didn't weird you out. I mostly came to watch them make idiots of themselves. Although you should know you look good, girl."

"Do you want to keep your eyeballs in their sockets, boy?" Her da had his hands on his hips, righteous indignation on his face. "Nate might be okay with you looking at her, but I'm not."

Nate grinned. "Which is why I'm okay with it."

Men. Daisy sighed and turned to her charges. "Boys, it's time for teeth brushing. If you're good, I'll let my da tell you a story about how he started a small land war in Africa once."

Things were going to be okay. Daisy carried Rani through the hallway toward the nursery. The older boys had sleeping bags they would lay out in the playroom, but she still put Rani in the nursery. She told her it was so she could watch over the littles, but it was mostly because Rani would talk all night to the boys about insect invasions and how bread was yeast and it was also an animal so it might eat them from the inside.

Weird kid.

Sweet kid.

Rani laid her head on Daisy's shoulder. The nursery was illuminated with night-lights, giving the place a glow.

Bri stood in the middle of the room. "I can't find Devi."

Daisy sighed and set Rani on her feet. "Hey, sweetie. You get into your PJs with Miss Bri and I'll be back to read you a story." She gave Rani a hug before turning back to Bri. "She's probably sitting on the back step regretting all of her life decisions. She thinks if she'd gone into the Army instead of college she might be in a better place. That better place being closer to Zach. You know she feels like the odd one out in her family even though Aunt Erin was thrilled she went to college."

"Talk to her," Bri said, holding Rani's hand. "I'll get Rani ready and then make us all some tea. I'll look around to see if I can feed the Aussies. They can eat."

They definitely could, and she might need something heartier than tea because she felt like she and her da were about to have a long overdue conversation.

She started for the back door when her cell buzzed in her pocket.

She glanced over at the security system and sure enough, it was off.

But Devi would have turned it off to open the door and back on when she closed it. She would never have left the alarm off. Devi was good with random numbers.

What Devi wouldn't have done was walked away from the door. She couldn't see her sitting on the steps where she sometimes took a break. Devi wouldn't have left that door unattended. Not ever. If she had to leave, she would have informed someone.

A chill went through her, and she backed up.

Something was wrong. She just knew it.

She raced back to the men she cared about most, eager to put this all in their hands.

Chapter Twelve

"Hey, Uncle Li, I just wanted to…" Lucas began.

Nate stepped back, wanting to watch how this scene played out.

"You wanted to what, Lucas? Do you think I don't have ears? What is your mother going to say when I tell her you wanted to defile my precious angel?"

It felt so good to have Li O'Donnell's outrage directed at someone else.

Lucas sighed. "She'll probably direct you to group therapy. My mom is very sarcastic. She'll give you a lecture on how defiling is my favorite activity."

When they'd shown up ten minutes before, his gut had tightened as he'd watch Li punch in the security code and let himself in through the front door. He'd watched as the man had avoided the kids' area. He'd known exactly where he was going. The security office, where Nate had settled in for the night. Only the addition of his father had made Nate think Li wasn't on an assassination run.

Liam had made his way to the office and then given Nate a rundown on what had happened in El Salvador.

It might take a few days, but Liam was absolutely certain someone from a rival cartel would handle the problem. He'd explained the work hadn't been rough. A little misinformation here and there and voila, Li O'Donnell had two rival cartels taking each other out. He was a perfectly ruthless bastard, and Nate approved.

Just a few more days and Daisy should be safe enough to be out and about in public, and what was Nate planning on doing about that?

His father had sighed and said something about Nate being young and he and Daisy just starting to date and Nate had been honest.

"Marry her as soon as she says yes," he'd explained.

Then real trouble had shown up. Before Li had been able to reply to his declaration of intent, those three lotharios had been invading and trying to take his honey. He'd known the minute those three had shown up Aidan had talked to the Doms and likely been an asshole who told them she was now on the market for a Dom.

Of course he'd heard the twins had been told what was happening and they'd unleashed a wrathful Lou on Aidan's ass. Aidan was being bombarded with emails about male enhancement drugs. It was a minor revenge, but then Aidan had been following his father's wishes.

This felt like malicious compliance at its finest.

The good news? He'd heard his girl explaining all the reasons she had no interest in any of these pretty, rich boys.

Gabriel Lodge was heir to a billionaire. Lucas's parents ran a restaurant empire. Hunter's folks were part owners of McKay-Taggart.

He was nothing but a soldier with a busted-up truck and barely a room of his own, but his Daisy didn't care.

He was so fucking in love with her.

"I think they understand now, Liam." Nate was perfectly calm since he knew where his Daisy's affections went. He also thought once he had a collar around her throat all the horny arseholes would back off. Well, the Doms would. He got the feeling he would have to explain to more than one besotted idiot that Daisy belonged to him.

And he belonged to her, and he'd figured out his place in the world. By her side.

"You truly marrying my girl?" Liam asked.

"As soon as she says yes," Nate replied.

His father put a hand on his shoulder. "I'm happy for you, son."

Liam breathed out a deep sigh and looked toward the heavens before making the sign of the cross. "Thank the lord. No take backs, Nathan. No matter how much trouble she causes."

Nate felt a grin slide across his face. "I can handle some trouble."

"Did you hear that, Brody?" Liam was all smiles now.

"I told you it would work out," his father said with a smile of his own. "And the best news is I've been talking to your mother and she wants to make Dallas our home base for a while. Elodie's safely in Sydney. So we'd like to be around friends again."

Liam's expression turned serious as he held a hand out to Nate's father. "We'll be more than happy to have you. I would bet Avery already has Steph looking for a place close to us. You want to be close to us and not the run-down place where Daisy's going to make Nate live. You're going to need to learn a lot about home improvement, son."

Was he about to get everything he wanted? His girl. His family. Knowing his sister was happy and fulfilling her dreams.

Daisy ran into the room, her cell in her hands. She looked at the boys who were still joking around and not getting ready for bed in any way. Daisy took a steadying breath.

Something was wrong.

"What is it?"

He and Liam asked the question at the same time, both moving in front of her.

Liam took a step back, giving Nate the chance to talk to her first.

Because she was his responsibility now. He reached for her hand. "What's happening?"

"The alarm is off, and I can't find Devi," she whispered.

His father cursed under his breath. "I'm on it. We've been away from the bloody security cams. I'll run them back. She couldn't have gotten out the front. We would have seen her."

"She went out back," Daisy replied, still surreally calm. "She was upset about something, and she sits on the back steps when she's upset. Lucas, I need you to get the boys into the nursery. Bri's there."

Lucas was suddenly all kinds of serious. "You need me to call my dad?"

She shook her head. "My father's already on it."

"Yeah, go get Ian," Liam was saying into his cell. "Tell him I want a sniper on the roof of the club, and they're looking for Devi on the east side of the Ferguson building. Keep this quiet. We don't know what's happening yet."

Lucas turned to the kids. "All right, guys. Let's get a move on."

Hunter was already in motion, gathering up the youngest. "Let's brush some teeth. Don't want them to fall out, do we?"

They weren't military but they were calm under pressure.

"We'll stay with Bri and the kids," Gabe assured them. "Let me know when the coast is clear. Until then, we'll keep everyone in lock-down."

The young men moved efficiently, getting the boys to cover without panicking them.

"I think they're calling my cell." Daisy's hand shook slightly as she passed it to him. "I didn't answer or look at the texts they sent."

"Smart girl." Her father still had his cell in hand. "Better to play dumb. The minute you answer you're on a timer."

Daisy nodded. "I also didn't get close to the windows. When I realized the alarm wasn't on, I made sure no one could see me. I would have loved to have seen her, but that would put me on a timer, too."

She hadn't panicked. She hadn't rushed out trying to save her friend herself. He was proud of her. His cell rang, and he slid his finger across the screen, putting it on speaker. "Dad? What have you got?"

Daisy leaned in.

"She went out the back and did exactly what Daisy said she would. She was drinking coffee, sitting on the back steps crying," his father explained. "And then two men with military-grade weapons dressed in all black took her. I think they're in a van on the other side of the Ferguson building. Liam, I told you I thought someone was following us."

Liam cursed under his breath. "I'm sorry. I didn't see it so I brushed it off." He looked to his daughter. "I was too eager to get home and tell you and your mother you're going to be safe. I just wanted to see my daughter and tell her how much I love her."

Daisy nodded. "I love you, too, Da. But we have to get Devi. I can't let them take her. We have to exchange me for her, and then you'll rescue me. It'll be fine. I'll be a perfectly good hostage."

There was only one problem with the scenario. "They don't want you as a hostage, love. They want you dead so you can't testify against their boss. So no, we're not exchanging you."

"I can be very charming," she replied, her shoulders straightening like she was actually getting ready to walk right into danger and expect to come out on the other side. Because she was charming.

Keeping her alive was going to be a full-time job.

"You are, my darlin. You are the most charming woman alive besides your sainted mother, but I think in this case, we should try to take the fuckers out before they lay hands on you." Her father was suddenly the voice of reason.

"Da, we can't let them take Devi." Daisy's voice wavered.

"Her mother is already on her way, and Boomer happened to be in the club tonight so he's got a high-powered rifle, and I assure you he only needs one shot," Liam explained. "However, we're going to have to start the timer or I worry they might kill her and try again later. I can't imagine Devi's being charming right now. She's probably proving she's Erin Taggart's daughter and giving them hell."

"She fought hard," Brody said over the line. "They roughed her up but good. However, she was alive when they put her in the van. Oh, wow, we've got incoming. Erin's moving around the back. She's clinging to the shadows. I don't think they can see her. She's in."

Erin Taggart strode into the room wearing an overcoat that absolutely did not fit her. She'd been playing at Sanctum so there was probably some fet wear under the men's jacket. She'd tugged on a pair of sneakers, too. "Li, where's my girl?"

"Brody's got eyes on a van across the street. They took her in there," Liam explained.

Erin simply nodded. "We need to get her out of the van. It's too close quarters to start a fight there. Have they contacted you?"

"They're trying to call right now," Daisy said, holding up her phone.

"Damn it." Erin's jaw tightened. "We need a couple of minutes to put people in place. Theo's having to move around the long way so they don't see him. Ian's with him. Brody, contact Big Tag and let him know they need to be behind the van."

"On it," his father said over the cell.

Nate could see the battlefield in his mind. One of the first things he'd done when he and Daisy had moved in was study the area around them. When her uncles came to visit, he would take a jog. Those long sessions were more about becoming acquainted with the area than actual exercise.

He was getting plenty of workouts because his Daisy was insatiable.

"So Theo and Big Tag come in from behind." He could see them moving into position. "We need the targets in the courtyard."

Erin nodded. "Boomer told me the courtyard would be perfect. He has an unobstructed view from the west side of Sanctum if they're in the courtyard."

"Li, I think you and Erin should ease out the front and stay in the shadows around the parking lot," his father explained. "Nate and I can use the west side exit to come around on either side of the building, and then they would be in a nice trap. Even if Boomer can't take them, they would be facing six of us, and there won't be any place to run."

His gut tightened. "How would we get them into place?"

He knew what was coming.

Daisy's eyes lit up. "Me. I'm bait." She actually smiled. "I think I can be good at this."

Her cell trilled again.

"You're going to have to answer them, sweetie," Erin said, her voice tight. "If you can hold them off even for a few minutes, it will be so helpful."

"So answer them but don't answer them." Daisy nodded and then slid her finger across the screen to answer the call. "Hello? Excuse me, who is this?" She giggled. "Sure, Hunter. Try again. Like you don't try to scare me all the time. I'm not some ditz who falls for it." She hung up. "That should buy us a minute or two. And I promise I can word salad them for a long time."

"Excellent, then maybe you won't have to be bait," Nate pointed out.

"Daisy, I know I shouldn't ask this of you, but they're going to have guns on Devi," Erin began.

Liam puffed up a little. "Now, Erin…"

"We can handle it without risking Daisy," Nate assured them.

"But this is all about me," Daisy argued.

"I'm worried about how close they'll keep Devi to them. If Boomer can't get a shot or if we end up in a standoff…" Erin began.

"Devi could get killed." Daisy shook her head. "I'm not letting anything happen to Devi."

"You're not allowing anything at all, girl," her father announced.

"Da, I can handle it," Daisy replied stubbornly as her phone went off again. "You're wasting time. Get into position."

Erin was already moving. "We need a distraction, Daisy. Something that will make those men drop their guard for a second or two."

A silent look was exchanged between the two women, some communication Nate didn't get, but Daisy nodded her aunt's way.

"I know exactly what to do, Aunt Erin," she said resolutely. "I won't let you down."

"Daisy, stay bloody well safe, girl." Liam moved out behind Erin.

They eased out of the building to get where they needed to be.

Nate's father came in from the opposite hall. "I've got Ian and Theo in position."

"Erin and Li just left." Nate checked his SIG. "Dais, you're going to answer now. It's time. If you have to walk out, you go with your hands up, and the minute I give you the signal, you take cover, all right?"

"I'm supposed to distract them," Daisy insisted.

"Cry," his father said, checking his own weapon. "Give them a good cry. It unnerves men sometimes. Don't worry. We're going to handle it. Now answer. We need roughly sixty seconds to get into position."

Daisy answered, and it was the hardest thing he'd ever done walking away from her, but he did it. Somewhere in the Sanctum building there was a whole team with eyes on the area. She had six trained operatives watching her.

"She's going to be okay, son," his father whispered as they snuck out of the building, taking the opposite route Li and Erin had. "She's been in tight positions before."

"Yes, that's what scares me." Nate moved behind his father. "She thinks she can handle anything. I'm worried about what she's going to think a distraction is."

He should have stayed with her. Should have ensured she didn't walk out of the building.

But then he saw the door to the van open and a tall man exit. He immediately turned and had a gun to Devi's head. In his other hand, he held a cell phone.

The second kidnapper exited the van and stayed at Devi's back. Naturally he had a gun, too, and it was pressed to Devi's side.

"That's right. You come out here and come out alone, and we'll let your friend go," the man was saying.

"They're too close," his father whispered. "If there were only one of them I would say Boomer can take him out, but if the other guy…"

If the other guy had enough time to pull the trigger, Devi would be gone and her whole family gutted. Daisy would never recover from watching her friend die in front of her.

His heart thudded, but Nate forced himself to remain calm.

"I can see Big Tag, but they can't. Is there anyone behind the wheel?" Nate asked.

"Can't tell." His father's back was to the wall, clinging to the shadows. "Bloody surprise op. I'm carrying comms from now on. I don't like not having someone in my ear."

But Nate knew comms could blow. His father had worked from the cozy comfort of a team with every possible technological advantage. Nate hadn't gotten comfy yet.

"I don't see you," the man was saying as he moved Devi along.

Devi started to stumble, but the second man held her upright, keeping a tight hold on her. "My mother is going to kill you."

The second man chuckled. "Sure. Your mom. I'm real scared, kid."

They should be. They had no idea they were about to be surrounded by Taggarts. The only question was could they get the shots they needed without endangering Devi's life.

"They're almost where we need them," his father whispered. "When Boomer takes his shot, I want you to roll out and get into position. We'll still have one to deal with. You'll be behind him."

Nate cautiously looked around the corner while the kidnappers were arguing with Daisy about why she was stalling. They kept Devi in between them. The good news? She was half a foot shorter than one of the men. It would make for an easy shot. The bad? She was as tall as her second kidnapper. She would be an excellent shield for him.

He would have to be careful. So careful.

"She's coming out," the taller one said. "I think your friend wants you to… Holy hell."

Both men stopped and their guns lowered suddenly, their eyes on whatever was happening in front of them.

Was Erin moving in early? He barely had time to register the grin that came across Devi's face when the tall guy's head snapped back. Boomer's aim had been true, but the second guy was a harder target. Nate's training kicked in. He strode out from behind the building and took the shot because Devi had been able to move away from him slightly. Nate fired, catching the guy in the head and ending the threat.

"Daisy O'Donnell!" Liam jogged over from the outer edge of the parking lot. "You put on some clothes right now."

What? Nate looked over, and Daisy was smiling wearing nothing but the glorious skin she was born in.

She shrugged one gorgeous shoulder. "They were distracted."

Erin ran in, grabbing her daughter and moving her away from the dead bodies.

Ian sat down in the middle of the parking lot and laughed his ass off while Theo joined his wife and daughter.

His future wife was still standing there. She was getting such a spanking. Nate tugged his T-shirt over his head. "Daisy O'Donnell, you know damn well that was not the distraction I was talking about."

"But, Nate, it worked," she replied. "Devi, you okay?"

"Thanks to you, bestie," she called out.

"Hey, Dais, you're looking good." Hunter stood behind her.

"Thanks. I totally work out," she said with a grin.

"Nathan." Liam managed to make his name a command.

A command to deal with the source of all the storms in their lives. He moved in, shielding her as he stuffed her head through the opening of his shirt. "Do you want to keep your eyeballs in your skull, mate?"

Hunter immediately averted his gaze. "I thought you said we could look. I'll go give the all clear to the rest of the guys."

He'd changed his bloody mind about that, but he wasn't going to argue with anyone but Daisy. "This is not the club. You were supposed to cry or something."

Her chin came up, and she was so fucking gorgeous his dick hurt. "This was way better. They actually lowered their weapons."

"I need a bloody drink," her father exclaimed. "Nate, she's all yours, son. Like I said. No take backs."

"I was good," Daisy insisted.

"Yes, you were, sweetie," Erin said as she helped Devi up the stairs. "You were perfect."

"I always knew Daisy's boobs would save the world at some point." Devi gave her a watery smile.

She'd put herself right in the line of fire. "You are never doing that again."

Her hands were on her hips, and she faced off with him. "You don't get to tell me what to do, Nathan Carter."

"I bloody well do since I'm the man who loves you. I'm the man who's going to marry you, and this right here? Hard limit, Dais. Hard fucking limit." He'd been calm, but now he realized how close she'd come to getting hurt.

"Well, I'm the woman who loves you and is going to marry you, and this is not the sixteenth century where you own me," she shot back. "So we should agree to disagree and then go inside and take out all of this adrenaline on each other before the cops get here."

"You honestly believe we're going to have sex now?" She was going to drive him mad. Utterly bonkers.

Her lips curled up. "Yep. See you inside, Nate."

"Hey, are we doing something with these bodies?" Big Tag stood looking down at them. "Also, Boomer says all the sniping made him hungry. My kitchen is not equipped for him tonight."

Nope. He had something else to attend to.

"I think we're letting the authorities handle this one," his father said, joining Big Tag.

Nate followed his future wife. His job wasn't done.

* * * *

"Did you have to do that?"

Daisy slid onto the barstool beside her father, feeling infinitely better. Well, mostly. Her backside was a wee bit sore because Nate had some things to work through. But oh, the orgasm after had been one hundred percent worth it. "I had to save Devi. O'Donnells get the job done. No matter what they have to do."

Her da raised a hand toward the man working Sanctum's bar this evening. "We need two. Make 'em doubles."

She was kind of glad Nate had taken his anxieties out on her backside because she needed to be loose for this talk. Despite the fact her da had told her he loved her, she was still nervous. "Da, I thought we should talk."

He shook his head. "Not until we're properly lubricated." He nodded as the bartender slid two glasses in front of them. He raised his toward her.

She picked hers up and they clinked glasses as they said *sláinte* in chorus and she tipped back for her first drink.

She sighed at the taste and realized her da had made the same sound.

Her mom was right. She was her father in feminine form. The question was could he accept her.

"Now, we should talk," her father said with a sigh. "I suppose this conversation is a long time coming."

She was confused, but then she was often confused. "Long time? I thought you just figured out I'm not some saint. You know I'm not evil either. I'm pretty normal for a woman."

"Normal? Ain't nothing normal about you." He snorted. "My darlin', did you honestly think I didn't see you all these years? Did you think I missed all the times you said you were going to Bri's or Devi's and you snuck out with some gangly boy who couldn't grow facial hair?"

There hadn't been too many times. "Why didn't you stop me?"

He took another drink. "Because I know what my relationship was like with my mum when she brought her foot down. Right on me neck. My mother put the raising of my brother on me and ignored us most of the time. She had other priorities. But when I did what most young men would do, like have any kind of a social life, she would ground me. I hated my mother a lot. Dreamed about being anywhere except her house. I couldn't stand the thought of you hating me, Daisy."

Her heart clenched. "I could never hate you, Da."

He seemed to let the words sink in. "I followed you most of the time. To make sure you were safe."

"A lot of those times Aidan came with us, or Cooper or the twins."

"Yes, I made sure of it," he confessed. "You weren't doing anything that's not natural for a young woman your age. But I always worried you would end up… I worried you would end up finding a man like me one night."

"What?" Her father was the best.

"Like I used to be," he said with a sigh. "Not now. Falling in love with your mum set me straight, but I wasn't the same man before."

"Momma says you went through women like they were chicken

wings." She and her mother had several long, painful conversations about her da's past.

"I really liked chicken wings." A wicked smile hit her da's face.

She could see his call. "I really liked bartenders."

Her da's head shook, but he laughed. "Oh, Daisy, you're my sweetest miracle and my worst nightmare." He reached out, cupping her cheek as he stared at her. "I was ready for Aidan. I'd practically raised my brother. I knew how to handle a boy. My brother went bad, but I figured your mum would offset anything nasty in my DNA."

"It wasn't in your DNA. It was in his. Your brother was a bad guy. He was selfish and mean. There wasn't anything you could have done to save him. I know you tried." She couldn't allow her father to think he'd been anything but wonderful. Even if he had apparently been the stud of choice amongst the Dallas chicken wing waitress scene.

"Then I found out we were having a girl." His expression went soft. "I can't tell you how scared I was at first. I didn't know how to raise a girl, but I knew Avery would teach me. When they put you in my arms and I looked down at the sweetest face I'd ever seen, I lost my heart all over again. I thought I was raising a little Avery."

"I'm not like Mom. I'm afraid that's Aidan." Her brother had their mom's temperament. He was patient and kind and knew how to stick with something. She was like their father. A bit mercurial until she knew what she wanted. Something of an imp at times.

"Yes, I realized you were like me when you were around twelve. And then I realized you had my sex drive, too, and that was when I started to choose delusion." He knocked back the rest of his whiskey resolutely. "Now, what you have to understand is delusion is not a bad place to be. Delusion can be nice. Just because a man chooses to park his RV in delusion and live there happily for a few years doesn't mean he doesn't love his daughter, doesn't mean he don't understand her."

"It means he needs time to process that his baby girl is a woman and she's going to make mistakes and go wild at times," Daisy said softly.

"But she's still my little girl," he replied. "And I'll always be her da. Daisy, you and Aidan are the best things I've ever done in my life. I'll always see you as a sweet baby who toddles around after me. I'll always feel the way you used to rest your head against my shoulder and sleep, and I would sit there no matter how much work I had to do because nothing was more important than letting you rest. This family… It's more than I could have imagined."

Tears pierced her eyes. "I love you more than you can know."

"You're just learning about love," he said with a smile. "And I'm happy for you. So Nathan Carter?"

She sniffled and decided to tease him a bit. "I don't know. Maybe."

Her father's face went red. "He told me he was going to marry you."

"Uhm, do we really need a piece of paper?" Yes, her imp was out today.

"You do," her father said, righteous indignation in his words. "You absolutely do."

"Hey, stop teasing your father." Her mom joined them, putting a hand on her father's shoulder. "I've been around them all week. Trust me. They'll be married far sooner than they should be, but when it's right, it's right."

Her father's gaze softened when he looked at her mom. He picked up her hand and brought it to his lips. "Well, we married within three weeks of meeting each other, so I think it can work out. Have I told you how much I missed you?"

Her mom ordered a whiskey of her own. "No. You were too busy starting a cartel war that led to your best friend's daughter nearly getting murdered and our own being forced to use all of her assets to save her."

"Now, Avery, you can't blame it on me," her da countered. "First off, it worked. As of an hour ago, the man Daisy is supposed to testify against is dead. Shanked in prison because someone started a very good rumor about him turning on another cartel and exposing their crimes. What's good for the goose and all. Brighton told us when we were explaining all the bodies. Kai's pissed, by the way. We got blood on the concrete or something and it could be triggering to patients. I say it's like immersion therapy."

"That's not a good therapeutic plan in the case of PTSD," Daisy pointed out. "Oh, and I'm going back for my master's in clinical psychology. I'm going to start a children's practice at the Ferguson Clinic. I told Uncle Kai all about it."

"No wonder he looked a little green," her father said.

"I think it's a wonderful plan." Her mom held her glass up. "To our Daisy."

"Hey, what the hell is happening?" Her brother was dressed hastily, his shirt not properly buttoned and…yes, it was inside out. "Gabe shows up at the club and tells me Devi got kidnapped and Daisy distracted the bad guys with her boobs and now everyone is dead, but you guys are drinking?"

Her poor brother. "Just another night for the O'Donnells."

"Get my son a drink, Matt," her father ordered. "And top me and my daughter off. Did I mention to you my sweet Daisy can drink anyone under the table?"

Aidan sank down beside her. "I have no idea what's going on."

"Daisy and I have agreed to be ourselves around each other from now on." Her father picked up his now full glass again. "The bad guys are all dead. Your sister has a career path that has nothing to do with danger, and both my kids are getting married. Nate hasn't formally asked yet, but he knows what happens if he doesn't. So let's have a toast, and then you two should stay away from the main stage unless you want to know how you were conceived."

"I'm going to need more liquor," her brother said.

Maybe her da was onto something. She lifted her glass. "I think we can stay a little delusional, Da."

He grinned and winked her way. "To delusion."

That was something she could drink to.

* * * *

Nate stared across the lounge where it looked like the whole O'Donnell family was now celebrating.

Damn, his woman was fine.

"You really think you can handle her, son?" His father stood beside him. The same way he'd been for as long as Nate could remember. Brody Carter might have missed the first couple of months of his life, but he'd more than made up for it.

"Of course he can." His mom wrapped an arm around his waist. "He and Daisy are a perfect match. Just like her parents."

He watched as Liam and Daisy managed to slap their shot glasses on the bar in time and drink in perfect synchronicity.

A terrible thought hit his brain.

"I'm the Avery, aren't I?"

His father patted his shoulder and sighed. "Yes, son, I'm afraid you are definitely the Avery."

"Hey," his mom said. "That's not such a bad thing to be. She's all kinds of awesome."

Nate threw his head back, laughter filling him. His woman was wild, and he would have to balance her. She looked over and smiled his way.

It wasn't a bad thing to be at all.

He led his parents into the bar to join their extended family.

Epilogue

Years later
Dallas, TX

"I'm going to run to the store, love."

Avery glanced up from her work. Casseroles. She'd already made three. One breakfast and two for lunches or dinners. Her daughter's freezer was going to be well stocked for the coming weeks.

Damn, but she loved Liam O'Donnell. He'd aged some, but she still saw him in the prime of his life. So gorgeous she could barely stand to look at him. Sometimes she still felt the moment her eyes had locked with his and she'd known she wanted to be with him forever.

Or maybe it had been more complex and the years had softened the actual history. Maybe it had been harder, but there was nothing hard about loving Liam O'Donnell now.

"Do you need anything?" he asked.

Anything she'd needed, she'd been given.

"Hey, love, what's this about?" Liam moved into her space, cupping her cheek, and when he looked down at her she was young again. He used his thumbs to gently wipe away the tears clinging to her. "I don't have to go to the store, but you know Brody and Steph are on their way from the airport right now, and Brody's been on a plane for twenty-four hours. He's going to be hungry. Besides, our Daisy asked for chicken salad."

Their Daisy. Their smart, funny girl who'd recently given them even more joy. She laughed. "I'm baking a couple of weeks' worth of food for her, but she needs chicken salad. Her postpartum cravings are worse than her pregnancy ones."

A brilliant smile crossed her husband's face. "Well, you have to admit she deserves it. Our little granddaughter is perfect."

Their first grandbaby. Wilhelmina Avery Carter. Billie.

Their first but not their last since they'd gotten good news the night before.

How new the world felt. She'd loved raising her family, but there was something so sweet about watching them go out into the world and find their places. Nate had moved up to an investigative team at McKay-Taggart, and he seemed to love solving mysteries with his partner, an intellectual guy who reminded Avery so much of Brody's friend Walter. Daisy had graduated with her master's, and she hadn't even burned down Kai's clinic yet. She was helping kids, and now she had one of her own.

"She is indeed." Avery went on her toes and kissed her husband. "Are they sleeping?"

Liam nodded. "They were up all night with Billie. Are you sure we should go home tomorrow?"

The birth had been hard, but Daisy had come through it like a champ. Like all new moms she needed help, so Avery and Liam had stayed for the first week ensuring all Nate and Daisy had to do was take care of themselves and the baby. They'd cooked and cleaned, and Liam had tried to hog the baby as much as possible, rocking her and singing her Irish lullabies. But it was time to let her other grandparents help.

"It's Steph and Brody's turn," she said firmly. "You know how much it killed them that they couldn't get here until today."

Steph's clinic in Sierra Leone had grown. She ran it with Faith Smith, and they'd recently opened a women's wing. Steph had been caught in a bureaucratic tangle when Daisy had gone into labor two weeks early. They'd only been able to arrange their travel in the last few days. They lived a block away when they were in Dallas, but Steph liked to be hands-on at the clinic several months out of the year.

He gave her one last kiss and stepped back. "Well, I suppose I can share. I'll be back as soon as I can. Billie's asleep in the bed in the nursery. Nate snores, and I won't have him waking my sweet granddaughter."

He winked and walked out.

The man never learned. Billie was already a saint of a girl. Just like her mother. She was fairly certain her granddaughter would end up as wild as Daisy. As troublesome as her grandfather. Trouble in the best way.

She heard him drive away, and then there was a chiming sound. Avery rushed to the front door because her husband was right. Daisy and Nate needed sleep.

She threw open the door and Steph stood there.

For a moment she saw another Stephanie. A teenaged Stephanie

Gibson who'd shown up at Avery's hospital bed, skinny because she hadn't eaten, wracked with guilt. She'd only met with the girl because Steph's mother had begged her. Stephanie had been driving the other car, the one that had plowed into hers. The one that had taken her first husband, Brandon, and her little baby, Madison, away from her. She'd been planning on telling Stephanie Gibson to go to hell.

She was transported to the moment when she'd looked at the girl who'd wronged her and known she had to make a choice.

A choice that brought her here. A life-changing choice.

"Hello, old friend," Avery said, her heart filled with love for this woman.

Tears streamed down Steph's cheeks. "I sent Brody to pick up some stuff from our place because I needed this moment with you. You feel it, too. I knew you would."

Avery held out a hand. "Of course I do."

They'd made a bargain once. Avery had told Steph she owed her a life. Two, really. Avery had used her inheritance money to get Steph through medical school, and Steph had tried to save the world. Over the years, she'd come to realize the life she'd demanded had been more than some singular debt. It hadn't been a debt at all. It had been a decision. To live. For Avery. For Steph.

For them all.

Steph moved inside, taking her hand. "Sometimes I still feel like this is a dream and I'm going to wake up and you don't forgive me."

She shut the door and pulled her friend in. "Never."

Steph hugged her close. "You are a miracle, Avery O'Donnell."

Avery stepped back and wiped away her tears. "Nope. Just me. But let me show you a real miracle."

Steph set down her bag and followed her through Daisy's house. Over the years she and Nate had fixed it up, laying hardwood floors and painting and building a home together. Her daughter was happy.

Because she'd made the choice to forgive so long ago. When she'd chosen to forgive Stephanie Gibson, she'd chosen to live, too. What she hadn't known at the time was she was choosing Liam. And Aidan and Daisy. She'd been choosing her friends. She'd been choosing an amazing career working with a woman she admired. She'd been choosing Billie.

She led Steph to the sweetly decorated nursery. Kangaroos were the theme, a nod to her father's homeland. "Meet your grandchild, Stephanie."

Steph put a hand to her heart, the tears flowing freely now. "She's so beautiful."

"She's got her mom's eyes and her father's smile." Billie was a unique mix of her parents. Like Aidan and Daisy were of her and Liam. Like Nate and Elodie of Steph and Brody.

A whole new generation. Beloved. They would grow in the shadow of their parents' love, learning from the generations before. They would make their own mistakes. Live their own magnificent lives.

Steph turned to her. "You said I owed you a life. I owe you so much more, Avery. This…this doesn't happen without you."

"We don't know that," Avery replied.

Steph nodded. "I do. I know what I was going to do. I had planned it. It seems so far away most of the time. Like it happened in a different life, but I feel it so strongly today because Nate wouldn't have been born. Billie wouldn't have been born."

"And Liam would have died without you," Avery pointed out. "Our lives entangled one night in a terrible way, and look at what we made. Look at her, Steph. I said you owed me a life, but what you gave us all was a future."

Billie opened her eyes, little mouth yawning.

"Hey, sweetheart. Meet your grandma Steph." Avery reached down, picking up the baby. "How many have you delivered?"

"Too many to count." Steph practically glowed as she stared at the baby and held her arms out.

"You made the world a better place for all of us." Avery handed over the baby and let Steph settle into the rocker. Emotion welled as she watched her friend fall madly in love with their grandbaby. "Thank you for our family."

Steph reached for her. "Thank you for our family."

They sat together in the warm light of day, rocking the baby and talking about the future. Avery couldn't wait to see what would happen next.

* * * *

Also from 1001 Dark Nights and Lexi Blake, discover Tempted, Delighted, Treasured, Charmed, Enchanted, Protected, Close Cover, Arranged, Devoted, Adored, and Dungeon Games.

Sign up for the 1001 Dark Nights Newsletter
and be entered to win a Tiffany Key necklace.

There's a contest every month!

Go to www.1001DarkNights.com to subscribe.

**As a bonus, all subscribers can download
FIVE FREE exclusive books!**

Discover 1001 Dark Nights Collection Eleven

DRAGON KISS by Donna Grant
A Dragon Kings Novella

THE WILD CARD by Dylan Allen
A Rivers Wilde Novella

ROCK CHICK REMATCH by Kristen Ashley
A Rock Chick Novella

JUST ONE SUMMER by Carly Phillips
A Dirty Dare Series Novella

HAPPILY EVER MAYBE by Carrie Ann Ryan
A Montgomery Ink Legacy Novella

BLUE MOON by Skye Warren
A Cirque des Moroirs Novella

A VAMPIRE'S MATE by Rebecca Zanetti
A Dark Protectors/Rebels Novella

LOVE HAZARD by Rachel Van Dyken

BRODIE by Aurora Rose Reynolds
An Until Her Novella

THE BODYGUARD AND THE BOMBSHELL by Lexi Blake
A Masters and Mercenaries: New Recruits Novella

THE SUBSTITUTE by Kristen Proby
A Single in Seattle Novella

CRAVED BY YOU by J. Kenner
A Stark Security Novella

GRAVEYARD DOG by Darynda Jones
A Charley Davidson Novella

A CHRISTMAS AUCTION by Audrey Carlan
A Marriage Auction Novella

THE GHOST OF A CHANCE by Heather Graham
A Krewe of Hunters Novella

Also from Blue Box Press

LEGACY OF TEMPTATION by Larissa Ione
A Demonica Birthright Novel

VISIONS OF FLESH AND BLOOD by Jennifer L. Armentrout and
Ravyn Salvador
A Blood & Ash and Fire & Flesh Compendium

FORGETTING TO REMEMBER by M.J. Rose

TOUCH ME by J. Kenner
A Stark International Novella

BORN OF BLOOD AND ASH by Jennifer L. Armentrout
A Flesh and Fire Novel

MY ROYAL SHOWMANCE by Lexi Blake
A Park Avenue Promise Novel

SAPPHIRE DAWN by Christopher Rice writing as C. Travis Rice
A Sapphire Cove Novel

IN THE AIR TONIGHT by Marie Force

EMBRACING THE CHANGE by Kristen Ashley
A River Rain Novel

Discover More Lexi Blake

Tempted: A Masters and Mercenaires Novella

When West Rycroft left his family's ranch to work in the big city, he never dreamed he would find himself surrounded by celebrities and politicians. Working at McKay-Taggart as a bodyguard and security expert quickly taught him how to navigate the sometimes shark-infested waters of the elite. While some would come to love that world, West has seen enough to know it's not for him, preferring to keep his distance from his clients—until the day he meets Ally Pearson.

Growing up in the entertainment world, Ally was always in the shadow of others, but now she has broken out from behind the scenes for her own day in the spotlight. The paparazzi isn't fun, but she knows all too well that it's part of the gig. She has a good life and lots of fans, but someone has been getting too close for comfort and making threats. To be safe, she hires her own personal knight in shining armor, a cowboy hottie by the name of West. They clash in the beginning, but the minute they fall into bed together something magical happens.

Just as everything seems too good to be true, they are both reminded that there was a reason Ally needed a bodyguard. Her problems have found her again, and this time West will have to put his life on the line or lose everything they've found.

* * * *

Delighted: A Masters and Mercenaries Novella

Brian "Boomer" Ward believes in sheltering strays. After all, the men and women of McKay-Taggart made him family when he had none. So when the kid next door needs help one night, he thinks nothing of protecting her until her mom gets home. But when he meets Daphne Carlton, the thoughts hit him hard. She's stunning and hardworking and obviously in need of someone to put her first. It doesn't hurt that she's as sweet as the cupcakes she bakes.

Daphne Carlton's life revolves around two things—her kid and her business. Daphne's Delights is her dream—to take the recipes of her childhood and share them with the world. Her daughter, Lula, is the best kid she could have hoped for. Lula's got a genius-level intelligence and a heart of gold. But she also has two grandparents who control her access to private school and the fortune her father left behind. They're impossible to please, and Daphne worries that one wrong move on her part could cost her daughter the life she deserves.

As Daphne and Boomer find themselves getting closer, outside forces put pressure on the new couple. But if they make it through the storm, love will just be the icing on the cake because family is the real prize.

* * * *

Treasured: A Masters and Mercenaries Novella

David Hawthorne has a great life. His job as a professor at a prestigious Dallas college is everything he hoped for. Now that his brother is back from the Navy, life seems to be settling down. All he needs to do is finish the book he's working on and his tenure will be assured. When he gets invited to interview a reclusive expert, he knows he's gotten lucky. But being the stepson of Sean Taggart comes with its drawbacks, including an overprotective mom who sends a security detail to keep him safe. He doesn't need a bodyguard, but when Tessa Santiago shows up on his doorstep, the idea of her giving him close cover doesn't seem so bad.

Tessa has always excelled at most anything she tried, except romance. The whole relationship thing just didn't work out for her. She's not looking for love, and she's certainly not looking for it with an academic who happens to be connected to her boss's family. The last thing she wants is to escort an overly pampered pretentious man-child around South America to ensure he doesn't get into trouble. Still, there's something about David that calls to her. In addition to watching his back, she will have to avoid falling into the trap of soulful eyes and a deep voice that gets her heart racing.

But when the seemingly simple mission turns into a treacherous race for a hidden artifact, David and Tess know this assignment could cost them far more than their jobs. If they can overcome the odds, the lost treasure might not be their most valuable reward.

* * * *

Charmed: A Masters and Mercenaries Novella

JT Malone is lucky, and he knows it. He is the heir to a billion-dollar petroleum empire, and he has a loving family. Between his good looks and his charm, he can have almost any woman he wants. The world is his oyster, and he really likes oysters. So why does it all feel so empty?

Nina Blunt is pretty sure she's cursed. She worked her way up through the ranks at Interpol, fighting for every step with hard work and discipline. Then she lost it all because she loved the wrong person. Rebuilding her career with McKay-Taggart, she can't help but feel lonely. It seems everyone around her is finding love and starting families. But she knows that isn't for her. She has vowed never to make the mistake of falling in love again.

JT comes to McKay-Taggart for assistance rooting out a corporate spy, and Nina signs on to the job. Their working relationship becomes tricky, however, as their personal chemistry flares like a wildfire. Completing the assignment without giving in to the attraction that threatens to overwhelm them seems like it might be the most difficult part of the job. When danger strikes, will they be able to count on each other when the bullets are flying? If not, JT's charmed life might just come to an end.

* * * *

Enchanted: A Masters and Mercenaries Novella

A snarky submissive princess
Sarah Steven's life is pretty sweet. By day, she's a dedicated trauma nurse and by night, a fun-loving club sub. She adores her job, has a group of friends who have her back, and is a member of the hottest club in Dallas. So why does it all feel hollow? Could it be because she fell for her dream man and can't forgive him for walking away from her? Nope. She's not going there again. No matter how much she wants to.

A prince of the silver screen
Jared Johns might be one of the most popular actors in Hollywood, but he lost more than a fan when he walked away from Sarah. He lost the only woman he's ever loved. He's been trying to get her back, but she won't return his calls. A trip to Dallas to visit his brother might be exactly

what he needs to jump-start his quest to claim the woman who holds his heart.

A masquerade to remember
For Charlotte Taggart's birthday, Sanctum becomes a fantasyland of kinky fun and games. Every unattached sub gets a new Dom for the festivities. The twist? The Doms must conceal their identities until the stroke of midnight at the end of the party. It's exactly what Sarah needs to forget the fact that Jared is pursuing her. She can't give in to him, and the mysterious Master D is making her rethink her position when it comes to signing a contract. Jared knows he was born to play this role, dashing suitor by day and dirty Dom at night.

When the masks come off, will she be able to forgive the man who loves her, or will she leave him forever?

* * * *

Protected: A Masters and Mercenaries Novella

A second chance at first love
Years before, Wade Rycroft fell in love with Geneva Harris, the smartest girl in his class. The rodeo star and the shy academic made for an odd pair but their chemistry was undeniable. They made plans to get married after high school but when Genny left him standing in the rain, he joined the Army and vowed to leave that life behind. Genny married the town's golden boy, and Wade knew that he couldn't go home again.

Could become the promise of a lifetime
Fifteen years later, Wade returns to his Texas hometown for his brother's wedding and walks into a storm of scandal. Genny's marriage has dissolved and the town has turned against her. But when someone tries to kill his old love, Wade can't refuse to help her. In his years after the Army, he's found his place in the world. His job at McKay-Taggart keeps him happy and busy but something is missing. When he takes the job watching over Genny, he realizes what it is.

As danger presses in, Wade must decide if he can forgive past sins or let the woman of his dreams walk into a nightmare…

* * * *

Close Cover: A Masters and Mercenaries Novel

Remy Guidry doesn't do relationships. He tried the marriage thing once, back in Louisiana, and learned the hard way that all he really needs in life is a cold beer, some good friends, and the occasional hookup. His job as a bodyguard with McKay-Taggart gives him purpose and lovely perks, like access to Sanctum. The last thing he needs in his life is a woman with stars in her eyes and babies in her future.

Lisa Daley's life is going in the right direction. She has graduated from college after years of putting herself through school. She's got a new job at an accounting firm and she's finished her Sanctum training. Finally on her own and having fun, her life seems pretty perfect. Except she's lonely and the one man she wants won't give her a second look.

There is one other little glitch. Apparently, her new firm is really a front for the mob and now they want her dead. Assassins can really ruin a fun girls' night out. Suddenly strapped to the very same six-foot-five-inch hunk of a bodyguard who makes her heart pound, Lisa can't decide if this situation is a blessing or a curse.

As the mob closes in, Remy takes his tempting new charge back to the safest place he knows—his home in the bayou. Surrounded by his past, he can't help wondering if Lisa is his future. To answer that question, he just has to keep her alive.

****

Arranged: A Masters and Mercenaries Novella

Kash Kamdar is the king of a peaceful but powerful island nation. As Loa Mali's sovereign, he is always in control, the final authority. Until his mother uses an ancient law to force her son into marriage. His prospective queen is a buttoned-up intellectual, nothing like Kash's usual party girl. Still, from the moment of their forced engagement, he can't stop thinking about her.

Dayita Samar comes from one of Loa Mali's most respected families. The Oxford-educated scientist has dedicated her life to her country's future. But under her staid and calm exterior, Day hides a few sexy secrets of her own. She is willing to marry her king, but also agrees that they can circumvent the law. Just because they're married doesn't mean they have to change their lives. It certainly doesn't mean they have to fall in love.

After one wild weekend in Dallas, Kash discovers his bride-to-be is more than she seems. Engulfed in a changing world, Kash finds exciting new possibilities for himself. Could Day help him find respite from the crushing responsibility he's carried all his life? This fairy tale could have a happy ending, if only they can escape Kash's past…

* * * *

Devoted: A Masters and Mercenaries Novella

A woman's work

Amy Slaten has devoted her life to Slaten Industries. After ousting her corrupt father and taking over the CEO role, she thought she could relax and enjoy taking her company to the next level. But an old business rivalry rears its ugly head. The only thing that can possibly take her mind off business is the training class at Sanctum…and her training partner, the gorgeous and funny Flynn Adler. If she can just manage to best her mysterious business rival, life might be perfect.

A man's commitment

Flynn Adler never thought he would fall for the enemy. Business is war, or so his father always claimed. He was raised to be ruthless when it came to the family company, and now he's raising his brother to one day work with him. The first order of business? The hostile takeover of Slaten Industries. It's a stressful job so when his brother offers him a spot in Sanctum's training program, Flynn jumps at the chance.

A lifetime of devotion….

When Flynn realizes the woman he's falling for is none other than the CEO of the firm he needs to take down, he has to make a choice. Does he take care of the woman he's falling in love with or the business he's worked a lifetime to build? And when Amy finally understands the man she's come to trust is none other than the enemy, will she walk away from him or fight for the love she's come to depend on?

* * * *

Adored: A Masters and Mercenaries Novella

A man who gave up on love
Mitch Bradford is an intimidating man. In his professional life, he has a reputation for demolishing his opponents in the courtroom. At the exclusive BDSM club Sanctum, he prefers disciplining pretty submissives with no strings attached. In his line of work, there's no time for a healthy relationship. After a few failed attempts, he knows he's not good for any woman—especially not his best friend's sister.

A woman who always gets what she wants
Laurel Daley knows what she wants, and her sights are set on Mitch. He's smart and sexy, and it doesn't matter that he's a few years older and has a couple of bitter ex-wives. Watching him in action at work and at play, she knows he just needs a little polish to make some woman the perfect lover. She intends to be that woman, but first she has to show him how good it could be.

A killer lurking in the shadows
When an unexpected turn of events throws the two together, Mitch and Laurel are confronted with the perfect opportunity to explore their mutual desire. Night after night of being close breaks down Mitch's defenses. The more he sees of Laurel, the more he knows he wants her. Unfortunately, someone else has their eyes on Laurel and they have murder in mind.

* * * *

Dungeon Games: A Masters and Mercenaries Novella

Obsessed
Derek Brighton has become one of Dallas's finest detectives through a combination of discipline and obsession. Once he has a target in his sights, nothing can stop him. When he isn't solving homicides, he applies the same intensity to his playtime at Sanctum, a secretive BDSM club. Unfortunately, no amount of beautiful submissives can fill the hole that one woman left in his heart.

Unhinged
Karina Mills has a reputation for being reckless, and her clients

appreciate her results. As a private investigator, she pursues her cases with nothing holding her back. In her personal life, Karina yearns for something different. Playing at Sanctum has been a safe way to find peace, but the one Dom who could truly master her heart is out of reach.

Enflamed
On the hunt for a killer, Derek enters a shadowy underworld only to find the woman he aches for is working the same case. Karina is searching for a missing girl and won't stop until she finds her. To get close to their prime suspect, they need to pose as a couple. But as their operation goes under the covers, unlikely partners become passionate lovers while the killer prepares to strike.

Discover the Park Avenue Promise series...

From Lexi Blake and Blue Box Press...

*Three young women make a pact in high school—
to always be friends and to one day make it big in Manhattan.*

Start Us Up
Now Available!

She's a high-tech boss who lost it all...

Ivy Jensen was the darling of the tech world, right up until her company fell apart completely after she trusted the wrong person. Her reputation in tatters, she finds herself back in the tiny apartment she grew up in, living with her mom. When a group of angel investors offer her a meeting, she knows she has to come up with the new big idea or her career is over.

He's an up and coming coder...

Heath Marino has always been fascinated with writing code. He's worked on a dozen games and apps and is considered one of the industry's more eccentric talents. But now he's back in New York to spend time with his grandmother. She was known as one of the city's greatest matchmakers, and he wants to know why. Surely there's some kind of code in his grandmother's methods, and he's going to find them.

When Ivy meets Heath it's instant attraction, but she's got a career to get back to and he just might be her on-ramp. It could be a perfect partnership or absolute heartbreak.

* * * *

My Royal Showmance
Now Available!

Anika Fox knows exactly where she wants to be, and it's not on the set of a reality TV dating show. She's working her way up at the production company she works for and she's close to achieving some of her dreams. The big boss just wants one thing from her. She's got a potential problem with the director of *The King Takes a Bride* and she wants Anika to pose as a production assistant and report back.

As the prince of a tiny European country, Luca St. Marten knows the world views him as one of the pampered royalty of the world. It couldn't be further from the truth. His country is hurting and he's right there on the front lines with his citizens. When he's asked to do a dating show, his counselors point out that it could bring tourism back to Ralavia. It goes against his every desire, but he agrees.

When one of the contestants drops out at the last minute, Anika finds herself replacing the potential princess. She's sure she'll be asked to leave the first night, but Luca keeps picking her again and again. Suddenly she finds herself in the middle of a made-for-TV fantasy, and she's unsure what's real and what's simply reality TV.

Sweet Little Spies
Masters and Mercenaries: New Recruits, Book 3
By Lexi Blake
Coming September 17, 2024

Since he was a kid, Aidan O'Donnell has known two things about the world. Tristan is his best friend, and Carys is the love of his life. Sharing her with Tristan was oddly easy. They both loved her deeply, and they never cared what anyone else thought. They were a team and everything was wonderful. Until the day it ended.

Carys Taggart has spent the last year and a half of her life living a lie. A lie Tristan forced on them all. She understands that it was meant to protect her and Aidan, but lately when Tristan says he doesn't love her, it feels more like the truth. The wedding she's dreamed of has been put off far longer than he promised. When he asks her and Aidan for another delay, she's ready to move on without him.

Tristan Dean-Miles has a good plan and the best of intentions. Go undercover as a ruthless arms dealer so he can find a deadly bombmaker at the top of the agency's wanted list. It might be taking longer than expected, but he's so close he can taste it. Unfortunately, getting this close meant getting in way too deep. He knows he will succeed, but if he can't convince the love of his life and his best friend that he's worth the wait, his victory will cost him everything.

About Lexi Blake

New York Times bestselling author Lexi Blake lives in North Texas with her husband and three kids. Since starting her publishing journey in 2010, she's sold over three million copies of her books. She began writing at a young age, concentrating on plays and journalism. It wasn't until she started writing romance that she found success. She likes to find humor in the strangest places and believes in happy endings.

Connect with Lexi online:

Facebook: Lexi Blake
Twitter: authorlexiblake
Website: www.LexiBlake.net
Instagram: www.instagram.com

On Behalf of 1001 Dark Nights,
Liz Berry, M.J. Rose, and Jillian Stein would like to thank ~

Steve Berry
Doug Scofield
Benjamin Stein
Kim Guidroz
Chelle Olson
Tanaka Kangara
Asha Hossain
Chris Graham
Jessica Saunders
Stacey Tardif
Grace Wenk
Dylan Stockton
Kate Boggs
Richard Blake
and Simon Lipskar

Made in the USA
Middletown, DE
04 August 2024